Dyan Sheldon is the author of many books for young people, including *Confessions of a Teenage Drama Queen*; *One or Two Things I Learned About Love*; *The Crazy Things Girls Do for Love*; *Tall, Thin and Blonde*; and *My Worst Best Friend*, as well as a number of stories for younger readers. American by birth, Dyan lives in North London.

Other books by Dyan Sheldon

bursting Bubbles

Dyan Sheldon

WALKER
BOOKS

First published 2014 by Walker Books Ltd
87 Vauxhall Walk, London SE11 5HJ

2 4 6 8 10 9 7 5 3 1

Text © 2014 Dyan Sheldon
Cover photographs © coloroftime/Getty Images,
Dean Mitchell/iStockphoto and fStop/Alamy
Cover illustrations © 2014 Nina Tara

This book has been typeset in Berkeley

Printed and bound in Great Britain by Clays Ltd, St Ives plc

British Library Cataloguing in Publication Data:
a catalogue record for this book
is available from the British Library

ISBN 978-1-4063-4910-8

www.walker.co.uk

Prologue
Something That Happened Last Christmas

There will be millions of things that Dr Kilpatiky will forget as time goes by, but the moment when she saw the set of golf clubs among the donations for the school's Christmas Adopt-a-Family appeal will not be one of them. That she will remember for the rest of her life.

"God help us!" Dr Kilpatiky spoke so loudly that everyone in the room turned around. "What the hell is that?"

"Golf clubs," answered Mrs Mahoney, who was unfortunate enough to be standing beside the principal right then.

"I can see that!" Dr Kilpatiky snapped back. "What I don't understand is what they're doing *here*."

"They came with the slicing machine and the caviar," muttered Mrs Mahoney. She might have added, "and the pairs of very expensive worn-once shoes", but didn't because she was already scurrying away.

Left to herself, Dr Kilpatiky examined the offerings more closely. The shoes were all designer labels. The slicing machine had never been used. The caviar had expired. The golf clubs were monogrammed.

Every year the local paper publishes a list of families in the county who have fallen upon hard times and need some special help at Christmas, and every year Shell Harbour High School "adopts" one of those families. Because Shell Harbour is one of the most affluent communities in the state, its students have shelves (if not closets and rooms) full of things that have barely or never been used, and they are encouraged to donate them. But it's always been understood that these should be practical things – things people struggling to get by can use: canned and boxed goods, towels and linens, jackets and trainers, toys and games, even small appliances or a sixth TV set that no one has ever plugged in. While there might be an argument that a slicing machine is practical (assuming the recipient has something to slice), Dr Kilpatiky didn't feel that the shoes, the caviar or the clubs fell into that category.

Thanks to the monogram, it took the principal no time at all to identify the donor: Marigold Liotta. Marigold Liotta was summoned.

* * *

Marigold was smiling as she stepped into the principal's office. Partly she was smiling because she had never been in even the most minor trouble since she started school and had no idea that anything was wrong. Partly she was smiling because Marigold smiles the way the sun shines. Always, unless hidden by something.

Dr Kilpatiky thanked her for coming.

"Oh, that's OK," said Marigold with her usual good humour. "Is it about the Christmas tea?" Traditionally, Marigold's sorority hosts a tea for the staff each December. That year Marigold was one of the organizers. "Because you don't have to worry, Dr Kilpatiky. I found a baker who can do gluten-free."

"No, it's not about the tea." Dr Kilpatiky gestured to the chair in front of her desk. "Please, have a seat, Marigold. I wanted to have a word with you about your very imaginative donations to our Christmas appeal."

Marigold's smile brightened. "I wanted to do something different."

"Well, you certainly achieved that." The principal's lips were as flat as the EKG of a corpse. "I don't think anyone's ever donated caviar before."

Marigold said she figured as much. "Everybody usually gives stuff like beans and spaghetti."

"Exactly. That's what I wanted to talk to you about."
Dr Kilpatiky folded her hands on her desk, leaning
forward slightly. "I was wondering, Marigold, if you'd
actually read the information on the family we adopted."

That year the school had chosen Family 898: two
adults, and three children under twelve; both parents
unemployed because of lay-offs and a debilitating illness;
deep in debt because of impossible medical bills and lack
of income; living in an emergency shelter since the bank
foreclosed on their house.

"Of course I did," said Marigold. "I feel really bad for
them. Those poor little kids."

"I see," murmured the principal, but she didn't. "Then
could you explain what you thought our family could do
with your gifts? Did you think Mrs 898 would wear the
Louboutins to the laundrette?"

Not one of the students at Shell Harbour High has
ever suspected the principal of having a sense of humour,
but Marigold laughed nonetheless. "Of course not. But I
know Georgiana – Georgiana Shiller? – I know she gave
her boots. And I know other people gave slippers and
trainers and stuff like that. That's why I gave shoes that
are nothing but pretty. And special. I thought they'd
cheer her up."

"But she's never going to use them."

"That doesn't matter," explained Marigold. "I mean, Christmas shouldn't be just about warm jackets and jumpers and boxes of macaroni and cheese, should it? It should be fun and joyous. I believe Christmas should sparkle."

Rather like the Louboutins.

"That's a lovely thought, Marigold." Dr Kilpatiky was starting to feel that staring at Marigold's smile was like staring at a naked light bulb. "Only—"

"And didn't Jesus say that you can't live just on bread?"

"More or less," murmured the principal. "But I doubt very much that he was thinking caviar and golf clubs were needed for a well-balanced life." She took a breath and tried again. "The point is that none of these things really help people who are hungry."

"Oh, but they do," Marigold protested.

Dr Kilpatiky raised one eyebrow. Archly. "Let them eat caviar? Have you become Shell Harbour's answer to Marie Antoinette?"

"No, that's not what I mean. What I mean is that they can sell all that stuff on eBay. And get whatever they want with the money they make."

"Expired caviar and monogrammed golf clubs."

Marigold nodded, causing the miniature reindeer hanging from her ears to dance merrily. "The caviar's only just expired, so it's fine, and those clubs are really expensive. Somebody'll buy them no matter whose initials are on them."

"And what if our family doesn't have a computer?" enquired the principal. It surprised her that she was actually having this conversation, but she couldn't seem to stop herself. "They're not going to be able to sell them on eBay without a computer."

"Oh, they'll have a computer," Marigold assured her. "You know Byron – Byron Locke? – he's always upgrading. He gave them one of his old ones."

Chapter One
Dr Kilpatiky's Bubble Speech

Almost a year has gone by since Dr Kilpatiky had her few words with Marigold Liotta about her Christmas donations. It is now the end of August, and today Dr Kilpatiky and the department chairpersons of Shell Harbour High are having one of their final meetings before the start of the new school year.

The last item on the meeting's agenda is the school's community service requirement. In order to graduate, every student must donate twenty hours a year to work that in some way benefits the public – such as picking up litter in the park, visiting care homes, raising money for charity, helping in a church charity shop or coaching an elementary school sports team. Dr Kilpatiky has been giving this requirement a great deal of thought over the summer, and has come to the conclusion that there is a flaw in the system.

"I don't really see any problem," says Mrs Mahoney. Not that she would. The community service requirement is managed by the social sciences department, which Mrs Mahoney heads. "We can't expect them to do more than twenty hours a year. Not and keep up our academic standards." Among other things, Shell Harbour is known for its high academic standards and competitive curriculum.

Several pairs of eyes glance quickly at watches. Dr Kilpatiky can almost hear ice cubes falling into glasses and lawn furniture being dragged into the sun. It's been a long meeting; everyone wants to go home. She smiles. Warmly. As if to say, *This won't take much more time and it won't hurt.* "Of course not, Gwen. It isn't the quantity I'm worried about; it's the quality."

"I'm afraid I don't understand." Mrs Mahoney's smile falters. "You know we have no control over what goes on in the placements, Irenie. If they don't find their own, we just provide a list of options. The organizations and the students do the rest."

"It's not as if they get graded on what they do," chips in Ms Sketz from maths. "They just get marked on attendance." No one has ever failed a community service position – not even the junior who was found sound asleep in a supply closet at the hospital.

"Yes, I am aware of that." A sledgehammer couldn't

shift Dr Kilpatiky's smile right now. "However, if I'm remembering correctly, the community service placements are supposed to expand our students' experience of the world." The only way Shell Harbour could have a wealthier and more privileged student body would be if it were a private boarding school. Along the lines of Eton. The majority of its students have about as much contact with ordinary people as the Queen of England does. Possibly less since their visits to hospitals and developing countries aren't as frequent as Her Majesty's.

"And that's what they do," says Mrs Mahoney.

"Not as well as they might." While others were relaxing at the beach, Dr Kilpatiky was looking into this quite thoroughly. Although all of the students are doing something that can be interpreted as community service, many of the projects are not exactly Everest-like challenges that catapult them out of their comfort zones or put them in touch with the less fortunate. "Something like picking up soda cans from the side of the road may be very helpful but it's not really stretching their capacity for compassion."

"We're not trying to create Mother Teresas," argues Mrs Mahoney. "Just open them up a little and encourage a sense of public responsibility. And in any case, you can't blame them for the less challenging options. The brief is necessarily rather broad."

"I'm not blaming them. But the majority of placements are within our township." Dr Kilpatiky absentmindedly twists her wedding ring around her finger. "Which means that many of our students have no idea how most people live."

Sebastian Marks from the language-arts department stops doodling at the bottom of his agenda and puts down his pen. "With all due respect, Irenie, 'most people' don't live in the United States. So even if you have them running a soup kitchen they're not going to know how most people in the world live."

Dr Kilpatiky's mouth looks like patience stretched to its limits. "I meant most people around here, Seb."

"Even so," says Mr Marks. "You can hardly blame them for that, either. This is their community, after all. They don't live in a trailer park or a suburban slum, they live in Shell Harbour." Where, besides the ocean and the bay for their boats, everyone has a pool. "As far as our kids are concerned, being poor means having one bathroom, one car and only two TVs."

Because she has years of training and experience, Dr Kilpatiky manages to sigh only in her heart. "I appreciate that, Seb, but I overhear things and I observe. And my general impression is that a lot of them believe that life is a meritocracy and that those who don't succeed have only themselves to blame."

"Be that as it may—" begins Dr Goldblatt from science.

"Be that as it may, besides this general impression of mine, several things happened last year that have convinced me that many of our students live in a bubble. A bubble of advantage. Which I believe it is our duty to burst."

"Are we talking about the war on poverty debate?" asks Mr Marks. It was in his class that Georgiana Shiller suggested that throwing a party could be used as a weapon against hunger.

Dr Kilpatiky does believe that if life were a candy bar Georgiana Shiller would eat the wrapper, but it wasn't Georgiana who started the principal thinking about reforming the programme. "Not specifically."

"Asher Grossman coming to the Halloween dance as a homeless person?" guesses Ms Sketz. Asher, dressed in clothes that obviously weren't his (they were cheap and well-worn), had sat himself near the door of the gym, a dog wearing a bandana on one side and a cardboard cup that held a few dimes and nickels on the other. On his lap he had a sign that said *GOD BLESS YOU*. When Dr Kilpatiky saw him Ms Sketz thought the principal might have a seizure. Her face turned a shade of red normally associated with over-ripe tomatoes, and her nose started twitching uncontrollably, a sign that she is very angry. "He was being ironic," adds Ms Sketz. Asher not only has the highest GPA in the school but is the star of her Advanced Placement Calculus class (and every other class he takes) and, therefore, deserving of her protection.

"That's one interpretation of what he was," says Dr Kilpatiky. "But to be honest, it was as much the dog as anything. You don't see that many people living on the street with a dog that costs over a thousand dollars. But, again, I wasn't thinking specifically of Asher."

"Oh," Mrs Mahoney sighs. "It's Marigold Liotta who's brought this on, isn't it?"

It is. If there is any one student who stands out among the scores whose comments and jokes and behaviour have caused the principal's eyes to narrow and nose to twitch like a hound on the scent of a hare over the last year, it is probably Marigold Liotta, who, though her heart is very much in the right place, wins the so-out-of-touch-she-might-as-well-be-in-orbit prize. Dr Kilpatiky really never will forget her first sight of the golf clubs, although it was probably the expired caviar that was the sliver of straw that would have had her flat on the ground and waiting for the ambulance if she were a camel.

"I'm still not sure what it is you want to do," says Mrs Mahoney. "You can't punish them because their parents have money."

"I don't want to punish them," says Dr Kilpatiky. "I want to help them become the sensitive and aware people I know they can be."

"What are you planning to do?" asks Mrs Moreno from foreign languages. "Pack them all off to dig wells in Africa?"

"I don't think we need to do anything quite that drastic. However, it won't do them any harm to broaden their definition of community a little. After all, we're not an island. There are other, less wealthy, towns and villages all around us, but very few of our students choose the placements they offer." She can't restructure the entire programme, but she can do something to redress the balance – even if only slightly. "What I'm suggesting is that we remove the element of choice, so those who would automatically choose the soft option won't be able to."

"You mean assign them placements?"

Guarded glances are exchanged and eyes roll. Choice is something the pupils of Shell Harbour think of as a constitutional right. The menu in the cafeteria is testament to that.

"I was thinking of something more random and

lottery-like." Dr Kilpatiky focuses her smile on Mr Jacobwitz, chairperson of IT. "I was thinking there must be a computer program that could make the selections."

"*No problema*," says Mr Jacobwitz. "We have the technology."

"What if they get something they can't do?" Mrs Moreno wants to know. "Something they aren't any good at? Let's face it, you wouldn't want someone like Georgiana cutting the grass in the park."

When the laughter finally stops, Dr Kilpatiky says, "Then we do it again."

"I don't think this is a good idea," says Mr Marks.

"They're not going to like it," warns Mrs Mahoney.

"They don't have to like it," says Dr Kilpatiky. "They just have to do it."

A statement that, though the principal has no way of knowing it, easily fits under the heading: Famous Last Words.

Chapter Two

A Conversation at the End of Summer

Six teenagers and a Yorkshire terrier lie on rattan loungers by a large swimming pool. The pool water is the colour of a tropical lagoon on a very good day in a very good year, and all seven are shaded by brightly coloured umbrellas (souvenirs, like the loungers, of a trip to Thailand the summer before). The pool has a view of the ocean and gives the impression that if you dived in and kept swimming you would effortlessly flow into the Atlantic (and, presumably, be washed out to sea). Three of the six – Marigold, Asher and Georgiana – are being discussed at this very moment by Dr Kilpatiky and her staff. The remaining three are Claudelia Gillen, Byron Locke and Will Lundquist. The Yorkshire terrier's name is Dunkin. Dunkin belongs to Will. The pool belongs to Georgiana.

Summer is almost over. Soon the leaves will begin

to turn colour and fall, and the days will grow shorter and cool. Even sooner, the pool, the swimsuits, the Ray-Bans and the sunblock will be replaced with classrooms, school clothes and iPads; the planning of beach parties and boat rides replaced with organizing what everyone's doing on Saturday night or after the game. Which is not a thought that makes them all happy.

Beneath the umbrella decorated with dragons, Georgiana sighs, a sound like someone trying to blow out a fire. "God, can you believe the summer's almost over?" It seems to Georgiana that it was only yesterday that she walked out of Shell Harbour High, free as a bird and full of anticipation and plans, and now here she is about to walk back in, the door slamming shut behind her. Caged again. "I had so many things I wanted to do that I never did, and already it's back to the old grind."

"But we did have some really good times." Marigold believes in positive thinking. There is no cloud so black that she can't find a silver lining in it – or, at least, a silver thread. "And there are a lot of fun things to look forward to in the fall and winter."

Byron grins. "What? Like flu and getting stuck in the snow?"

Marigold laughs in her good-natured way. "You know what I mean. It's not all gloom and doom, is it? There are dances and parties. Homecoming. Christmas. Skiing. All that cool stuff."

"Yeah, sure there is. And I love all that, too." Georgiana absent-mindedly twists a strand of hair around one finger. "But, I don't know – the winter's not like the summer. It's all routine and schedules and regular life. In the summer it's like anything could happen." By "anything" Georgiana means romance and adventure. Not that there has been much of either in her life so far. This summer the most exciting thing that happened to her was nearly drowning in the undertow swimming at her aunt's house in Baja. Last summer all Georgiana got in Thailand was dysentery.

"Let's not start talking about snow yet, OK?" says Claudelia. "I mean, I've only just gotten my tan even and soon it'll be all leggings and sweaters and boots."

"I wasn't even thinking of that stuff." Georgiana sighs again. "You know, sometimes I really wish I lived in LA. I know it has its downside..."

"You mean like the weird people, the earthquakes and the terminal pollution?" asks Will.

"Don't forget the Godzilla traffic," chips in Byron. "We were stuck in a jam so bad it would've been faster to walk back to the hotel over the cars."

"But at least it's always warm and sunny," says Claudelia.

"Permanent summer." Georgiana looks wistful. "I could do that. It'd be awesome."

"But you'd still have to go to school," points out Will.

Georgiana scowls at him. "Like I could forget that, right?" Georgiana is not the biggest fan the education system has ever had. She believes that life is for living, not sitting in a room being taught a whole lot of things she's never going to have any use for. Does she need to understand *Hamlet* to shop? Grasp the basics of quantum mechanics to play tennis? Master quadratic equations in order to have a bank account? No, no and no. People spend a lot more time under the ground than above it. Life's too short to read Proust. That's what Georgiana thinks.

"Oh, come on," says Marigold. "School's not so bad. I like it." Which is true. Marigold is a straight-A student with a special passion for literature. She's already read Proust.

"I wonder if there's any place in California where you can go to school in a bathing suit." Claudelia is still thinking about her tan. "I mean, if there's anywhere on the planet where you could, that would have to be it, right? Or maybe Florida. Florida's pretty laid-back."

"Oh my God!" Something has finally made Georgiana smile. "Can you imagine the cow Dr Kilpatiky would have if you showed up in a bikini? She wouldn't shut up about it for months!" Georgiana's laughter makes her lounger tremble and wakes up Dunkin on the chair beside her (though not for long).

Will, who has been lolling, sits up, straight as a bolt. "Wow! That'd be so awesome. Can't you just picture it? I'd pay to see that. I really would."

"Never mind paying," says Asher. "We could sell tickets. Make a fortune."

Too-funny-for-words tears fill Georgiana's eyes. "Oh God, wouldn't it be fantastic?" she gasps. "The old witch would be so outraged! And you know how her nose twitches when she's really upset? I bet she'd go into lift-off."

"Oh, man!" Byron is in danger of falling off his chair. "I don't know how, but I forgot about the twitching nose! The twitching nose is phenomenal. Can you grasp the total wonderfulness of what would happen if we got it on camera? Put it on YouTube?" He turns to Claudelia. "Come on, Claudelia, why don't you do it? Show up the first day wearing what you're wearing now." Three small triangles of material and several lengths of string. "Just to see the Killjoy's reaction."

Claudelia knows exactly what the principal's reaction would be. "Yeah, in your dreams." She jerks her head towards Asher. "Why don't you get Ash to do it? He's the pro at dressing down."

Asher pretends to laugh. Hahaha. "You're very funny." When it comes to wearing inappropriate clothes and causing the Kilpatiky nose to twitch so much it looked as if it were trying to wrest itself from the Kilpatiky face, Asher, of course, has history. It is, however, a history he'd rather not repeat. Not a year away from graduation. "I still can't get within a yard of the old bat without her making some crack about last Halloween."

"Halloween!" Will falls back against the cushion again. If a bull could laugh, it would sound like Will. "Now that was truly awesome. It was like you created the Legend of Shell Harbour. We should probably write a song about it. No one's ever going to forget it."

"Well I wish the Killjoy would." Even wearing swimming trunks and a T-shirt, Asher manages to give the impression that he's wearing a suit. An immaculate and well-pressed suit. This ability of Asher's to always look as if he's going to an important interview, no matter what he has on, was noticed by Dr Kilpatiky at the Halloween dance. Which didn't make her like his costume any more. "I don't really think grudge-holding is a desirable trait in an authority figure. It shows a lack of flexibility. She needs to learn how to let go of things. Crissake, it was just a joke." Which is where he went wrong, of course. If you converted the Killjoy's sense of humour into money she wouldn't be able to buy a small cup of coffee. Not even at twentieth-century prices.

"Grudge-holder is right," says Georgiana. "Unlike you, Ash, I didn't actually do anything. I just *said* something. In a debate, for Pete's sake. In language arts." Which is about the same as saying something silently and to yourself in an igloo in the middle of the frozen tundra. The only person who was actually listening was Dr Kilpatiky. "Look at the dumb things politicians say on TV and nobody gets on their case, do they? But boy, just say one little thing about parties helping fight poverty and she acts like I was arguing to bring back slavery."

Byron smirks. "I guess she's old-fashioned enough to think that the last thing somebody living in a cardboard box needs is a party."

Georgiana rolls her eyes. "Um-duh, Byron. I didn't mean throw *them* a party. I meant as a fundraiser. Gees Louise, everybody does stuff like that. It's called charity."

Which, of course, is what she told Dr Kilpatiky. Not that that cut any ice with the nose-twitcher. The woman single-handedly redefines the meaning of "party pooper". Dr Kilpatiky said that charity isn't an effective weapon against poverty because it treats the symptom, not the cause. "You might as well put a Band-Aid on a bullet wound," said Dr Kilpatiky.

"Like all of a sudden she's what's his name?" gripes Georgiana. "That Communist. The one with the beard."

"Castro?" guesses Asher.

"No, the other one."

Will tries Che Guevara.

"No." Georgiana shakes her head. "The one we did in history last year. He wrote that thing."

"Are we talking about Karl Marx?" asks Byron.

"That's him!" Georgiana snaps her fingers. "All of a sudden she's Karl Marx."

This is a comparison that would surprise both Mr Marx and Dr Kilpatiky, but the only one around the pool who disagrees is Byron. "More like Stalin, really. She who must be obeyed or it's off to the Gulag."

Marigold has been quiet throughout these tales of woe and injustice, but now she says, "Well, she is the principal. I mean, it is her job to enforce the rules." Marigold, of course, has had her own difficulties with Dr Kilpatiky and charity but she believes in being reasonable and fair. She also doesn't like to dwell on unpleasant or upsetting things. What you don't talk about doesn't really exist. That's what Marigold thinks.

"And anyway, it doesn't matter, does it?" Georgiana

gazes at the strip of ocean on the horizon as if she will never see it again, and effortlessly returns to the beginning of this conversation. "Even if Dr Kilpatiky gave birth to twin cows, it still wouldn't make up for summer being over. I mean, seriously? How are you supposed to have a life when you have to go to school every day? It is such a drag."

"It beats working at McDonald's," says Byron.

Will whoops with derision. "How would you know, Locke? You've never been in a McDonald's in your life." As it happens, Will, who is hypoglycemic and will eat just about anything that can be considered edible, is the only one here who has.

"And?" Byron raises an inquisitive eyebrow. "I've walked by dozens of them. Hundreds of times. Smile, scoop. Smile, box. As jobs go, Lundquist, it's not exactly the great challenge of our times."

Georgiana peers at Will over the top of her sunglasses. "Yeah, but I'm not going to wind up scooping fries in McDonald's, am I, Willem? That chapter is not in the book of my life."

"You don't know," says Asher. "You might if you don't go to school." There are times when he sounds so much like his father, he might have been cloned from him. "Especially if you don't do well." The most important

29

thing in life is to get ahead, and the way to do that is through hard work, ambition and being better than everyone else. That's what Asher thinks.

Georgiana makes a not-again face. "Please. Spare me the lecture on the joys of education."

Will takes the damp towel hanging over the arm of his lounger and throws it at Asher. "From the mouths of anal-retentive, over-achievers…"

"I'm just saying," says Asher.

He throws the towel back at Will, but it lands on Dunkin.

Dunkin doesn't notice.

Chapter Three
Marigold Tries Reason

Mrs Mahoney finishes packing her briefcase, shuts it and picks up her bag. This was the last day of the first week of classes, and it's been a long and stressful one. The community service placements were handed out this morning, and it seems Mrs Mahoney was right when she suggested that Dr Kilpatiky's change would be greeted with less celebration than an outbreak of skin fungus. People who are used to getting their own way seldom shrug philosophically when they don't. They carp and grumble. They follow you down the corridor defining the word "unfair" for you, since you clearly have no idea what it means. They interrupt conversations you're having with other teachers to explain their human rights. Mrs Mahoney is looking forward to getting home. Which is why when she hears a knock her immediate impulse is to duck under the desk. "Yes?" Mrs Mahoney holds her breath as the door slowly opens.

"Mrs Mahoney?" Marigold Liotta appears in the opening, smiling like good news. Smart, motivated, outgoing, conscientious, and always pleasant and upbeat, Marigold is a favourite with the staff of Shell Harbour High. Indeed, ever since kindergarten, Marigold's report cards have always included the information that it was a real pleasure to have her in the class. Mrs Mahoney starts to breathe again. Golf clubs and caviar aside, if more students were like Marigold Liotta, fewer teachers would quit because of pressure and stress.

Marigold steps into the room. "I was wondering if maybe I could talk to you for a minute?" If sunshine were a teenage girl, this is definitely the teenage girl it would be. "I mean, if you're not real busy."

"I was just leaving," says Mrs Mahoney. "Why don't you walk me to my car and we can talk on the way?"

"Oh, that'd be great." Marigold makes it sound as if this was exactly what she wanted. Still smiling, she waits for Mrs Mahoney to turn off the lights and lock the door.

"I hope you don't already have a problem this term," says Mrs Mahoney as they walk down the hall.

"Oh no, not a real problem." Beside all her other virtues, Marigold is not in the running for Drama Queen of the Year – unlike many of the teenagers Mrs Mahoney has known. "More like a minor glitch."

The "minor glitch" has to do with the new system for community service placements.

"I'm very in favour of innovation and not doing things a certain way just because that's the way it's always been done," explains Marigold. "And I think using a computer program is really cool. I mean, this is the twenty-first century. Why have all this technology if we don't use it? But in my case I really don't think the computer's made the right choice."

"Even computers can make mistakes." There has been one instance already of it doing just that. Mrs Mahoney laughs. "Don't tell me it has you coaching football."

Marigold joins in the laughter. "Oh no, nothing like that. It's just that I really believe my old placement makes much better use of my talents and interests."

Mrs Mahoney shakes her head. Regretfully. "I'm afraid I can't help you then, Marigold. If you were given something you're obviously not suited to we could get you another placement, but if it's just that you don't like what it gave you, it's out of my hands."

They cross the central foyer, empty as a ghost town. Their footsteps echo.

Marigold continues to radiate good cheer. "Well, whose hands is it in?"

Mrs Mahoney glances towards the principal's office. "That would be Dr Kilpatiky. She's the only one with the authority to make a change based merely on personal preference."

Marigold stops so suddenly that Mrs Mahoney takes a few more steps before she realizes she's walking alone and looks back.

"I guess I'll have to talk to Dr Kilpatiky then." Marigold waves cheerfully if dismissively. "Have a good night, Mrs Mahoney. And thanks for your help." She turns away.

Marigold continues to smile as she makes her way to the principal's office, though not because the prospect of talking to Dr Kilpatiky makes her happy. Her last serious discussion with Dr Kilpatiky is still vivid in her mind, the one in which the principal accused her of acting like Marie Antoinette – a comparison Marigold found a little harsh.

The office staff have already left for the day, but the principal's door is open. Marigold knocks. "Dr Kilpatiky? Can I talk to you for a minute?" Marigold still looks as if this is something she's looking forward to.

One of the reasons why Marigold acts more like the goodwill ambassador from the planet Perfect than a normal adolescent from the dark and dangerous kingdom of Teen is that she believes that life is what you make it. Not in the sense that you can have anything you want if you work extremely hard and go to Harvard, as Asher does. In the sense that if you think and act as if everything is good, then it will be. The glass is always half full – and never with anything unpleasant. Things may be bad right now, but it's all going to be just fine very soon. There is nothing so wrong that wishing can't make it right; nothing so impossible that persistence can't make it happen.

Although this doesn't seem to be a philosophy that Dr Kilpatiky shares.

"No, Marigold, I'm sorry," says the principal when Marigold has finished explaining what she wants. "I'm afraid we can't change your placement on a whim."

"But it's not a whim, Dr Kilpatiky." If Marigold were a summer day there still wouldn't be a cloud in the sky. "Literature is one of my major passions and my last placement was at the library, so that was perfect for me. I really learned a lot, and I don't want to sound like I'm waving my own flag or anything, but they kept telling me what an asset I was. Only, this term, with this new system, the computer gave me a tutoring programme. In Half Hollow. You know, for kids who are innumerate and practically illiterate? I mean, not only is that really a job for qualified teachers, I think you'd agree that it's a waste of my abilities and talents."

Dr Kilpatiky, however, wouldn't agree. She repeats that she is sorry. "I'm sure you were a valuable asset to the library, Marigold, but I don't really consider shelving books a specialist skill. If, for example, you were a basketball prodigy and wanted to swap your placement for coaching kids hoping for a college scholarship, I would certainly consider that."

"Books are just as important as basketball, you know." Marigold continues to look as if this conversation is going the way she planned. "And it's not just shelving, Dr Kilpatiky, it's my knowledge of both fiction and non-fiction, as well. It's very extensive. I help people."

"Well, now you can help the students in the tutoring programme." Dr Kilpatiky's nose twitches involuntarily. "As you said, many of the children who attend are functionally illiterate. Which means that someone with a major passion for literature is exactly what they need to inspire and encourage them." Her smile is an afterthought. "You can be a role model."

"I don't want to argue with you, Dr Kilpatiky." In fact, Marigold doesn't like arguing with anyone. Ever. "But I do think they need something much more basic." She gives a light, non-argumentative laugh. "You know, Richard Scarry, not Richard Ford. Or phonics. That's it. They need someone who knows phonics."

"I appreciate that, ideally, this is a job for qualified teachers, but I'm afraid there isn't any funding for that. Everyone who works in the programme at Half Hollow is a volunteer."

The summer sky begins to darken ever so slightly. "But that doesn't mean I should be one of them." You might think that Marigold is so determined to get her old placement back because her friends won't be able to visit her at the tutoring programme as they did at the library, but that isn't actually why. There are, in fact, two reasons why she doesn't want to change. The first is that Marigold doesn't really want to deal with children. She has one sister, eight years older, who lives in Australia, which means that the only time she's ever been around little kids was when she was one. The second is that Marigold really doesn't like anything unpleasant or depressing. She wants the world and everything in it to be bright, shining and pleasant, if not actually filled with music and joy. She has never been to Half Hollow but she knows that, compared to Shell Harbour, it is virtually a slum. Busted. Depressing. Children from a busted, depressing slum aren't going to be bright, shining, pleasant or filled with music and joy. What they're likely to be is dysfunctional, difficult and miserable. "I've never taught anyone to read, Dr Kilpatiky. So sending me there just isn't the best deployment of resources."

The principal's nose twitches some more. "This isn't a career we're talking about here, Marigold; it's a few hours of community service. I'm sure the library will survive without your input. Just as I'm certain that the tutoring programme will benefit from it." She pushes back her chair and gets to her feet.

Marigold stays seated. "But Dr Kilpatiky—"

Dr Kilpatiky is already at the office door. "Marigold, I do have some other things to do before I can go home…"

With less speed than a slow loris moving from one tree to the next, Marigold stands up and crosses the room. "I really think this is a big mistake," she says as at last she reaches the door.

"I know you do," says Dr Kilpatiky. "And if it's the end of civilization as we know it, you can most certainly blame me."

Chapter Four
Georgiana Grumbles

Georgiana and Will sit at a window table of the Bay Cafe, recovering from the traumas of the first full week of school – though the way Will eats it is more like he's refuelling than recovering.

From the expression on Georgiana's face as she watches him chomp on his sandwich you might think that what he's actually doing is dismembering a very small bird with his bare hands – a parakeet, or, possibly, a wren – and tossing the tiny feet onto the table.

"It's nice to see your appetite hasn't been affected," says Georgiana.

Will gazes at her over his seeded bun. "By what?"

"By what?" Georgiana tilts her head to one side and frowns. "I'm sorry. Was I dreaming? I thought today was the day the community placements were handed out."

"Yeah. And?" Will wipes ketchup from his mouth

with his napkin. "It's not like we're being sent into combat." He spears a few fries with his fork. "We always do community service. We just didn't get to pick for ourselves this year, that's all." Which apparently bothers him about as much as not getting to choose the day's weather.

Georgiana stirs her coffee as if she's trying to dig a hole in the bottom of the cup. "I'm glad it was such a non-event for you, Willem. But, personally, I feel like I've been ambushed. I can't believe Dr Killjoy's done this to me."

"To *you*?" Will's voice is slightly muffled because his mouth is filled with fried potato. "What'd she do to you?"

"What do you mean, what'd she do?" There is nothing muffled about Georgiana's voice. It rings through the cafe like a very large bell. "You know what she did. She deliberately gave me a placement she knew I wouldn't want."

"What are you talking about?" Many people believe the world is manipulated by conspiracies and ulterior motives, but Will isn't one of them. His is an easy-going nature. If Will had a motto, it would probably be "whatever". "Why would she do that?"

"Why?" Georgiana, however, is a look-under-the-bed-and-check-the-closet kind of person, whose nature is as easy-going as an arctic winter. "Because of that stupid debate, that's why. She hasn't forgotten it, and she hasn't forgiven me, either. She wants me to pay." Georgiana's spoon clatters to the table. "In blood, preferably."

"Aw, come on, George. You can't be serious. Dr Kilpatiky's got a lot more to do than lie awake at night coming up with ways to punish you." Will's smile is less disarming than usual because of the piece of lettuce lodged in his teeth. "And besides, she didn't give you the placement. The computer did. It was random. Luck of the draw. You know, like being hit by a chunk of space debris or winning the lottery."

Georgiana's lips remain as flat as a meat cleaver. "You really believe that?" It's clear from Georgiana's tone that she's starting to wonder if Will is as clever as she's always thought. "That's what she wants us to think. But I know her. She watched me like a surveillance camera all last year—" She breaks off suddenly, slapping the table so hard that coffee sloshes out of its cup. "Good God! Now it's all making a really horrible kind of sense." She leans forward. Earnestly. "You know what I just remembered?"

Will, who is definitely clever enough to spot a rhetorical question when he sees one, says nothing.

"Last spring? Right before school ended? She actually asked me what my community placement was!" Georgiana's eyes shine with righteous triumph. "What do you think of that? You still think this is just a coincidence? She came right out and asked me! She was hatching this plot even then."

Will is beginning to wish he'd said no when Georgiana invited him to stop for a bite on the way home. They've been friends since sixth grade; he knows her well enough to understand that there is nothing so small that she can't turn it into an earth-shaking event. And it's always an earth-shaking event aimed at her. In the world of Georgiana Shiller, it never simply rains, it's always a tropical storm especially created to ruin her new shoes. Normally, Will doesn't mind the drama and emotion – he has two sisters and plays basketball: drama and emotion are part of his life – but this afternoon what he really wanted was to chill out, not hot up. He also suspects that the moment is coming when he gets some of the blame. It's what his sisters always do. So he doesn't wave his fork at her and say, *And? Your point is? She's the head honcho – she's always asking stuff like that. She has to prove that she's interested in all her students.* Which is what he would like to do. Instead, he tries to look sympathetic and says, "You mean, like, out of the blue, for no good reason she asked you what your placement was?"

"Yes! Out of the blue! Pointlessly!" The muffin Georgiana isn't eating jumps as she slams her hands down on the table again. "Can you believe it? Apropos to absolutely nothing, Will! Like she'd been festering about it for months and finally pounced!"

He swallows the last fry. He should have gotten onion rings as well. "You mean you were just walking along and all of a sudden Dr Kilpatiky came charging down the corridor and demanded to know what you were doing for community service?"

"Pretty much an instant replay," says Georgiana.

Will rattles the ice in his glass of soda. He isn't sure he believes her. Not that Georgiana lies exactly, but she does have a way of making reality agree with what she thinks, rather than getting what she thinks to agree with reality. As it happens, he is right to be sceptical. The only similarity between what he described and what actually happened is that Georgiana and Dr Kilpatiky are in both versions. "I still don't see how that means she had anything to do with you getting the nursing home. And even if she could've fixed it, how would she know you'd hate it so much? If you ask me, it's a pretty cushy number."

"Oh, really?" Georgiana's smile is almost as sweet as vinegar. "Well, I'd give anything to do what you're doing. At least yours is fun."

"No, you wouldn't, and no, it isn't. I'm doing maintenance work at the park." Georgiana has never trimmed anything except her nails. "The only reason you even know what a lawnmower looks like is because your gardener uses one."

"So? It's not rocket science. You just sit on it and go. And mowing lawns is a lot better than working in an old people's home."

"No, it isn't," says Will. "It's just boring manual labour. And I'll be out there, shovelling walkways in the snow. At least yours is indoors."

"So is jail."

"Anyway, I don't see what's so bad about working in the home," Will goes on. "Besides being warm and dry, you may have a good time. Old people can be really interesting and cool. Look at Keith Richards."

"Who?"

"He's a famous rock guitarist. He's one of the coolest dudes on the planet. My grandad has all his albums."

Georgiana sighs. Patience isn't her strongest quality. "Will, Keith Whateverhisnameis isn't going to be at St Joan's with his guitar. It's just going to be full of regular old people who are all wrinkled and bent and dying." Georgiana squinches her nose in distaste. "I don't like death."

"You mean, unlike everybody else?" Will's smile is amused. "'Cause if you're under the impression that death's more popular than YouTube, George, I think you may be wrong about that."

Georgiana does know that few, if any, of us could be said to like the idea of death, but for her it's more of a phobia. She hates to think of anyone dying and closes her eyes whenever she passes a cemetery, a funeral parlour or a funeral procession. In fact, death frightens Georgiana so much that she has never had a pet, not so much as a goldfish; she couldn't face finding even something that small floating at the top of its bowl, its empty eyes staring at the ceiling. All of which makes the thought of working in a place where the residents have no future to look forward to but the grave particularly unappealing. Georgiana thinks of nursing homes as death's waiting rooms. What if someone actually dies while she's with them? What then?

"I don't know why I couldn't stay where I was," grumbles Georgiana. "I told Dr Killjoy I like dogs." Which is exactly what she did tell the principal.

This is how Dr Kilpatiky really discovered what Georgiana's community service placement was. It happened by chance one Saturday. Dr Kilpatiky was weeding the flower-bed in front of her house when Georgiana walked by with a dog named Desmond. The principal had her back to the street and didn't see them, but Desmond saw her cat, perched on the railing of the porch. Desmond feels about cats the way sharks feel about fresh blood. After they got the cat out of the tree and Desmond out of the hydrangeas, Dr Kilpatiky started talking about pets, and Georgiana explained that Desmond doesn't belong to her, he's a rescue dog at the animal shelter and she was just taking him for a walk. Dr Kilpatiky then politely asked her how she got involved in that. "I'm working there for my community service placement," said Georgiana. "I really like dogs."

"So get a dog if you like them so much," says the ever-practical Will.

Georgiana glowers. He really can be exasperating. She wonders if he does it on purpose. "I don't want a dog, Will. I just want to help them. They're much easier than old people." And usually much more attractive. "I really don't think I can be around old people. Not for more than a couple of minutes. They really creep me out. They're so fragile. Like soap bubbles. And they fall down." She stares at the empty air behind him. "They're always falling down."

"*Always?*" Will laughs. "I don't think that's true. I think some of them manage to walk a few feet without landing on the sidewalk."

Georgiana shakes her head. "No, you're wrong. One minute they're fine, and the next thing you know they're dead. They just fall down dead."

"Oh, come on, get real here." Will is still laughing. "Anybody can fall down dead. You don't have to be ancient for that to happen. Young people die all the time. What about that football player?"

"Football?" She looks as if she'd like to throw a football at him. "How did we get onto that?"

"All I'm saying is I think you're blowing this way out of proportion. Anyway, I bet not everybody at this place is there because they're old."

"Oh no?" Maybe not a football. Maybe a boulder. "Then why are they there? They got lost going to their wrestling class?"

Although his nose isn't twitching, Will gives her a look very similar to the one Dr Kilpatiky gave her during the poverty debate. "You didn't read up on this place, did you?"

"What for?" Georgiana is not a girl to take two steps when one will do. "I know what a nursing home is."

"Apparently you don't."

Georgiana laughs but not because she's amused. "And you do?"

"Well, more than you do. My sister did her community service at Ocean View. You know, that big place out by the water? Lucy said it's majorly awesome." The grounds are like a private park with fountains, lakes and gardens; the amenities include a gym, beauty parlour, indoor pool and tennis court; every room has a flat-screen TV. "And lots of the residents there were convalescing from operations or getting some kind of therapy. She said there was even a bunch of kids and teens. She said most of them were having a ball."

"Yeah, I'm sure they were. The zombie ball. Warm milk and the Beatles' greatest hits."

"I'm serious. And in case you want to know, they don't even call them nursing homes any more. They call them nursing centres."

Georgiana being Georgiana, she is not convinced. A skunk by any other name, is still a skunk. "And what'd she have to do there? I bet she had to push old people around in their wheelchairs and stuff like that."

"Not Lucy. She played the violin."

Georgiana's first thought, of course, is that she doesn't play the violin. Or anything else except the radio and the stereo. Her second is, "They let her do that?"

"They practically begged her. They had concerts every Sunday, and on special occasions like Christmas and Easter. She said it was fun."

"Oh, I'm so sure." Fun. Fun is definitely not something Georgiana associates with people who are about to fall over and die.

"I'm just telling you what Lucy said."

Georgiana's frown is thoughtful. "And you think St Joan's will be like that? With concerts?"

"What am I now, psychic? I don't know if it will or not. But you can't tell what something's going to be like till you do it. St Joan's may not be as bad as you think."

"Or it could be worse." Georgiana is nothing if not consistent.

Will takes a deep breath. Georgiana also doesn't respond well to criticism. "For the love of cheese, George, you know, it wouldn't hurt you to be a little more like Marigold."

"You have to be kidding me! Little Miss Sunshine?" Georgiana, of course, couldn't be less like Marigold if they belonged to different species. Marigold always looks for the good; Georgiana has X-ray vision when it comes to seeing the bad. "Don't get me wrong, Will, I love Marigold. She's great. But you know... Sometimes it's like she's in a musical and is about to burst into song."

"That would be *Singin' in the Rain*," says Will. "But what I meant was that you could try to be a little positive." Just to break the routine. "Marigold doesn't like her placement, either, but you don't see her winding herself up about it. She just makes the best of it. I mean, it's not like you're going to be there every day. It's just an hour every week or two."

Georgiana purses her lips. "An hour can be a long time if you're at the dentist."

"And a short time at a party," counters Will.

"St Joan's is not a party. That I'm sure of. And no matter what they call it, there's still going to be lots of old people there. They're going to be in the majority."

Will isn't the type of person to bang his head on the table, but for a second he is tempted. He's captain of the basketball team and good at strategy – good enough to know when to retreat. So instead of continuing the argument – or banging his head against the checkered tablecloth – he points to her untouched muffin. "Are you going to eat that or what?"

"Don't tell me you're still hungry."

"Well, if you don't want it, I'd hate to see it go to waste…"

"You mean, unlike my breath," says Georgiana, and shoves it towards him with so much force that it might be a hockey puck and Will the goal.

Chapter Five
Asher Attempts Negotiation

"Oh, come on, Claudie," pleads Asher. "Please? For *me*?"

She should have known when he offered her a ride home – disrupting his afternoon schedule – that he wanted something. Asher always has an angle.

"No." From the way Claudelia shakes her head it's clear that if they weren't sitting in his car and there were a door between them she'd slam it shut. "I won't do it. And that's as final as the end of the world."

Asher's expression is so guileless he'd make a saint look shifty. "But why not?"

"Because it's a stupid idea, that's why not."

"I'd do it for you."

Claudelia smirks. "No, you wouldn't."

He decides not to get into that argument. They've been officially going out together for almost a year. There may be too many precedents for him to win it. Asher isn't a mean or ungenerous person, but he is a numero-uno kind of guy.

"It's not a stupid idea," he insists. "It's sound as Fort Knox. I have the technology. Even you won't be able to tell the difference between the printouts." Asher is known for his smile, as charming as a magic spell. "I swear, Claudie. They'll be identical twins."

Claudelia scowls. Today Asher's smile isn't charming her. "Except the names will be changed."

He winks. "To protect the innocent."

Which, of course, is Asher.

"But it's not going to protect the innocent," says Claudelia. "It's going to hang the guilty."

"No, it isn't. I'm telling you, they won't be able to tell it didn't come from the school. They'll just think there was some glitch in the system. That kind of thing happens all the time. That's why firms like my dad's have an IT guy on the payroll."

"Asher." Claudelia puts her hands on his shoulders as if this will help him understand what she's trying to say. "They will find out. At some point, someone's going to look in their file or whatever and wonder how Asher Grossman turned into Claudelia Gillen."

"Maybe," he concedes. "Maybe there's a tiny

subatomic-particle kind of chance that that'll happen. But even if it does, it'll be too late by then. Nobody's going to bother switching us around again. It'll be a *que será, será* situation."

"No, it won't, because it's not going to happen. I'm not getting involved in one of your great ideas. What about Will? At least he's a guy."

Asher shakes his head. "Will won't do it. He likes raking leaves." This is only half of the truth. The other half is that Claudelia isn't the only one who doesn't want to get involved in one of Asher's great ideas. Will got in trouble for letting Asher use Dunkin in his Halloween costume. "But it's not like we're doing anything wrong," insists Asher. "Fair's fair, Claudie. You got my placement. We're just putting things back the way they should be."

"Oh, *your* placement. I'm sorry." She sounds as sorry as a drone bomber. "I guess I forgot you owned it. I guess you must have the deed in your safe."

Asher pretends to laugh. Hahaha. "You know what I mean. My dad set that placement up. Mayor Duggin did it as a special favour." Working in the mayor's office may not be an internship in DC, but it's a step in the right direction. Asher's father thinks he should consider a career in politics. It's what he would do, if he had his life to live over. "It's part of my professional strategy."

Just about everything Asher does – the classes he takes, the grades he gets, his hobbies, interests and extracurricular activities – are part of his "professional strategy". "Working in the mayor's office is going to look a lot more impressive for law school than working in the community centre."

"Not if you wanted to work for the ACLU, it wouldn't."

"But I don't want to work for the ACLU. Corporate law, that's what I want."

Claudelia sighs. Two of the things she likes about Asher are that he is ambitious and he is focused. Everyone else, including herself, is about as focused and ambitious as a dust mote. There are times, however, when they are also two of the things she likes least about him. This is one of those times. "Your dad must know someone high up in the school system. Couldn't he get your placement changed?"

The simple answer to this question is: yes, of course he could. Albert Grossman knows someone high up in every system in the country – bankers, businessmen, generals, administrators, judges, politicians. In this instance, he is a friend of the superintendent of schools.

"I don't want to bother him with this." One of the things Asher likes about Claudelia is that, unlike Georgiana (who's a major drama queen) and Marigold (who could find something good to say if they were all on a sinking ship in an ice storm), she's so logical. Though today it's a quality he's finding annoying. "He's really busy right now."

Claudelia makes an um-duh face. "Oh, please. That's like saying water is wet. Your dad's always busy. He probably works in his sleep."

He would, if he slept more than a few hours a night.

"Which is why I don't want to go to him with something this dumb. I want to handle it myself."

Handling things himself has been a recurring topic of conversation between Asher and his father lately. Albert Grossman has high expectations of his son. Indeed, when Asher talks about "my professional strategy" he really means his father's, planned almost as soon as Asher was born. Albert Grossman is extremely successful, but Asher is going to be more extremely successful – perhaps even President (or, at the very least, in the Cabinet or Senate). Which is why he's decided Asher needs to take more responsibility for himself. Act with the maturity and dignity of his calling. Dr Kilpatiky wasn't the only one disappointed by Asher's choice of Halloween costume, though for different reasons. It didn't bother Albert that his son bought some second-hand clothes in the charity shop (washed three times then dry-cleaned) and tied a bandana around Dunkin's neck. Impersonating the much less fortunate didn't offend his sense of moral rightness. Albert Grossman is a lawyer, not a spiritual leader. What bothered him was that Asher misjudged what the principal's reaction would be. He should have known better. In the future, that kind of mistake could cost him an election.

"So maybe you should get Byron to help you." Claudelia laughs. "He's the computer wizard. Maybe he can hack into the school's system for you. Change the placement at source." Claudelia is joking.

But Asher isn't. "He won't do it." She should have known he'd already asked Byron. Asher is nothing if not efficient. "He thinks he'll be arrested."

She shrugs. "Then I guess you're going to be working at the community centre."

Asher doesn't want to work at the community centre. He's never actually been in a community centre, of course, but he has no trouble picturing it. There will be fluorescent lighting, fourth-hand furniture and one of those gigantic coffee urns that no one ever washes properly. The place will be filled with do-gooders being chirpy and wearing cheap clothes, middle-aged women doing Pilates and T'ai Chi, and kids who can't read or have nowhere else to go. With poor people; people who don't try hard enough or work hard enough to succeed. People who don't want to work, don't want to succeed; who just want handouts. People things happen to, not people who make things happen. His father wouldn't want him to work in the community centre, either. What does that have to do with corporate law? With the people who do make things happen? His father will be disappointed in him. He'll think that it's Asher's fault; that he didn't make enough of an effort; that this is what he gets for being immature and annoying Dr Kilpatiky. The last thing Asher wants is to disappoint his father.

"You never know." Claudelia smiles like a pat on the shoulder. "Maybe the centre won't be that bad."

"Oh, it will be that bad, that's guaranteed," says Asher. "It's in Queen's Park, Claude. Queen's Park is so busted it's like the graveyard of hope."

Claudelia suggests that that might be why they have a community centre. "You know, because people need help?"

"It used to be a supermarket. A small one." Asher says this as if it's conclusive proof of just how bad the placement is going to be. "I checked it out online."

Of course he did. Asher wouldn't buy a ballpoint pen without checking it out online first.

"And that means what?" asks Claudelia. "It was a

supermarket, not an abattoir. An abattoir could have some really bad vibes from all that blood and screaming animals. But a grocery store? What's the problem? You're afraid of finding an expired can of peas?"

"You know, you could be a little more sympathetic," says Asher. "This is really hard for me."

"And you could be a little more like Marigold," says Claudelia.

Even Asher can't help but smile at that. "You mean grow my hair and wear short skirts?"

Claudelia nods. "And nail polish. Colour-coordinated to match what you're wearing. And fake lashes."

"OK, I can do the polish, but I draw the line at the eyelashes. I don't know how she sees through those things, they're like awnings. One day they're going to fall into her soup and she's going to choke to death."

"Seriously, though," says Claudelia when they stop laughing. "I think you should. Not the skirts, but her attitude. She doesn't want to teach reading any more than you want to help out at the community centre, but she's not acting like it's the biggest tragedy anyone's ever experienced in the history of civilization. She's just making the best of it." This time Claudelia does pat him on the shoulder. "I know this is hard for you, Ash, but you're not making it any easier."

"Yeah, but it's different for Marigold," argues Asher. "It doesn't really matter to her what she does."

It is different for Marigold. She gets good grades without staying up till three in the morning and falling asleep over her homework. She doesn't have to be the best at everything she does; she's happy enough to be good. She has no interest in being even a minor town official, never mind President of the United States.

"You mean because she's not an obsessive workaholic?"

"No, Claudelia, that isn't what I mean." Asher is starting to feel as if he's dealing with a difficult witness. "Because she thinks life's some kind of buffet. You try a little of this and a little of that, and if you wanted salmon but they only have herring, you have herring. She doesn't have a career strategy like mine."

"Asher," says Claudelia, "even Napoleon Bonaparte didn't have a career strategy like yours."

Asher doesn't smile this time.

"And, anyway," she continues, "just because you're focused doesn't mean you can't float with the tide now and then. Give yourself a break." *And everyone else*, she thinks.

"I have a goal trajectory," says Asher. "You don't float when you have a goal trajectory. That's like trying to get to Istanbul by getting on the first plane you see and hoping that's where it's going."

"I just think that you shouldn't go into this expecting the worst."

"I'm not. I don't think it's going to be like a high-security prison in Texas. That would be the worst. Or in South America. A high-security prison in South America, that would definitely be the pits." Asher watches a dog trot across the road. "What I think it's going to be is boring. Probably irritating, too. And I know for sure that it's going to be pointless."

"For your goal trajectory."

"For everything. It's not going to be any use to me, but it's no use to these losers, either. Like my dad always says, you can't help people who won't help themselves."

Claudelia is saved from having to argue any more by the alarm on Asher's phone going off.

"I have to get a move on," says Asher, "or I'll be late for my fencing class."

"Right." She leans over and kisses his cheek. "See you tomorrow."

Asher broods about the placement on and off for the rest of the day. His father is in Washington doing something very important. Should he call him and ask for his help? He was told not to. That's how important whatever his father's doing is. He was told that if there's an emergency he should call Albert's assistant and that she would pass on the message. Unless Asher's arrested; then he can call his father directly. So maybe he shouldn't bother his dad. The housekeeper's out for the night, so Asher blitzes himself a pizza in the microwave and sits in front of the TV in his room to eat it. His father's probably in a meeting. Sometimes his meetings go on for days. At ten o'clock, Asher finally breaks down and decides to call. Then imagines his father's face, serious and disappointed. This is not taking responsibility. This is not handling things himself.

He disconnects before it starts to ring.

Chapter Six

Marigold Starts Weaving a Tangled Web

Marigold's mother is in a good mood this morning. This is as big a relief to Marigold as not seeing any white people riding through their territory would have been to the Lakota two or three hundred years ago. Eveline Liotta is delicate. She has a sensitive nature and is easily stressed out. She spends a lot of time in bed.

Her mother is another reason why Marigold acts more like the goodwill ambassador from the planet Perfect than a normal, moody teenager. Living with Eveline is like living in the shadow of an active volcano. There is nothing that can't upset her (including absolutely nothing). She may hide it from the outside world, but her family knows that her cheerfulness is as fragile as a glass ball in a hurricane. She can lose her temper over the smallest things – the wrong look, the wrong greeting, a dish left on the table, a bar of soap left in a sink. She can suddenly burst into tears because the mail is late or she's spilled something on her blouse or it happens to be Tuesday and raining. She can get one of her migraines because the washing machine broke or her lunch plans were cancelled. Life – and every person and every thing in it – is always disappointing her. Her husband and her daughters are either pitted against her or letting her down. No matter what they do, it's never enough. No matter what they give her, they should have given her something else. No matter what they say, they should probably have kept their mouths shut. Marigold's father suffers the most. If the Liottas' marriage had a historical equivalent it would be the Hundred Years War (with Mr and Mrs Liotta on opposite sides, of course). The only day when they don't have a fight is the day when they don't see each other. Which is the reason Marigold doesn't like to argue. She gets enough of that at home.

Marigold's father spends a lot of time working – either in the office, or out with a client, or away on business. Since Marigold doesn't have the advantage of somewhere else to be, she tries hard to keep a low profile and do nothing to upset her mother. And to always pretend – even after the worst tantrum, argument or tears – that nothing is wrong. Just as her mother does.

This morning, however, Mrs Liotta is genuinely

happy. Marigold can tell the difference. She's making pancakes and laughing along with the audience on the breakfast show she watches. Marigold glances out the window as she sits down. Her father's car is in the driveway. She wasn't woken up by fighting, so that must be a good sign.

Mrs Liotta puts a plate in front of Marigold, then takes the seat across from her. "You're working in the library this afternoon, aren't you?" she asks. "Would you like me to pick you up?"

"Thanks, but that's OK." Marigold hasn't told her mother that she is no longer working at the library because she knows that her mother won't like the idea of her volunteering in Half Hollow any more than she does. Possibly less. Half Hollow is not her mother's kind of town; she has heard her joke with her friends that the only professionals who live there are the police. "It's not that far. And anyway someone usually gives me a ride home."

"You could take my car if you want. I don't really need it today."

Her mother usually doesn't like anyone using her things. Especially her car. Marigold's sister, Rose, once borrowed it without permission and backed it into a wall, an event that sent her mother to bed for a week.

She is in a really good mood if she's offering her the car. Marigold darts little glances around the room, looking for flowers. And then she notices the pin her mother's wearing, a silver angel holding a diamond that Marigold's never seen before. Eveline Liotta loves both angels and diamonds. It must be a peace offering.

"Thanks, but I'll be fine, Mom." And here is something else Marigold hasn't told her mother. Marigold has shied away from driving since May, when she hit a pigeon. Even Marigold couldn't find anything positive about that, especially not from the pigeon's point of view. She felt so guilty (even though it was really the pigeon who hit her) that she thought she might have nightmares about it for the rest of her life. "And anyway, you might need it after all."

"Might need what?"

They both look up as Marigold's father strides into the room, wearing his usual suit and tie, his briefcase in one hand. He's in a good mood, too.

"How are my girls this morning?" He kisses first one, then the other, but puts up a hand when his wife jumps up to get him a plate. "Sorry, darling, I'd love to hang out with you two, but there's no time. Forgot I have an early meeting. Just coffee to go." He fills his insulated mug and kisses them both goodbye.

As the front door shuts behind him Marigold's mother picks up her own mug. "Well, call me if you change your mind about the ride, honey. I'm having lunch with Meg and Jessica, but other than that I have no plans."

Marigold says that she will.

Over lunch Asher tries to commiserate with Marigold about her first day at her new service placement. "It's like we're in a battle and you're the first one over the hill," says Asher. "I don't start mine till Saturday." An event he's looking forward to about as much as his own funeral.

Marigold pretends to look almost puzzled by his sympathy. "It really doesn't bother me, Ash." By now, she's almost managed to convince herself that this is true. "Actually, I'm kind of looking forward to it." Instead of sinking into a Slough of Despond because Dr Kilpatiky is as immune to reason as a charging rhino, Marigold is trying to think of the tutoring as a new and exciting learning experience for her as well as her student. "It's not my first choice. We all know that. I'd much rather hang out with books than challenged children. But what can you do? It's what I got. I figure I have to make the best of it or I'll just make it worse." She doesn't see the look Claudelia gives Asher, or the look that Will gives Georgiana. "And, you know, it could be super interesting." She beams over her sandwich like the sun over a hill. "It's important to step outside your comfort zone now and then. I think it'll help me grow as a person."

If anyone else talked like a self-help book, the girls would roll their eyes and the boys would groan or pretend to throw up. But they don't; they all look at their lunches and nod. Except for Georgiana (who also didn't see the look Will gave her).

"Yeah, but I don't want to make the best of it," says Georgiana. "I want it to be good to begin with."

Marigold smiles. Sadly but wisely. "Only life isn't like that, George. You have to think of everything as an opportunity. You can't always get what you want."

"I don't see why not," says Georgiana.

"Me neither," says Asher.

Patience shuffles beside sadness and wisdom in Marigold's smile. "I think because sometimes what you want isn't really what you should have. Things always work out for the best."

"No, they don't," says Georgiana.

"Maybe they do if you have a good lawyer," says Asher.

Byron gives Marigold a ride to Half Hollow.

"Shoot, man," laughs Byron. "The only time I've been

out this way was when I was going somewhere else and I got lost."

Marigold has never gone anywhere that would take her out this way, no matter how lost she was. "It's kind of like a treasure hunt, isn't it?" she says gamely. "We don't really know what we'll find when we get there. It'll be a surprise."

This is only true up to a point. The closer they get to the town the more what they can expect to find when they get there becomes fairly obvious. With every yard they travel, the smaller and older and more run-down the houses are; the more rusting cars and busted appliances decorate the porches and lawns; the more people stare at the late-model, candy-red sports car as if it's an alien spaceship. Until, eventually, the lush lawns and sprawling homes of Shell Harbour are so far away they really might be on a different planet. And not necessarily a friendly one.

"Better lock your door," advises Byron.

By the time they reach Half Hollow, even Marigold is feeling about as upbeat as one of those Irish ballads where the hero accidentally murders the only woman he will ever love and then throws himself in the river. Nor does their first glimpse of the town itself make either of them feel any better. When the nation was growing and industry was booming, Half Hollow was a thriving mill town where people came for jobs and a decent life. But now that the country's streets are paved not with gold but potholes and burger boxes, the mill is derelict and half the stores on Main Street are empty. Now it's a town that people leave. If they can.

The elementary school is at the top of a steep hill behind Main Street. It was built at the turn of the twentieth century, and the years have been no kinder to it than they've been to the rest of Half Hollow. In most towns, it would have been torn down decades ago and replaced with something modern, or turned into the local historical museum. But not in Half Hollow. Half Hollow has no money for new schools, and no one interested in visiting a museum about its history.

Byron pulls up in front of the dingy, brick building and peers dubiously through the windshield. "Man, it looks like something out of a horror movie."

"It makes me think of *Oliver Twist*," says Marigold.

He looks over at her. "You want me to wait for you?"

"Don't be ridiculous." Marigold would love for him to wait for her. She'd like it even better if he'd go in with her, and hold her hand. "You can't sit here for an hour and a half. People will think you're up to no good."

"You really think so?" If you ask Byron, this is the kind of place where everyone looks like they're up to no good. And probably are. What difference could one more sketchy-looking person make? He stares out at the road as if expecting the ground to suddenly open up and release an attack of ghouls. "But how will you get home if I don't wait?"

"No problem. I checked and there's a bus from Main Street. It'll get me home in no time." At least she hopes so.

Byron is still looking dubious. "A bus? You sure?" Why would there be a bus between Half Hollow and Shell Harbour? It's like having a bus between Beverly Hills and Last Ditch, Arkansas. "I really don't mind waiting. I have my phone. I have stuff to do."

"Don't be silly. The building isn't empty, Byron. There are people inside. I'll be fine." Marigold gets out of the car, waves cheerfully and marches up the concrete steps. The reinforced door is locked. She rings the bell, smiling at the camera on the security system. "Hello!" she chirps into the speaker. "I'm Marigold Liotta? I'm here for the volunteer programme." Someone buzzes her in.

The woman in charge of the tutoring is barely five feet tall and bone-thin with a cloud of grey hair and eyes like black stars. But, although she has the body of a child, she has the presence of a brigadier general. One in the middle of a war.

"Bonnie Kupferberg," she says, pumping Marigold's

hand. "I can't tell you how glad I am to meet you." She winks. "I've heard all about you from your Mrs Mahoney."

"Mrs Mahoney?"

"Don't look so shocked. This is a very demanding job you've volunteered for."

"Oh well, I didn't exact—"

"Enthusiasm only gets you so far in this game. I had to make sure you'd be up to it." She shakes her head; it's like watching the sky shift. "Many aren't, believe me. But Mrs Mahoney says you are. She says you're one of the best students in your class. And not just academically. She had nothing but good things to say."

"Oh well, I—"

"She says you're positive, intelligent, responsible, persevering and highly motivated."

"Oh, well I—"

"I tell you that's bang on the head of the nail of what we need here. A lot of the kids who come to us are about as motivated as mashed potatoes. They need a strong role model. Someone who doesn't just yack at them. Someone who can be an example to them. Can inspire them."

Having failed with her attempts at modesty, Marigold changes tack. "Oh, really?" she says. "I thought the kids here came because they wanted to. You know, because they need a little help."

"Oh, they need help, all right. But that doesn't mean that they want it or are going to ask for it. That's the last thing they're going to do." Bonnie Kupferberg's laugh rolls down the corridor like bricks. "One or two do. Because they're failing everything or they're going to be suspended if they don't shape up, so they cut a deal. And one or two come because they have nowhere else to go till their mothers can pick them up. But mainly these kids have to be dragooned into coming."

"Dragooned?"

"Practically shanghaied, really. We use every threat, bribe and form of coercion we can come up with."

Marigold says nothing to that. She has an image of children in chains.

"But you understand that we do that because this is so important. If we lose these kids now, in elementary, chances are we'll never get them back."

Marigold's laugh floats like dandelion fluff on a breeze. "I just thought I was helping with reading. I—"

"Oh you are, you are. That part's pretty straightforward. Mrs Mahoney has given you the basics on what to do, right?"

"Oh, yes, she—"

"Just don't get conned into actually doing the work. Show and explain, but don't do it." By now they are

striding down the hallway, the short legs of Bonnie Kupferberg setting a pace with which a jaguar would have
trouble keeping up. "But reading and maths are the keys
to the kingdom, aren't they? Without those skills what
do you have?"

"Nothing?" guesses Marigold.

"That's right. Bubkes. The giant zero."

Marigold was prepared for this placement being
boring and even depressing, but suddenly it's sounding
like the challenge of the century. "Well I hope I—"

"And Mrs Mahoney also says you are totally passion-
ate about books. She says you love literature the way
most teenagers love their iPads."

"Oh, I do. I used to work at the—"

"That is fantastic. Seriously. Because these kids –
these kids would rather watch cartoons in French with
bad reception than read a book. They'd probably be happier shearing sheep."

"Oh, I—" bleats Marigold.

"Here we are!" Bonnie stops in front of Room 21. "I've
given you Sadie Hawkle to tutor. She's nine, but she can't
read more than a picture book without help. And not
always that."

"Nine," repeats Marigold.

Bonnie opens the door to a room where desks have

been arranged side by side in twos. There are several students and tutors already at work. "And she's very reluctant," adds Bonnie. "She's not going to make it easy for you."

Marigold is wondering if there's any chance that Byron is still waiting for her in front of the school. If she ran back outside would they be able to get away before Bonnie caught her and dragged her back?

"And one other thing before I introduce you," says Bonnie. "She doesn't always talk much."

"Doesn't talk?"

"Not always."

Sadie Hawkle is a narrow child – narrow shoulders, narrow body, narrow face, even her hair seems particularly thin. As if she were made of leftovers and there weren't quite enough. Only her eyes are large and round; the eyes of a dead fish. Everything she's wearing – including the two plastic hair clips on either side of her head – looks worn and defeated. Her smile is so narrow it doesn't exist.

"Sadie, this is your new tutor, Marigold." Bonnie sounds as if she's offering Sadie a box of candy. "Marigold's been really looking forward to meeting you."

Sadie looks as if she's about to be force-fed.

Marigold smiles as if meeting Sadie is an event as

major as the junior prom, minus the formal dress and the corsage. "Hello, Sadie. How're you doing?"

Sadie stares back at her, looking worried and wary, as if she doesn't know what the right answer to Marigold's question is. If Marigold really were a box of candy, Sadie would probably throw her across the room.

"You going to say hello to Marigold?" prods Bonnie. She has the patience of a mountain.

Sadie continues to stare like a rabbit that has wandered out onto an eight-lane highway.

"Mrs Kupferberg says you need a little help with reading," says Marigold. "Did you bring something with you that you want to read?"

Sadie doesn't blink.

Because someone has to, Bonnie eventually answers for her. "I'm sure Sadie must have something she's reading in class. If not, we have a shelf of books over there that she can choose from."

"Well, Sadie?" Marigold's voice bubbles with the false cheer of a game-show host. "Do you have a book to read, or should we go over to the shelf and pick one?"

Sadie just stares. Mrs Kupferberg isn't the only one with some of the qualities of stone. Unless the child's gone into catatonic shock.

Maybe she doesn't speak English, thinks Marigold. *Is*

that even possible? Wouldn't Bonnie mention that if it were true? "Not only can't Sadie read, Marigold, but she doesn't even speak English!"

Bonnie reaches up and touches Marigold's shoulder. "I'm afraid I have a million things to do. I'll leave you two to it."

"Thank you," says Marigold, and so hard is she smiling, and so desperately is she trying to be positive, that for a second she actually means it.

There is a cheap, pink backpack hanging from Sadie's chair.

Marigold points to it. "Is that yours?"

From the way Sadie's eyes gaze ahead blankly, it's possible she only communicates through telepathy. Which is not an ability Marigold has.

"Is that your backpack, Sadie?"

A few more minutes pass as slowly as camels crossing the desert in wellies.

Finally, Sadie nods, a movement so slight it's a wonder that Marigold sees it.

"I thought it must be!" crows Marigold. "Do you have a book to read in it?"

This, too, is a question Sadie feels she can't answer hastily. It takes another five minutes to establish that there is a book in the backpack, and another ten to get the book out of the backpack.

"Wow," enthuses Marigold as Sadie drops the book onto the desk in front of her. "I haven't read this before. It looks really interesting."

It's a picture book about a family of elephants.

"Do you like elephants, Sadie?"

Sadie is no longer staring at Marigold but at the cover of the book.

"Why don't we open the book, and start from the beginning," suggests Marigold. "You know, since I haven't read it before?"

If Sadie heard her, she obviously feels this is not a question that requires any response in word or deed.

Marigold tilts her head and leans forward so that she is looking right at the little girl, even if the little girl isn't looking right at her. "Sadie? Why don't we open the book?"

When it is clear even to Marigold that Sadie has no more intention of opening the book than she has of reciting the Gettysburg Address, Marigold folds back the cover.

"OK," she says, pointing to the first word. "Why don't you start? I'm right here if you have any trouble."

The first word is "the". But it isn't a word that trips lightly off the lips of Sadie Hawkle.

"Come on." Marigold's smile shines with encouragement. "You can do it."

Sadie's scowl – now aimed at a point several feet in front of their desks – is more like a black hole.

"What's the 'th' sound?" prods Marigold. "Th... th... th..."

Sadie yawns.

"And then when you add an 'e' it's ..."

Sadie yawns again.

"... the!" exclaims Marigold. Triumphantly. "The 'th' sound with an 'e' gives you 'the'."

Sadie rubs her eyes.

Is the child a narcoleptic? Is she actually going to fall asleep sitting up?

"OK, now how about the second word?"

Time continues on its painful way.

All around them voices murmur and heads bend over books and notebooks. Faces frown in concentration. Chins rest on fists. Erasers move furiously back and forth. Now and then someone even laughs. But not where Marigold and Sadie sit. Sadie has her arms folded in front of her and Marigold smiles vaguely at the desktop. She asks Sadie if she doesn't really like the elephant book after all. They could try something else. Or write a story. But if there is one thing you can say about Sadie

Hawkle, it's that she isn't easily pressured; she doesn't utter a word.

At last, in desperation, Marigold picks up the book and starts to read it out loud herself. "The elephants lived in an ancient temple, deep in the jungle," she begins. At the end of each page she asks Sadie a question about the story. Which, needless to say, goes unanswered by Sadie.

It's not that long a book. When she's finished, Marigold sets it down in front of the little girl. "Your turn," she says brightly.

Sadie gives the book a shove that sends it flying to the floor.

Marigold is having a hard time trying to figure out what the bright side of this situation might be, or how to make the best of it.

"You're picking that up," she says, but her mouth looks as if it's saying something else. Something pleasant and possibly full of praise.

Sadie yawns.

At last people start getting to their feet and putting the desks back in rows, and Bonnie charges into the room. "No problems? Everything OK?"

"Yeah, fine," says Marigold. "But she is very quiet."

"She's shy," says Bonnie. "It'll take a little while for her to get used to you."

Marigold lowers her voice, assuming that Sadie isn't deaf and has heard every word she's said. "I don't know, Mrs Kupferberg, I don't think I'm very good with Sadie. Maybe someone el—"

"There is no one else." Bonnie Kupferberg, it seems, can also smile with delight while imparting bad news. "You're my last hope. Everybody else has given up on her. Even the teachers."

"Oh, but—"

"If you don't try, she'll just sit there like she did all last spring till her mother finally shows up to take her home."

"But I only have to do twenty hours a year," Marigold explains. "And I—"

"You will come next week, won't you? Besides everything else, I've lost six volunteers since last year." She runs her hands through her cloud of hair, as though that's where they might be. "I'm really desperate."

She looks desperate. Which makes Marigold feel guilty.

It is only twenty hours, Marigold reminds herself; she's already done more than two. And it's not like she has to work; all she has to do is sit there. Possibly read a book. She might even read a book she wants to read. And at last Marigold finds a thin but glowing silver lining in this particular cloud: the sooner she puts in her time, the sooner she can stop coming at all.

"Well, I guess I could make it next week."

It isn't just her mother that Marigold doesn't like to disappoint.

Chapter Seven
No View of the Ocean, Either

When the bell rings at the end of the school day Georgiana usually is off like a horse at the Kentucky Derby. Today, however, Georgiana lingers as if she's been at a party that she doesn't want to end. She double-checks that she's written down the assignment; she carefully gathers up her books and zips them into her backpack; she rises from her seat only when every other student has left the room. Mr McCrimber finishes erasing the board and looks over, surprised to find her still behind him. Mr McCrimber has taught her before: Georgiana is always the last one to take her seat, and the first one to jump out of it. Maybe she's not feeling well. Maybe she's being bullied and is trying to avoid a confrontation.

"Are you all right, Georgiana?" She smiles and says she's fine. He watches her drift across the room and out the door, to where Claudelia is waiting for her with a bored expression on her face. But when Mr McCrimber leaves himself the two of them are only a few feet from the classroom. Maybe it's drugs.

Claudelia shuffles along beside Georgiana. "Can't we go a little faster? I'm getting a cramp in my calf."

"You go on. You don't have to stay with me." Georgiana waves her ahead. "I'm not in a hurry."

"I got that part," says Claudelia. "If you went any slower we'd be going backwards. But I thought you start your community service this afternoon. You don't want to be late on your first day."

"Why not?" Georgiana would like to be so late she never shows up. "What are they going to do? Fire me?"

Claudelia laughs. "Holy Mother, don't tell me you're still moaning about your placement."

Georgiana looks over at her, her mouth in a knot. "Yes, Claudelia. I am still moaning about my placement. And I intend to continue moaning about it until I've put in my twenty hours of penal servitude and don't have to go any more and can forget about it for the rest of my life."

"You're going over the top, as usual," says Claudelia. "It's not that big a deal."

Georgiana, of course, has already had this pointed out to her. More than once; and by more than one person. "That's what everybody says."

"Well, everybody's right. Quit acting like you're going to your own hanging. You're just going to sit and talk to some old lady for an hour. There's nothing hard about that. Pretend she's your grandmother."

"You mean already dead?"

Give me strength, thinks Claudelia. Aloud she says, "You don't have a grandmother? Not even one?"

Georgiana comes to a complete stop at her locker. "No grandparent of either sex."

"Not ever?"

Georgiana rolls her eyes. "Um-duh, Claudelia. Obviously my parents didn't just drop out of the sky. But their parents all passed away before I was born. Except one grandmother." With the attention of someone defusing a bomb, Georgiana turns the dial on her combination lock. "But I don't remember her. She died when I was little."

"OK, but it's not like you've never seen a grandmother. You've met other people's. You've met mine. You talked to her all right. You said she was awesome."

"Claudelia…" Georgiana yanks off the lock. "Your grandmother isn't a wrinkled old bag who doesn't know what day it is. She runs her own company and she goes hunting. She is awesome."

"She's still my grandmother. And she does have

wrinkles. Plus, it's not a big company and she's not that good a shot."

Georgiana takes her jacket from her locker. "You know what I mean."

"And you know what I mean," counters Claudelia.

The locker door bangs shut. "Yeah. Be more like Marigold."

Despite the fact that Georgiana has a better chance of becoming a prima ballerina than a twin-soul to Marigold Liotta, she does try to improve her attitude before she arrives at St Joan's. It can't hurt. Georgiana knows that she can both overreact and exaggerate. Even her father, who is very fond of her, has been quoted as saying she could make the Andes out of a pebble. She also knows that if she continues to wind herself up like this her skin will break out.

As she drives, she thinks about what she's been told. Maybe Will and Claudelia and everybody else she's complained to about the placement (which is just about everyone she's seen in the last week, including Mr Malachay at the gas station and some woman who had the misfortune of stopping Georgiana to ask for directions) are right after all and St Joan's isn't going to be as bad as she imagined. Maybe there will be young people and middle-aged people and people who are totally healthy except they broke something or had a stroke and have to learn how to walk again. Besides that, it's not solitary confinement, is it? They don't lock them in tiny, dark cells and shove a tray of food through the door three times a day. So there probably will be lots of different things to do. Georgiana can't play the violin, but she can play tennis, dominoes and bridge. She's also a pretty terrific square-dance caller. And maybe Will is even right about some old people being interesting and cool. It's not impossible. It's not just ordinary, boring people who get old – celebrities get old, too. As for the inmates at St Joan's who are doddering around in that space between life and death, someone with special skills will be taking care of them. They're not going to be left to the care of a high-school student who doesn't even iron her own clothes. They won't be roaming through the corridors on their walking frames either. They'll be tucked up in their rooms, safe and sound. Which means that, statistically, the chances of Georgiana being present when someone does fall over and/or die are so small as to be non-existent.

Georgiana turns off the main road, slowing down when she sees a large sign that says *ST JOAN'S NURSING CENTRE*.

Nursing Centre, thinks Georgiana, *Centre, not Home. So far, so good…*

It takes no time at all for her to spot some differences between the centre Will described and what she sees looming at the top of the circular drive. For starters, the grounds don't look like a private park. There are a few trees the bulldozers missed, a small, defeated lawn and a few hardy shrubs but no sign of gardens, lakes or fountains – and nowhere to put them if there were. Ocean View, where Will's sister worked, was once the mansion of a wealthy railroad man; St Joan's was once an elementary school.

As Georgiana approaches the main building, a middle-aged woman and an elderly man come through the door. He has yeti eyebrows and leans on a cane, wobbling noticeably and walking as if he's paying for each step. The woman has an arm through his, and is talking to him in the sticky-sweet voice some people use with very young children. *He can't fall, she's holding on to him,* Georgiana tells herself, and puts on a Marigold Liotta God's-in-His-heaven-all's-right-with-the-world smile. The woman ignores her; the old man starts coughing. Georgiana hurries past them; she doesn't want to see him hit the ground.

It's a busy afternoon at St Joan's Nursing Centre. The desk plate says that the receptionist's name is Alice Einhorn. Alice is on the telephone; another telephone is ringing. From somewhere come the sounds of music (not the violin) and TV voices. It could be someone on the television, but Georgiana thinks she also hears sobbing. A nurse hurries past looking worried. Another rushes by from the opposite direction, talking into a cell phone. White-haired people shuffle along the hall – some in robes and slippers, some dressed as if they have some-where to go. A woman with a walking frame comes towards her, singing in Italian.

In the blink of time between putting down one phone and picking up another, Alice Einhorn looks question-ingly at Georgiana.

Georgiana ups her smile. "I'm Georgiana Shiller? From Shell Harbour High? I'm here to start my commu-nity service placement today?"

Alice holds up one hand. "St Joan's Nursing Centre," she says in a voice intended to inspire confidence. *Your aged relatives are safe with us.* "How can I help you?" The other phone starts ringing again.

The person Alice is talking to has a lot to say. She covers the receiver and whispers to Georgiana, "Our administrator will see you as soon as he's free. He likes to induct the volunteers himself, but he's in a meeting." She waves her hand. "Why don't you just wait over there?"

"Sure," Georgiana whispers back. "Thanks."

But "over there" is not the waiting area of chairs and a

table full of magazines that she expected. "Over there" is a wall. Georgiana props herself against it – under a sign that says *No Cell Phones In This Area* – smiling as if she's the welcoming committee.

People come and go. Except for the staff in their uniforms and soft-soled shoes, and the visitors in their hats and jackets and looks of somewhere else to be, everyone Georgiana sees is really old. Clapped out. Decrepit. If they walk, they walk slowly. Stooped. Shaking like leaves in a slight wind. Hair from which the years have sucked all colour and skin as wrinkled as a raisin. She can tell from the way they look at her that it's been a long time since most of them saw a teenager. Can they even remember what a teenager is?

The phones keep ringing. An ambulance pulls up and the crew jumps out, urgently pushing a stretcher. Georgiana flattens herself against the wall. *Somebody's died*, she thinks. *And I only just got here.* Two grim-faced women come in, wanting to pick up their mother's things. *Their dead mother's things.* An elderly man in a golf cap shivers up to the desk shouting that there's something wrong with his phone – it never rings. "Mr Maisel, I told you," the receptionist shouts back. "We checked it. Your phone is fine." *His friends are probably all dead, too.* A couple walk past, tense as a tightrope. "I can't stand to see her like this," says the woman. The man takes her hand. "It won't be much longer." *Because soon she'll be dead.* The ambulance crew leaves, now carrying what is obviously a corpse. *Good God, are they keeping them alive or killing them here?*

The administrator of St Joan's is Mr Papazoglakis. Mr Papazoglakis is tall and solidly built. His hair is dark and thinning and flecked with grey; his skin so pale you'd think he must live underground. Georgiana has witnessed a second ambulance's arrival and departure, and the sudden collapse just inside the entrance of an elderly woman returning from a walk with her daughter before Mr Papazoglakis finally emerges from his meeting. By which time Georgiana has almost forgotten why she's there.

Mr Papazoglakis has a green folder in one hand. "I'm sorry to keep you waiting," he says. "And you are–" he peeks into the folder – "Georgia. Georgia Shiller."

"Georgiana," she corrects him.

"Most people call me Mr P, Georgia." He says this without disturbing the even features of his face with a smile. "It's easier than trying to remember all those consonants."

And most people call me Georgiana. It's easier than using someone else's name.

"Georgiana," she corrects once again.

Mr Papazoglakis takes her on a tour. They go to the dining hall, the common room, the guest lounge with its almost-comfortable chairs and vending machines, the auditorium, the activity room (which, to Georgiana's amazement, includes a row of computers) and the gym. He points out the therapy rooms, kitchen and swimming pool and the corridors of private rooms, and introduces her to several reassuringly cheerful-looking people in white uniforms whose names she will never remember even though they wear ID cards around their necks. They don't go above the first floor; the second is only bedrooms and the third is a locked unit for those who "don't really know where they are". Georgiana doesn't ask for details.

While they walk, Mr Papazoglakis explains that the main concern of St Joan's Nursing Centre is quality of life. Dignity. Respect. Comfort. Security and safety.

"We here at St Joan's believe that a person's last days should be as pleasant as possible."

"I thought a lot of people are here for other reasons than because they're going to die," she says. "You know, like recuperation and stuff like that."

"We are, of course, an excellent care facility with very high ratings, but we do deal primarily with the elderly." Mr Papazoglakis's shrug is so slight it's barely a twitch. "And everybody does die eventually."

This is when Georgiana realizes that what Mr Papazoglakis in his dark suit and sombre expression most reminds her of is an undertaker. He may smell like Armani and not embalming fluid, but he looks as if he was born to sit behind the wheel of a hearse.

"Well, yeah." She giggles nervously. "But not all at once, right?"

"Of course not." Mr Papazoglakis still doesn't smile, but he does make a sound that could be the first half of a laugh. "We're a nursing centre, not a plague hospital."

Georgiana nods. *Well, thank God for that.* So she won't have to help dig any mass graves.

What she will have to do, Mr Papazoglakis explains, is socialize. She'll be given a resident to visit regularly. She can read to her, play a game or even just talk. Do the little things she might not be able to do herself – thread a needle, iron a blouse, change a light bulb. Take her for walks. Do a little shopping. Depending on her limits and abilities, Georgiana may even be asked to accompany her on a short outing. The centre's staff is overworked as it is; they have no time for any of the extra niceties.

As they come back to the reception desk, Mr Papazoglakis opens the green folder. "Now, let's see what we've fixed up for you." He runs one finger down the page. "Ah, yes." He looks up, his face still an undiscovered land as far as emotion is concerned. "We've given you Mrs Kilgour."

"Mrs Kilgour," parrots Georgiana.

"Mrs Kilgour doesn't have any family," says Mr Papazoglakis, "so her visitors are few and far between."

Georgiana guesses that this means she has none.

He looks back at the folder. "Room 10a." He points to the left. "Just down that corridor. Come with me. I'll introduce you. Naturally, she'll have been told that you were coming. I'm sure she's been looking forward to it."

Room 10a is a cheap envelope of a room with a bed, a night table, a small dresser, a chair that belongs somewhere larger and homier – somewhere with knickknacks on the mantel, a rug on the floor and a cat – an ancient television set, which is on too loudly, and a window, which is closed. There is a folded wheelchair in one corner and a four-footed walking stick next to the chair. The floor is linoleum and the walls are painted a sad shade of blue. The window looks out on a paved courtyard and a few dead pot plants. The only personal touch is the photograph on the dresser of a youngish woman in a long, flower-print dress holding a bouquet of roses and smiling as if she invented happiness. If this room were a person it would probably run away.

Mrs Kilgour is slumped in the armchair in front of the television, with her head on her chest and wearing only one slipper, looking like an abandoned doll. She is sound asleep.

"She's a very interesting woman," says Mr Papazoglakis. "But, like many of our residents, she does have a tendency to live in the past."

Georgiana glances at the room. And who could blame her for that?

"Mrs Kilgour." Mr Papazoglakis taps her arm. "Mrs Kilgour. You have a visitor. You remember the young lady from the high school was coming today?"

Mrs Kilgour mumbles something unintelligible, but doesn't open her eyes.

"Mrs Kilgour. Have you forgotten you were having a visitor today? This is Georgia."

"Georgiana," whispers Georgiana.

Mrs Kilgour mumbles again, her eyelids closed.

Mr Papazoglakis's phone hums softly. "Now what?" He pulls it from his pocket. "I'm afraid I have to go," he says. "I'm needed elsewhere. She does have a touch of narcolepsy." Which sounds like she takes drugs to Georgiana, but apparently means suddenly falling asleep. "Don't you worry, though, these spells never last very long. She'll wake in a few minutes. She does know you're here." He extends a hand for shaking. It's as warm as a can of soda out of the fridge. "Good luck."

Georgiana stands staring at the old woman in the chair for several minutes. If walnuts wore fuzzy pink bathrobes and had hair dyed a red normally associated with circus clowns, Mrs Kilgour would be easy to mistake for one. Georgiana is repelled by Mrs Kilgour. By her lined and sagging face. By her mottled, bony hands, the skin like crumpled tissue paper. She sniffs. Even the air in Mrs Kilgour's room smells like it's rotting. If anyone is going to suddenly drop dead, that anyone is sitting right in front of Georgiana with her mouth slightly open and her glasses askew.

She holds her breath, waiting for Mrs Kilgour to wake up as Mr Papazoglakis said she would, but she doesn't. Exactly what is Georgiana supposed to do? Throw cold water on her? Or just stand here, like a peacock stuck on a desolate marsh? She knew this wasn't going to work out. Didn't she say that? Didn't she say it was a bad idea? Everybody said she was wrong. Too negative. Too pessimistic. But she wasn't. She was right. She'd much rather be fishing paper cups and food containers out of the shrubs in the park. If it were Dr Kilpatiky asleep in that chair, Georgiana would be very tempted to push her through the window. Not for the first time in her life,

Georgiana wonders why she's always being punished for things she didn't do.

As she stares out of the window, her last bit of optimism dissolves like sugar in water. It's now that Georgiana might think of the words of Dante Alighieri describing hell. *Abandon all hope, ye who enter here.*

But she doesn't. She's thinking that, on top of everything, there's no view of the ocean, either.

Chapter Eight

Asher Is Dragged Away from His Career Strategy with Something of a Vengeance

Albert Grossman likes to boast about his son. There are no concerns about sex or drugs or rock and roll where Asher is concerned. No teenage inertia or teenage angst. No moodiness or sullenness. No plummeting grades or dropping out. Albert never worries about where Asher is or what he is doing. He knows where he is: working. He knows what he's doing: more than anyone else. "He's a chip off the old block," Albert Grossman always says. "Being a high achiever's in his genes." This is an understatement. If achievement were a mountain range, Asher reached the summit of the lowest mountain when he took his first summer college course in seventh grade. And never looked back. Five years later, Asher has a 4.0 GPA, is president and will be valedictorian of his senior class, and is involved in enough extracurricular activities to keep six-normal achievers busy, including fencing, archery and martial arts. (Albert Grossman, who was once attacked by an investment banker, learned the hard way that even a corporate lawyer has to know how to defend himself.) Saturday mornings, when other boys are still sound asleep, Asher has his kung-fu class. After today's class he has his first session at the community centre. You couldn't say that he's looking forward to it.

Right now, the high-achiever is sitting in his car in the small, potholed parking lot behind the centre. Or, as Asher thinks of it, the supermarket. Asher is preparing himself. Mimicking a crane hasn't given him quite the physical and spiritual strength he needs to meet the do-gooders and the do-nothings of Queen's Park, so here he sits, sipping black coffee from an insulated mug, feeling sorry for himself and running through a mental check-list to make sure he has everything he'll need to get him through the next hour and a half.

He does. At least he's pretty sure he does. It's all on the seat beside him in his leather messenger bag – which is what high-achievers with presidential ambition use instead of a backpack. Usually it holds his laptop and school things, a bottle of spring water, several energy bars, a bag of trail mix, breath spray, tissues, a travel toothbrush and toothpaste, a roll of dental floss, several individually wrapped hand wipes and a spare pair of socks. Today the laptop has been left at home for security reasons (he's sure someone at the centre will steal it) and been replaced by a bottle of antibacterial hand gel and disposable latex gloves (he's sure the centre has enough germs to wipe out Los Angeles).

He sighs. Asher's always been lucky, although he doesn't think of it as luck, of course. He thinks he gets no more than he deserves. But he doesn't deserve this. Of all the possible assignments the computer could have given him, why did it give him this one? Maybe Georgiana's right. Maybe Dr Kilpatiky rigged the whole thing. Trying to teach them all a lesson. Bureaucrats have small and petty minds.

Asher's watching a plastic bag wave in the branches of a solitary tree like a flag of truce and thinking of texting Will to meet him for lunch when the alarm on his phone goes off. Time to go in. He makes sure that he's also set it for an hour and half from now (time to go out), and steps from the car and crosses the lot with the lightness of step of prisoners of war on a forced march.

The back door doesn't open and no one answers Asher's knock, so he walks around to the main entrance where a handmade sign (a badly handmade sign) says: *Queen's Park Community Centre.* This door does open, but the handle comes off in his hand.

Asher steps inside. The place is a dump by anyone's standards; even someone far less fastidious than Asher Grossman. Asher's father has taught him that presentation is extremely important – you wear expensive suits, you drive an expensive car, you exude success – but no one has told that to the people who run the centre. Cheap white paint has been aimed at the walls, but it doesn't cover the scars of age and of what was there before (the Church of Hope, a temporary licence office when the town hall was being renovated, a bargain store, a hardware store, a paint store, a five-and-ten, a supermarket in a time before supermarkets became the size of airplane hangars). The false ceiling is missing sections; the light fixtures are missing bulbs. The blinds in the front windows don't fit and are broken. There's a crack in the glass that has been patched with tape. The only decorative touches are cobwebs and dust. The seats in the front area are a mishmash of old school chairs, very old wooden folding chairs and an oversized old sofa. Someone is asleep on the sofa, covered with a crocheted quilt that looks like it was made in the nineteen sixties and not washed since. There's a pillow under the sleeper's head. The dented coffee urn is in a corner by the window. The linoleum looks older than Asher's father. An attempt has been made to create separate rooms with makeshift partitions that double as bulletin boards. Asher can see a couple of people at the far end of the centre, but not one of them looks his way.

It has just occurred to him that, if they don't care that he's here, he might simply turn around and leave when he sees a very large woman bearing down on him, moving amazingly quickly for someone her size. She's wearing baggy work pants, a handmade sweater with a standing hare on it, the hair slide of a popular cartoon character in her short, curly greying hair, and, although it hasn't been raining, extremely orange wellies. Besides the barrette, there's a leaf in her hair. The partitions tremble as she passes.

"I'm guessing you're Asher Grossman." She has a voice that could scare off coyotes. She takes the door handle from him as if it's his ticket of admission, and with her free hand shakes his as if she's trying to get something out of it. "I'm Mrs Dunbar."

Mrs Dunbar is the wife of the minister of the local Methodist church, but that isn't what she looks like to Asher. She looks as if she's probably married to a mountain man – the kind who lives in a one-room cabin and picks his teeth with a knife.

"Mrs Dunbar." Smiling politely, Asher glances behind her, hoping to see someone who looks like the person in charge. "Nice to meet you."

"Not as nice as it is to meet you, believe me. It's Hell here today and the Devil's in a filthy mood."

Asher continues to smile. "Well, here I am, but I'm not sure who I report to."

"That would be me." She finally lets him have his hand back.

"Right," says Asher. "So ... so are you in charge of the centre?"

Mrs Dunbar laughs, causing even more coyotes to scamper for the hills. "We don't really have a ruling hierarchy here. We're more like an anarchist cell."

Asher nods. *Of course you don't. Of course you are.* He should have guessed. This place looks like a ship whose captain abandoned it long ago.

"Since we're all volunteers, we make major decisions as a group. Real democracy in action. Not this political hogwash the governments practise." She laughs again, emptying every tree in the county of birds. "But I guess for most day-to-day things I'm kind of the person who makes things work." She laughs again, waving the doorknob in the air. "Or tries to. Only today nothing wants to work. Today the basement's flooded, which is where we have the computers and the pool table and our little library for the kids. Carlin usually takes care of stuff like that for us but, unfortunately, he's not up to it this morning."

"Carlin?"

Mrs Dunbar nods in the direction of the sofa. "That's Carlin over there."

"Oh," says Asher. The passed-out drunk. He should have guessed that, too.

"I'll have to get him up soon, but only to move him so the new mothers' group has somewhere to sit, since downstairs is out. And on top of everything else, we're two people short and it's food bank this afternoon." She claps her hands together, and a used tissue falls out of her sleeve. "Which is why I am so glad to see you! This economic crisis has really hit this town hard. And with all the budget cuts…"

Asher, aware of the economic crisis in the way that he's aware that there are quite a few countries in Central Asia whose names end in "stan", says, "Um."

Mrs Dunbar shakes her head and the leaf falls to the floor. "Lord knows what'll happen when the new round of cuts comes. These politicians are determined to make every stone in the state bleed." Her smile is philosophical. "But that's the way it goes, isn't it? The more folks need, the less they're given. It's always the victim that gets the blame."

Asher, more a believer in the saying that when the

going gets tough the tough get going, again says, "Um."

"But complaining doesn't solve anything, does it?" She grabs his arm and starts back the way she came, pulling him along like a toy on wheels. "We just have to do what we can." Mrs Dunbar comes to a sudden stop. "Here give me that." She can't mean his satchel, can she? He automatically takes a step back. "You can't be walking around with that. We'll put it somewhere safe." But she isn't just quick on her feet. Before he can stop her she's yanked his bag from his grasp, opened the door to the nearest cubicle, and thrown it onto a chair. She shuts the door again, which must be what she means by safe. It would take a lame kitten to get in there. "Now, that's better. Come on, I'll show you what to do first."

There are two people in the back room, a middle-aged couple who are filling shopping bags with cans and boxes of food with the earnestness of missionaries handing out missals.

Mrs Dunbar introduces them. The Henleys, Irene and Nate. They smile serenely. *Jesus loves you.*

"This is Asher! Asher Grossman." Mrs Dunbar slaps a hand on his shoulder with such force that he flinches. "Didn't I say God wouldn't leave us in the lurch?" Not breaking the rhythm of their packing, the Henleys murmur their agreement. "He'll be back to help you in a little while. Right now I need him in the basement."

And she propels him to a door on one side of the room and down a flight of wooden stairs, talking the whole time. He is vaguely aware that she's back on the economy, but Asher isn't really listening to her; he's still hearing her tell the Henleys that he'll be back to help them in a while.

"Mrs Dunbar, you do know that—" What Asher intended to say was, "You do know that I'm only here for an hour and a half", but the sight of the basement distracts him from finishing the sentence. Christ. God may not have left her in the lurch, but maybe it would have been better if he'd ignored her completely. The basement looks like a rice paddy, but with furniture rising out of it instead of plants. There is no floor to be seen.

"What'd I tell you?" Mrs Dunbar splashes into the ankle-deep water. "There's never an ark around when you really need one."

"But what happened?" He doesn't remember rain last night. Unless the centre has its own microclimate, which wouldn't surprise him.

Mrs Dunbar picks up a sodden book. "I guess we have a leak."

Or an underground river that's rising. Asher might be looking down at Niagara Falls, he's gripping the banister so tightly.

She beckons him forward. "Come on. First thing you have to do is unplug the computers and get anything that's not going to benefit from a bath out of the water."

He hears the pronoun "you", but he can't believe it. She expects him to bail out the basement? Him? Does he look like a handyman? Does she have no idea how much his trainers cost? Or his jeans?

"Asher, come on. I have a million things to do before people start arriving."

Apparently she either doesn't know or doesn't care. Asher looks down at his trainers, so well taken care of that this might be the first time he's ever worn them. "But I don't have boots."

"Just take off your shoes and socks," she instructs him. "Leave them on the stairs."

Asher looks down at the water. Things are sitting in it. Books. Papers. Toys. Filthy fourth-hand furniture. Bugs and clumps of dust float on the top. And some kind of scum. She can't seriously want him to put his feet in that. God knows where it comes from. Probably the sewer. If he steps in that he'll be lucky if he doesn't come down with cholera. The first case on the East Coast in a hundred years.

"Snap! Snap!" Mrs Dunbar splashes forward. "You don't make butter by staring at the cream."

Asher could say that he's never had any desire to make butter, but Asher has been raised to respect authority, and right now the person in authority is the large woman in the handknitted sweater and neon wellies, so instead he reacts like a dog whose master has shouted "Come!" He takes off his socks and shoes, rolls up his pants and forces himself to step off the stairs. Which is when he remembers the spare socks and disposable gloves in his bag. But it's too late now.

The computers in his father's firm are all the same make and all state-of-the-art. These computers are all different makes and every one so old the only state any of them are in is pathetic.

"Where did they come from?" Asher wonders out loud. "I've never seen anything like them before."

"I know." Mrs Dunbar's smile is full of pride. "Two of them were donated, and the rest came from the street." It's like being proud of living on Welfare. "It's truly amazing what people throw out," says Mrs Dunbar. "But you know what they say." Asher has no idea. "The Lord provides."

"I wish the Lord would provide me with insulated gloves," mumbles Asher.

Mrs Dunbar laughs as if he's made a joke. "Don't worry, no one's been electrocuted yet," she assures him.

"You just get everything unplugged and out of the way." She points to a door under the stairs. "The garbage bags are in there for things that can't be salvaged. I'll turn on the pump and then I have to get back upstairs pronto. The mothers and babies will be arriving soon."

"Pump?" echoes Asher. "You have a pump? You mean this has happened before?"

She beams. "It happens all the time."

By clamping his mouth shut, Asher manages not to squawk with outrage. If God's going to help anyone, it better be him. He watches Mrs Dunbar mount the stairs, wondering if she'll come back. She doesn't. He's only just arrived but already he isn't surprised. Over his head the floor shakes, dislodging cobwebs and dust, while Asher does as much as he can. He can't shift the old pool table, not by himself, but he moves chairs and bookcases and tables, and makes sure the computers and other electrics are unplugged and out of danger. Then he picks up his shoes and socks and pads back upstairs.

The Henleys are still on their own, smiling and packing; Mrs Dunbar is at the front of the centre with the new mothers.

Asher tries to sneak to the cubicle to get his things without Mrs Dunbar seeing him, but even though she's facing the window she turns like an antelope that smells a lion. "Asher!" she shouts. "Come and meet everyone! Don't be shy! I've been telling them all about you."

Asher drops his hand from the doorknob and, smiling like a dead man, walks to the room at the front of the building. God knows what she's done with the body, but there's no sign of Carlin now. At least a dozen women sit in a cramped circle in the waiting area with cups of tea and coffee and a plate of cookie crumbs. For some reason it didn't occur to Asher that the new mothers would have new babies with them, but they do, most of them making some kind of noise. They also have older children. The older children are running around as if ghosts are chasing them. One of the new mothers, apparently unconcerned about hygiene, seems to be nursing. Asher blushes and looks away.

"I was just saying that I don't know what we would have done without you today." Mrs Dunbar holds one arm out towards him. "Ladies, this is Asher. Our godsend."

There is a general murmur of hellos.

One of the new mothers says, "You look like you've been fording a river."

The one with the baby clamped to her breast says, "He looks more like he fell in it."

The room bubbles with laughter.

Until one minute ago, Asher hasn't blushed since he

answered a question in second grade and got it wrong; and now here he is turning red for the second time. His pants are still rolled up and his shoes and socks are still in his hands. If his father saw him, he'd disown him.

When the laughter stops, Mrs Dunbar explains, "The cellar's flooded again."

This surprises no one.

This is Asher's chance to make his escape. "I think it's all under control now." He starts to edge away. "So I'm going to go—"

A small child runs into his legs, its sticky hands on his skin. He jumps back into the partition next to him.

Mrs Dunbar doesn't seem to notice either that he's trying to leave or that he nearly knocked over the wall. "Oh, that is wonderful!" she enthuses. "Now you can give the Henleys a hand. The poor things are beside themselves. No one else has shown up and the food bank opens in half an hour."

"Oh, I—" begins Asher.

But suddenly there's a woman in front of him, thrusting something into his arms.

"Just hold him for a minute," she says. "I have to get Angie before she does something."

Asher looks down. A small face with very dark eyes is looking back at him. It isn't true that all babies are cute.

"Oh, no, I——" begins Asher.

In his shirt pocket, the alarm on his phone goes off: time's up. Which is when, without so much as a cough or sound, the baby throws up all over him. He can practically feel the germs seeping into his skin. Where the cholera bacteria are waiting to greet them.

Dr Kilpatiky's plan has already worked. Asher has learned an important lesson: things can always be worse than you thought they'd be.

Chapter Nine
Another Week, Another Wednesday Afternoon

Every Wednesday at lunch Asher asks Marigold how her community service placement is going. Asher, of course, is hoping that hers is going as badly as his, but Marigold always says it's really good. "It's not easy," she'll admit. "Sadie has some problems. But I like the challenge." She gives the impression that she looks forward to their sessions. That, slowly but surely, she and Sadie Hawkle are bonding as seamlessly as atoms. Except for the part about it not being easy, none of this is especially true. Sadie has so many problems that, were they steps, you could build a stairway to the stars. Marigold has accepted the fact that Sadie is a challenge, but that isn't the same thing as liking it. She looks forward to Wednesday afternoons almost as much as she would major dental surgery. *Oh God*, she thinks when she wakes on Wednesday morning. *Not already...* They aren't bonding either surely or even slowly, they're just stuck with each other.

As an example of why Marigold would prefer a root canal to teaching Sadie Hawkle to read, on this particular afternoon they sit side by side in the centre of the room, an island of stillness and quiet in the middle of a sea of busyness and talk. Marigold is reciting a few lines of original verse in her head: *We sat there in silence, we sat there we two, I looked at the time, Sadie looked at her shoe...* Which do a fairly good job of summing up her Wednesdays in Half Hollow. Next to her, Sadie, shoulders hunched and mouth so tightly closed she may never be able to open it again, stares angrily into space. It's like sitting next to a clenched fist.

Marigold isn't sure how she came up with this little poem – she's never written so much as a limerick before. It simply popped into her brain not long after she sat down next to Sadie. As she always does, Marigold smiled brightly and warmly, and greeted Sadie with a cheerful, "Hey there, Sadie. How are you this week?" Sadie's reply (as always) was to bang her heels against the legs of her chair and glower. Summer sun meets with dark winter night on a deserted mountain road in a hailstorm.

Sadie brings the same elephant story to every session. Both of them know it so well that Marigold could recite it in her sleep and Sadie, when she's willing, can read it without hesitation. Possibly with her eyes closed. Today, however, Sadie isn't willing. She read two sentences and stalled like a car that ran out of gas. Sometimes she stops because she has a headache. Or she has a stomachache. Or her eyes hurt. Today she can't read any more because she's tired. If she doesn't stop yawning Marigold's going to take the apple left over from lunch and stuff it in her mouth.

Not really, of course. She can't do that. What would the others think? What would Marigold think if she saw someone stuff an apple into a yawning child's mouth? She'd think the apple-stuffer had lost her mind, that's what.

A second verse forms itself in Marigold's head. *I sit here with Sadie, she stares at the floor, I wish that a wizard would stroll through the door…*

Marigold sighs. It doesn't have to be a wizard. That's only one option. It could be almost anything as long as it's spectacular and fun, not frightening or dangerous. Jugglers, or a giraffe, or a nursery of baby orang-utans. It could even be someone on stilts dressed as Uncle Sam and whistling "Yankee Doodle Dandy". Anything to shake things up a little. Anything rather than sitting here with the black hole that is Sadie Hawkle beside her, arms folded, mouth a straight line. Marigold has yet to see Sadie really smile.

"Come on, Sadie," she coaxes, sounding as far away from being annoyed as she is from the moon. If nothing else, living with her mother has given Marigold an enormous amount of patience. "Why don't you finish reading? There are only a couple more pages."

Sadie looks at her out of the corner of her eyes. "I don't want to."

Last week Bonnie Kupferberg waylaid Marigold as she was leaving to ask how she and Sadie are doing. "How's it going with you two? You making any progress?" Marigold said yes. Which actually isn't a lie. Progress has been made. Sadie is reading, even if it's only the one book and she reads it with all the enthusiasm of someone digging her own grave. And sometimes Sadie will speak. No one could accuse her of talking too much – she usually limits her conversation to things such as "yes", "no", "don't mind", "OK" and "don't know" – but she has been known to make whole sentences.

As if to reward Marigold for her fortitude, she makes one now. "What'll you give me if I do?" asks Sadie.

Marigold, however, has progressed even more than Sadie. Besides being upbeat and positive, it is also her nature to stick to things and persevere. As it has to be. Anyone as determined as Marigold is to keep her mother happy and make the world a place where everything always turns out all right would have to have the willpower of the Roman Empire just to get out of bed in the morning. And Sadie Hawkle, the Mount Everest of children, has made that resolve even stronger. There will be no golf clubs or expired caviar this time, but to the sweetness and patience that make up her arsenal of weapons Marigold has added bribery. A candy or a pack of gum; a novelty pencil or some stickers. Bribery and the intransigence of a dictator.

"I have an apple in my backpack. If you finish the book it's yours."

"I don't want an apple." Sadie is a master of stubbornness herself. "I want potato chips."

"I'm not a store, Sadie. All I have today is the apple. But if you finish the story maybe I'll bring chips next time."

"It's boring." Sadie's heels bang against her chair again. "It's always the same."

So are you, thinks Marigold – but continues to smile. "Well, we can't just sit here like we're waiting for a train." Which is totally untrue; it's something they do very well. If it were an Olympic event they'd be famous. "Why don't we try a different book?" One that she hasn't read two hundred times might be an idea. "Why don't we see if we can find something new to read? Something really fun."

Sadie looks as if Marigold's suggested that standing on one leg in the rain would be fun, but she shrugs, which, loosely interpreted, means "OK". "And next week you'll bring chips? Mesquite?"

"Deal." Marigold pushes her chair back. "Let's see what we can find."

Marigold goes through the books on the shelves one by one. They might as well be looking for fish in the desert. They all seem to be either too young or too old; either too easy or too hard. Some of them have been scribbled in or have pages missing. Many of them would make the nutritional panel on a box of cereal seem exciting. Everything Marigold picks, Sadie rejects because they have too many words. Everything Sadie chooses, Marigold rejects because they have fewer words than Mr Liotta's business card. In the last fifteen minutes of the afternoon they finally reach a compromise, and return to their desks to read the book about the family of elephants for the two hundred and first time.

Marigold is going to be late getting home. Again. Although Half Hollow is only some fifteen miles north-west of Shell Harbour as the crow flies, the bus doesn't follow the route of a crow. It weaves and winds and back-tracks as if it's trying to find the longest possible way; or possibly never arrive at all. To make the journey even longer, it stops whenever someone suddenly steps out of a clump of trees waving, or whenever someone on the bus shouts out, "Hey, could you pull over by those mail-boxes?" Last week she forgot to text her mother with an excuse and Eveline was wringing her hands with worry by the time she got back. Where was she? Why was her phone off? Why didn't she call her to come and get her? Marigold is ungrateful and doesn't appreciate all her mother does for her. She thinks about nobody but her-self. She doesn't realize how upsetting it is not to know what's happening, to be left to imagine the worst. One voice was raised, and many tears were shed.

That isn't the problem tonight. When Marigold texted on her way to Half Hollow to say she was hanging out with friends after school, she got her mother's voicemail. This either means that she's at the gym or the health spa and isn't taking calls, or it means that the day has proved too much for her and she's gone to bed. Either way, Mari-gold doesn't have to feel anxious about being late. Nor does the slowness of the journey bother her as it often does. Her mind is so occupied that if it were a motel the *No Vacancy* sign would be lit up. She can't stop thinking about Sadie. There must be some way of reaching her. Marigold has seen enough movies and TV shows, and read enough books and magazines, to know that kindness and determination always win in the end. Children aren't eggs. Children who have been abused, or abandoned,

118

or disliked by their parents – even children who have been left by the side of the road or locked in a closet for years – have been put back together again because somebody cared. Marigold doesn't love Sadie – indeed, it's hard enough to try to like her – but she remembers what Bonnie Kupferberg said to her that first afternoon. *If we lose these kids now … chances are we'll never get them back.* If Sadie gets any more lost she'll simply disappear.

When Marigold does finally arrive home, although Eveline's car is in the garage, the house is quiet and dark when she steps inside. There is a note on the kitchen table, propped up against the salt and pepper shakers: *Have a really bad migraine. See you in the morning. Love, Mom.*

Marigold isn't sure if her mother really gets migraines or not. When things get too much for her and she's depressed she says she has a migraine and goes to bed. But the migraine may only be an excuse. It sounds better than writing: *Clinically depressed. See you in the morning if I can face getting out of bed.* Whatever the reason, Marigold has learned that the best thing to do is to leave her mother alone when she's like this. Don't ask if she's all right or if she needs anything; don't offer to get her a cup of tea or something to eat. Just leave her be. Let people with serious mood disorders lie.

In much the way that a hunter will know it's going to

snow, Marigold knows her father won't be coming home tonight. She makes herself a sandwich and goes to her room. She does her homework and checks her emails; she calls first Byron and then Claudelia. All the while she's doing these things, part of her brain is still thinking about Sadie. Marigold put a reminder about the mesquite chips on her phone, but mesquite chips aren't a solution. What to do about Sadie, that's the problem. Sadie is difficult, surly, pricklier than a rosebush, not as cute as a chicken, and far less charming than a sinkhole. Why does Marigold care? That isn't a question she can answer. But she can't give up on Sadie the way everyone else has. She just can't. Even if it means spending the rest of the year with the elephant family and their difficulties with furniture.

Marigold gets into bed and takes the book she's reading from the bedside table. Reading for fifteen or twenty minutes before she turns out the lights is something she's been doing for as long as she can remember. It's as that thought comes into her head that Marigold finally has a useful idea. Her books! The books she loved when she was little. The books she'd turn to when her parents were fighting to make everything all right. She'll bring her own books for Sadie to read.

As she falls asleep the thought in Marigold's head is: *So now I know where that verse came from.*

Chapter Ten
The Kilgour Wakes

Georgiana offers Claudelia a ride home after school. "It's on my way," she says. "I'm going to St Joan's."

"Again?" laughs Claudelia. "Didn't you go last week?"

Georgiana nods. "Yeah. I go every week."

Claudelia smiles like someone who ordered a chocolate ice-cream cone and was given a cow. "Really? *You*? Every week?"

"Yes, *me*. Every week. I don't see what's so astonishing about that."

She doesn't? Claudelia is still smiling at the cow. "I guess I figured you'd wait till the end of the year and then do the whole thing in a couple of weekends."

"It's only an hour a week," says Georgiana. "It's not really a big deal."

"Oh right. Of course it isn't." Has Claudelia's smile always been so sarcastic, or is Georgiana only now noticing? "What happened to working at the nursing centre being like stoking the fires of hell with a teaspoon?"

"I never said that," says Georgiana.

"Maybe not in so many words..." And the eye-rolling. Has Claudelia always rolled her eyes as if she's in some amateur play? "But you definitely gave everyone the impression that you'd rather stock shelves in Walmart for eternity than spend time with your old lady."

"Yeah, well, I wasn't happy about it. Everybody knows that." Georgiana shrugs. "But I guess maybe Marigold's onto something with her making-the-best-of-it thing. Because, you know, once I started it turned out not to be as bad as I thought."

"Really?" Claudelia looks at her as if she's committing every detail of Georgiana's face to memory so she can go home and paint her portrait. "Even with all those old people falling like bowling pins at a league championship?"

Georgiana can do a sarcastic smile, too. "It doesn't stress me, Claude, because I keep away from them. I just deal with Mrs K, and pretty much stay in one room."

Which makes it sound as if she stays with Mrs Kilgour in her room, keeping her company. But she doesn't. The one room Georgiana stays in is the bathroom, while Mrs Kilgour dozes in her chair by the TV. On that first afternoon, abandoned by Mr Papazoglakis and thinking about the lack of ocean, Georgiana finally noticed that there are three doors in the old lady's room. One leads to the hallway, one is a closet – and the third? If only it were the portal to a parallel world, thought Georgiana, one where she could do whatever she wanted whenever she wanted and no one ever died. Which, oddly enough, it almost was. It opened onto the bathroom, an oasis of quiet with a lock. Even if someone came looking for her (and, really, who would do that when everyone is so busy with people dying and complaining?) they'd just think she was using the facilities, not taking up residence.

"And you're OK with your old lady?" Claudelia sounds dubious. She's been friends with Georgiana long enough to know that she doesn't really do patience. "She doesn't crash to the ground or nag or get on your nerves or anything like that?"

"She's an angel." How could she not be? She's always asleep. "She doesn't really walk much and she has one of those canes with the feet, so she can't fall down, and she never gives me any trouble at all."

"So what do you do with her?"

"Oh, you know... She doesn't have many visitors, so mainly we just hang out. Talk. Watch TV. Sometimes I read the paper to her."

Georgiana sits on a cushion in the bathroom, plugged into music and checking out her friends on Facebook while Mrs Kilgour snores and snorts in the bedroom.

"Wow." Claudelia's smile is no longer sarcastic, now it's almost envious. "That sounds great. It's a lot better than what I'm doing at the mayor's office. Which is mainly answering the phone. Snoring boring with bells on! I mean, really, if I wasn't so bored I'd probably think I was dead."

"It's better than walking rescue dogs, too," admits Georgiana. Which, of course, it definitely is. "I don't have to go out in the rain or the cold or anything, and I don't have to worry that Mrs K's going to chase a cat or get into a fight with a German shepherd." Also, dogs are awake and demand attention, and although you can talk on the phone while walking most dogs it's difficult to text, surf the net or watch video clips or movies. It is because the St Joan's placement has worked out so well that Georgiana has committed herself to coming every week. The few extra hours this involves aren't a waste of precious time – she does exactly what she'd be doing at home, only in the bathroom between Rooms 10a and 12a – and it looks good on her college applications. Even Georgiana is aware that "chair of the dance decoration committee" might not clinch her a place at a decent school. Not that she mentions any of these things to Claudelia.

"I'm impressed," says Claudelia. Shocked and awed might be a more accurate description. Georgiana is not loved for her reliability or selflessness. "I really am."

Claudelia isn't the only one. Dr Kilpatiky has been keeping an eye on how the new system is working, and was pleasantly surprised to see that Georgiana Shiller not only had a glowing report from St Joan's but is putting in more time than she has to as well. Dr Kilpatiky commended Georgiana on this only last week. The principal is rather pleased with herself, too; she thinks it's proof that she was right.

When they pull up in front of Claudelia's, she says, "Thanks, George. And have fun this afternoon."

"Don't worry." Georgiana smiles back. "I will."

Which turns out to be, if not a lie, a misconception.

Life may not always be a party, but Georgiana can't help thinking that, if you try and, yes, let's use a word more normally found in Marigold Liotta's vocabulary, persevere, you can make most days the run-up to the party – when you're full of plans and anticipation (before you ruin your favourite dress or catch your date flirting with another girl).

As proof of this theory, Georgiana is humming a

catchy, upbeat tune from the radio as she pulls into the parking lot at St Joan's. It would be an exaggeration to say that she's been looking forward to this afternoon the way a hungry girl looks forward to lunch, but she is far from unhappy. It certainly isn't the torture she was expecting. If all her classes could be like her community service placement, Georgiana would never complain about school again. Not ever. (Or not much.) Indeed, if she could get credit for sitting at the back of history or language arts while on her phone, she'd be one of the best students Shell Harbour High has ever known. This is the life. It's almost as good as getting paid to go shopping.

Georgiana gives Alice at reception a cheery wave as she strolls up to the desk. She fills in her time of arrival on her sheet, and, with another cheery wave, heads down the corridor to Mrs Kilgour's room, smiling at everyone she passes, no matter how decrepit and likely to fall over they are. She takes hold of the doorknob to Mrs Kilgour's room, and, without bothering to knock or call out, walks in, her phone already in her hand.

Georgiana screams. It is an attention-grabbing scream. If Georgiana were in a movie she would have screamed because there was a scene of blood and horror or a mob of zombies behind the door. But she isn't in a movie, she's at St Joan's, and behind the door is Mrs Kilgour. She is sitting in her chair in front of the soap opera playing on the TV, wearing her pink robe over a white T-shirt and red plaid flannel house pants, and her Yankees baseball cap. An unsuccessful attempt has been made to apply lipstick to her mouth and rouge to her cheeks, making her look like a very old doll. A very old doll that has come to life. Because instead of facing the set, Mrs Kilgour is facing the door; and instead of being sound asleep, Mrs Kilgour is wide awake. Being awake does nothing to improve her looks.

She points the remote at Georgiana as if it's a gun. "Who the hell are you?" Her voice is surprisingly strong and clear for a woman of her age. "Who said you can just barge into my room like the FBI?"

Georgiana has as many faults as anyone else, but rudeness isn't one of them. "I–I'm sorry," she quickly apologizes. "I–I thought you were sleeping."

"Do I look like I'm sleeping?" No, she certainly doesn't. "Although it is obviously a disappointment to you, I am very much awake. The question is: who in creation are *you*?"

"I–I'm your volunteer visitor." Georgiana is far from recovered from the shock of finding Mrs Kilgour wide-eyed and angry, but does manage to shut the door behind her so the old lady's shouting doesn't bring a nurse or aide rushing to her rescue.

"My *what?*"

Georgiana may have no experience with the elderly, but she does know that you have to speak to them slowly and loudly. Slowly and loudly, she repeats, "Your volunteer visitor, Mrs Kilgour."

"My volunteer visitor." Mrs Kilgour's lips curl in what Georgiana takes for a smile. There is lipstick on her front teeth. "You mean as opposed to my involuntary visitor?"

Georgiana has no idea what she's talking about. "Your involuntary visitor?"

It isn't as hard to confuse a smile with a sneer as you might think.

"Yes, dear. You know. The one who shows up because evil forces in the universe make her come here against her will."

She must be senile. She probably doesn't even know where she is.

"I come from the school. The high school? From Shell Harbour?"

"This isn't Shell Harbour," snaps Mrs Kilgour. "We're miles from Shell Harbour. What are you, lost?"

So she does know where she is.

"No, I'm not lost. I go to school in Shell Harbour, but I'm

here for my community service. I'm your volunteer visitor."

Mrs Kilgour's voice becomes high and childish. "Oh, you're here for your community service. Aren't you a Good Samaritan. Your parents must be very proud."

Georgiana has never been mocked by an octogenarian wearing a baseball cap before. "Yes, I... No, I mean... We do it as part of our curriculum. I—"

"And that's *me*, is it? I'm not a human being. I'm not flesh and blood and a beating heart? I'm a community service? Like picking up soda cans on the highway? Is that what I am, a rusting can of Coke?"

"No, of course not. I—"

"You want some advice? Never get old. This is what happens when you get old. Strangers barge in on you whenever they want, trying to stick you in a garbage bag because you're no use to anybody any more."

"Look, I'm sorry I didn't knock. I'm..." She takes a deep breath and tries again. "I'm Georgiana. Georgiana Shiller. I'm here to visit you. You know, to be a little company for you. Didn't they tell you I was coming?"

"Of course they told me." She softens her voice, speaking in very much the same talking-to-a-small-child tone that Georgiana's been using to her. "Ooh, Mrs Kilgour, you're going to be having a visitor. A spoiled teenager who thinks life is a shopping mall. She's from Shell Harbour, where the rich people live. Won't that be nice? You'd like to see a rich person up close before you die, wouldn't you?"

"Mrs Kilgour—"

"But that was weeks ago." Her voice is normal again. Normal being brash and sarcastic. "What'd you do? Walk here via Tibet?" Then she shakes her head, arguing with herself. "No, that's ridiculous. I doubt you could find Tibet even by accident. You were probably just busy on that Web thing, telling everybody what you had for lunch."

"Mrs Kil—"

"Time may mean nothing to you, but I don't have a lot of it left at my age. I gave up waiting. I figured you'd had a better offer or found some other poor soul to torment." She eyes Georgiana's right hand. "Or lost your phone and didn't know how to get here."

There's no use making up some excuse, since the old bag doesn't listen. And anyway she wouldn't believe her if she did listen; she has her mind made up. "I'm not here to torment you, Mrs Kilgour," says Georgiana with a patience no one who knows her well would recognize. And loudly and slowly. "I'm here to help you. Be your friend."

"Help me? Be my friend? How could you be my friend? You're not even old enough to vote."

Georgiana clamps her mouth shut. *And you probably voted for Lincoln.*

"Look at you!" Mrs Kilgour jets on. "You couldn't look more like a princess if you were wearing a crown."

Look at you! You couldn't look more like an evil troll if you were hiding in a cave.

"Princess La-di-dah. Clutching that damn contraption in your hand like a second of silence would kill you! And all dressed up like you're going to a ball. You wouldn't last five minutes in the jungle. Not five lousy minutes. What are you going to help me do? Shop? Pick out a pair of shoes? Throw a party?"

Georgiana puts the hand holding the damn contraption behind her back. "Well, luckily for us, we're not in the jungle, are we, Mrs Kilgour? So there are lots of things I can help you with. And shopping's one of them. You know, if there's anything you need." *A life ... a personality...* "Or if you want me to do something for you."

"Do something? Do something like what?"

Georgiana pulls at her hair with her free hand. *Like lock you in the closet, you old bat. And throw the key into the ocean.*

"Well ... there must be lots of stuff you can't do yourself." *See well, or climb a ladder, or remember what you had for breakfast...* "I can help you. Like maybe if you need a needle threaded or—"

"A needle threaded?" She sounds so indignant, you'd

think Georgiana suggested teaching her to break dance. "Why would I want you to do that? I haven't sewn a damn thing since nineteen eighty-five."

Well, excuse meeee…

"We could play a game…" Hide-and-seek. Georgiana could be back in her car before Mrs Grumbles counted to three. "Do you like games?" Not tennis, obviously. "Cards or board games?"

The eyes behind the smudgy glasses look at her with new interest. "Poker? You play poker? Stud or Draw?"

"No, no, I don't play poker." Georgiana's only knowledge of poker comes from movies in which a bunch of overweight men sit around smoking, wisecracking and occasionally threatening each other's life while they shove plastic chips into the middle of the table. Not a bunch of old ladies. "But I do play bridge."

"You play bridge. With two people you play bridge?" The interest is gone and the sarcasm is back. "And how does that work? Do we get dealt double hands? Do we have to keep switching our seats?"

There are other people in the building, thinks Georgiana. *Not that any of them would want to play with you. You miserable kvetch.*

Just as Robinson Crusoe, marooned on his island, continued to behave as a civilized man, Georgiana Shiller, stranded in Mrs Kilgour's rudeness, continues to be polite. "Well, what about rummy? Do you play rummy?"

"Animal rummy? Is that what you play? Do you play it on your genius phone?"

"Or Scrabble." Robinson Crusoe raised his crops, and built his house, and read his Bible. Georgiana smiles. "I'm pretty good at Scrabble. I could bring my set next time."

Mrs Kilgour smiles, too. "I'm sure that's very kind of you, but to me that almost sounds like a threat."

Georgiana clamps her mouth shut for a second so the words that popped into her head – *Don't worry, you'll know when I'm threatening you* – don't actually come out.

"Well, if you don't want to play a game we could go for a walk." Georgiana would like to walk. She'd like to walk out. Just turn around and go home. Would she have to come back? Would she get into trouble? But what about Dr Kilpatiky? Would Georgiana lose the Brownie points she's earned? Would Dr Kilpatiky give her a placement that's even worse?

"A walk?" A laugh is not always happy. "And what do you think that thing over there is?" The thing over there is a wheelchair. "Do you think if I could walk more than a few feet I'd have one of those?"

"I meant that I'd walk, and push you." Straight into traffic, if she could.

"And where would we walk?" She waves towards the window at the concrete courtyard, dressed up today by a covering of colourful if dead leaves. "Out there in the prison yard? Or I suppose we could walk in the building – it depends on how fascinated you are by hallways."

"What about the common room Mr P showed me? There'll be—"

"Nothing to do but watch TV. Which I can do here. And which I'm going to do here. You can do what you want." She turns towards the set. "And stop shouting at me," she shouts. "I'm not deaf."

Georgiana can't leave for another forty-five minutes. "So what am I supposed to do if you're just going to watch TV?"

"Maybe you could thread a needle."

She sticks out her tongue at Mrs Kilgour's back and sits down on the edge of the bed. Gingerly. And turns on her phone.

Chapter Eleven
If You Won't Embrace the Chaos, the Chaos Will Embrace You

It's starting to seem to Asher that there are more Saturdays in a week than there used to be. He barely survives one than another is looming up in front of him like a three-headed, fire-breathing monster wearing a necklace made from the skulls of its victims. The fact that Asher's skull isn't yet on the necklace is a testament to something, but he's not sure what. Dumb luck maybe. A desire to prolong his suffering probably.

Today it is already dark by the time Asher leaves the community centre and staggers to his car. "Goodnight, Asher," Mrs Dunbar calls after him, loudly enough to have everyone with that name in the county look around. "See you next week!"

Not if I see you first, thinks Asher.

What really hurts – besides his back, his arms and his pride (the backed-up toilet was really disgusting and not a job for a future leader of the nation) – is that he used to love Saturdays. Saturdays were laid-back days – that pause in the week when not every minute of his time was accounted for. Sure, there was his kung-fu class first thing, but after that the day was pretty much his. He could go to brunch or lunch with Claudelia. Go to a game or throw a few baskets with Will. Play computer chess or do an hour of Mandarin online. Go for a swim. Work out. Some afternoons there would be a fencing competition. He might even do nothing for a whole hour, just sit in his room listening to music or catching up on the sudokus in the week's newspapers. But not any more. Now his Saturdays belong to Mrs Dunbar and the Queen's Park Community Centre. It's as if he sold his soul to the Devil.

When Asher gets home the lights of the Grossmans' house burn brightly along the driveway, over the front porch and behind the living-room window and the upstairs hall, welcoming him home. Which makes them the only things that do welcome him home. Albert is in Brussels this week – or somewhere like Brussels – and Mrs Swedger, the Grossmans' housekeeper, has weekends off. The lights are all on timers.

But despite the lack of anyone to greet him, Asher is as glad to be home as Odysseus was when he finally arrived back in Ithaca after ten years of harrowing adventures.

Partly he's glad to be home because Will's coming over to watch the Saturday game, something he's been looking forward to all week; but mainly he's glad because he would be glad to be anywhere that's not the Queen's Park Community Centre. Even a Greyhound bus, awash with germs and contagious diseases, would be better.

He opens the door, turns off the alarm and steps inside, suddenly aware of how truly tired he is. The centre may be a falling-down hole-in-the-wall, but it's a busy one. You'd think that people would drive right by it, assuming that any help it offered would be counter-productive, but they flock to it. Not just the ones getting free food, either. Besides the new mothers' club, it has a youth club, a senior citizens' club and a story hour for under-fives. It offers classes in English as a second language, and tutoring in reading and maths. It gives advice on your rights as both a citizen and a tenant, advice to women in abusive relationships, advice to parents with problem children, and help in filling out forms, applying for jobs, writing résumés and dealing with debt. According to Mrs Dunbar, they have to do so much because the government is doing next to nothing and cutting the funding it gives to the organizations that do try to do something. Also according to Mrs Dunbar, every week more people lose their jobs, their homes or both, while homeless and women's shelters, libraries and programmes to help the desperate are forced to close.

"Doesn't the Bible say that God helps those who help themselves?" asked Asher.

Mrs Dunbar said no. "The Bible doesn't say anything like that."

That isn't what Asher's been told.

"It was the Greeks. Check it yourself if you don't believe me," said Mrs Dunbar. "God doesn't concern himself with the material world. It's the government who helps those who help themselves. The bankers get bailed out and the unfortunate get thrown out. Jesus said you should love your neighbour as you love yourself, and, if you ask me, that doesn't mean foreclosing on his house and making him and his family homeless."

There isn't a Saturday that Asher isn't as busy as a doctor in a war. Because everyone who works at the centre is a volunteer, most of them are over sixty-five, and there are limits to how much they can heave, haul or carry, and to how high they can climb and how low bend. Which makes Asher very much in demand. They all keep telling him how nice it is to have an able-bodied young man on the team. Though if he keeps this up, he won't be able-bodied for long. Every time he finishes doing one thing, Mrs Dunbar – who always knows the second he stands still – pops up like some manic genie to give him another task. But even by the centre's high standards of chaos, today was special. Today was a Saturday that was handmade in Hell. Handmade and gift-wrapped with a big bow on top.

Someone threw a small stuffed pig into the toilet, causing it to back up and flood the bathroom. Today's workshop was housing advice, and at one point there were three people in the waiting room crying. The woman who runs the story hour couldn't get her car started. There was one epileptic fit, a violent drunk and a small child who fell down the basement stairs and had to be taken to the hospital. Mrs Dunbar dealt with the crying, the fit and the drunks, but the bathroom, story hour and the child were left to Asher. He's never dealt with waste matter, read to small children or been in Emergency before – which doesn't mean that any of them were experiences likely to make him a better person. On top of all that, they ran out of food boxes, which caused even more tears to fall.

He goes upstairs to shower and change. Besides sewage, he smells like a combination of sweat and the musty, never-really-clean odour of the centre itself, and has a funny taste in his mouth from an unwise cup of coffee he took from the urn. Asher is still getting dressed when Will arrives. "I'll be five minutes!" he calls, and tosses the keys to him from his bedroom window.

The Grossmans' family room features an enormous flat-screen TV, a top-end pool table (unlike the one at the centre that last saw better days in the nineteen-fifties), a ping-pong table, two oversized sofas and four matching armchairs. Looking at it, you would think that the family who uses it is a large one, not just two people – one of whom is rarely home. Will is on the sofa in front of the set, and leans back with a satisfied sigh as Asher comes in, carrying a tray of snacks and drinks.

"Man, this is the life," says Will. "You don't know how lucky you are not to have sisters. The house to ourselves and football. Heaven couldn't be any better than this."

"Yeah, it's cool." Cool but sometimes a little lonely. Will's sisters are pretty high-maintenance, but there are times when Asher would prefer any company to none. Asher's father is away so much that Asher has the house to himself more often than not; when Albert is home he's usually busy. And Mrs Swedger wasn't hired as a mother substitute, not even when Asher was younger; she was hired to keep the house running smoothly. She works a set number of hours a day, has her evenings off as well as weekends and has her own apartment over the garage. But Asher doesn't say anything about being lonely to himself, never mind to Will. What he says is, "Don't start pulling out the tears and violins, Lundquist. You don't have it that bad. Your sisters do have friends. And some of them are pretty all right."

"And what good does that do me?" demands Will. "You don't seriously think I could go out with one of my sisters' friends, do you? Trust me, dude, they've all seen that picture of me pissing on the side of the car when I was three. None of them thinks that highly of me. And even if I did date one of them, you can bet my sisters would tell her stuff about me even I don't know. Every time I belched or farted they'd be on the phone telling her how loud or how much it stank."

"Oh, man..." Asher laughs. "They'd take pictures of you sleeping, with your mouth open and drooling. And pictures of your room with your dirty boxers piled up on the floor and all those plates under the bed."

"Exactly. That's why I keep my door locked at all times." He pats Dunkin, sleeping loudly beside him. "And why I'm glad I have my guard dog here."

Asher sets the tray down on the coffee table and drops onto the sofa next to Will. "You're quite a team. He's hardly ever awake and you never stop eating."

"We'll ignore that unkind jibe, won't we, Dunk? Because we know you don't really mean it."

Asher winks. "You believe what you want."

Will reaches for a handful of chips and stuffs them into his mouth, sprinkling crumbs all over himself and the sofa. "So how was it today at the salt mines of Queen's Park? Drain any lakes? Feed the multitude with a couple of packages of hot dogs and a bag of rolls? Have anybody puke all over you?"

"Hahaha," says Asher.

Will thinks it's hilarious that Asher Grossman, the boy who was born wearing a suit and shoes with a spit shine, is doing menial tasks and manual labour. He has said – repeatedly – that he'd give a hundred bucks for a picture of Asher with a mop.

"I know this'll be a big disappointment, but there weren't any major floods or barfing babies like on my first day."

"You see?" Will punches him in the arm. "What'd I tell you? It's getting better, isn't it?"

"It depends what you call better. I did have to spend half a lifetime sitting in Emergency with a kid with a broken arm. And unblock the toilet and clean up the crap."

"Eww…" Will wrinkles his face in distaste. "You don't mean that literally, do you?"

"Oh yes, I do," says Asher. "We don't deal with meta-phors at the centre." They just deal with hopelessness and despair.

"So it's not getting better?"

"It's never going to get better. The most you can hope for is different." Every day a new crisis; every week a fresh disaster. "I know you think I'm exaggerating. Because I'm me." Someone who thinks civilization is collapsing if a fuse blows or his flight is delayed. "But I'm not. That place is total chaos. And if you think that there's any order in chaos, I can tell you straight up that there isn't. Not a subatomic particle of the stuff." Asher also takes some chips, but, unlike Will, he sets his down on a napkin. He's a neat eater. "There are always at least four things going on at the same time, and everybody running around like they're in a disaster movie." Which, if he's honest, they technically are. The disaster movie of life. "When anybody bothers to show up." Asher's father is right. No matter what Mrs Dunbar or the Bible says about loving your neighbour (he did check it out, she was right about God not helping the ambitious), without the profit motive, very little gets done. Either people don't come at all, or they come and achieve less than the paint on the walls – which, at the centre, at least is peeling. "And every five minutes something goes wrong. The power's always going out. There's always a partition collapsing." Though his theory is that Mrs Dunbar knocks down the partitions. Graceful as a bulldozer. "Today, besides the sewer taking over the bathroom, we had an angry ex-husband stinking of beer looking for his wife and threatening to set us on fire. I'm not even going to get into the rest of it."

"At least it's not boring. Unlike, for example, raking leaves."

Asher pours his soda into a glass. "No, it's not boring." It's a lot more like a psychiatric crisis unit than a community centre. "It's stressful. It's messy. And it's exhausting. But, no, you're right, Will, I honestly can't say that it's boring."

Will grins. "And I have to say that as awesome as I thought it was that this woman got you to stand in dirty water in your bare feet and mop up the cellar, I think it's a hundred times more awesome that she had you unblock the toilet. I assume you wore your surgical gloves." He tosses some more chips into his mouth. "Asher I-get-manicures Grossman! I really would pay to see that."

Asher jabs him with his elbow. "Lay off, will you? It was only the one time." His father took him to a VIP party and insisted on the manicure. "And anyway, you're not going to see it. Not in this lifetime."

Will pops the top on his soda with a flourish of spray. Asher never bothers offering him a glass. He's seen Dunkin drink out of a glass more often than Will.

"So, the multitudes still coming for the handouts?"

"Are you kidding?" Freeloaders, his father would call them. Wanting something for nothing. "You'd need barbed wire and dogs to keep them away. We actually ran out today." It surprised him that no one shouted or complained. Most of them just turned around and walked off with blank faces.

"So why did you even bother going?" Will takes a slug of his drink. "You must've done most of your twenty hours already. Just stop. If you have a couple more hours to do, do them in April or May."

But here's the weird thing. It doesn't seem that Asher can just quit. Not even for one weekend.

"I tried to." He really did. At least he thinks so. "But, I don't know, somehow it didn't work."

"Somehow it didn't work?" Will almost chokes with laughter. "What'd you do, fall through the rabbit hole or something? You're the slick-as-oil future lawyer. You could talk a moose into shooting itself."

"Yeah, I'm great with moose." Asher takes a few more chips. He chews them singly and well. "But Mrs Dunbar isn't a moose."

Will grins, waggling his eyebrows. "What is she? Some hot babe? Is that why you can't say no to her? Why as soon as she looks at you, you grab your plunger and wade into the muck? Because she makes you melt with her big blue eyes?"

Mrs Dunbar is a *femme fatale* only in the sense that she might knock him over and trample him to death. What she is, as far as Asher can figure, is a force of nature. Like a tornado. Something you can't really say no to. Not with any success.

"Man, are you on the wrong page, you doof. Mrs Dunbar's in her fifties, built like a black bear and married to the minister over at the Methodist church. She's just got this way about her."

"What way? She carry a gun?"

"She doesn't need a gun." Weak people may need to be armed, but not people like Mrs Dunbar. She would have made a great dictator. "And it's not like she's really bossy or anything like that. She just makes you think she's agreeing with you and then the next thing you know you're doing what she wants."

This is the literal truth. Last week, Asher kept saying he was finished for the day and was going home, and Mrs Dunbar kept saying how hard he'd worked and what a good job he'd done as if she was thanking him and telling him to go in peace, and the next thing he knew he was carrying someone's groceries to her car. Then he tried to tell Mrs Dunbar that he wouldn't be in this week, and she asked him why, and he heard himself saying, "Yeah, OK, I guess I can make it." The same thing happened this week. The woman doesn't seem to hear "no".

Will frowns. "Shoot, man. Does that mean you're not going to have any free Saturdays for the rest of the year? What about the games? And our climbing? We have to get one more climb in before the snow."

"There's no way I won't be free for that stuff, dude. We're going to do everything we always do. This time I really mean it. That woman's not going to see me again till the spring."

Famous last words. Again.

Chapter Twelve
Marigold's Favourite Book

"What is all this, honey?"

Marigold stops in the middle of the staircase, and automatically smiles. She left her mother alone for a few minutes to get something in her room, and here she is in the hall, peering into Marigold's opened backpack. Why isn't she still at the kitchen table, drinking coffee and watching TV?

"Oh, nothing." Smile solid as cement, Marigold continues her descent. "Just a couple of old picture books I'm taking to the library."

Her mother looks at her. "Books? You're taking books to the library?" She's wearing a smile, too. The happy Liottas. But she sounds as if Marigold has pulled a gun on her. "Isn't that like taking chocolate to Nestlé?"

"It's just books I don't need any more, Mom. I thought the library could use them."

"You mean you're *giving* them to the library? You're giving your childhood books away?"

Marigold chooses to misunderstand. "The library won't think it's weird, Mom. They're in really good condition." There has never been any scribbling or bending down corners in this house.

"Well, that goes without saying, honey. Of course they're practically like new. That wasn't what I meant. These were your books when you were a little girl. They have sentimental value." Mrs Liotta pulls out a hardback with a blue cover. "Look! This was your favourite book. You must have read it a thousand times. Remember? Remember how you loved it?"

The book her mother holds is *The Cat in the Hat*. When she was little and frightened of her parents' arguments Marigold would get into bed with her sister if one happened at night. But if it was in the day, she would hide in her closet and read until the shouting, the sobbing and the sound of things smashing stopped. To Marigold it was like disappearing into a different – and better – world. The book in her mother's hand is the only one she remembers reading the Christmas That Almost Never Was. The Christmas they didn't open their presents until the evening, because her parents had such an awful fight that her father left the house and her mother went to bed.

Marigold sat in her closet all afternoon, eating dry cereal and reading it over and over. Wishing the Cat in the Hat would come and rescue her and Rose.

"Yeah, of course I remember," says Marigold. "But I'm not a little kid any more. Now I never even look at them. They just sit on the shelf ."

"Aw, but honey…" Her mother pulls the other two books from Marigold's bag. "These are special. Don't you want to read them with your own daughter some day?"

Unexpected, unasked and definitely unwanted, a random thought flutters into Marigold's head. If this thought were a person, it would be sullen, scowling and wearing beat-up trainers. What if she has a child like Sadie Hawkle? What then?

"I can take her to the library and we can read them there," says Marigold.

"If you don't have room for them, we could put them in with Rose's."

Marigold's sister's room has been kept exactly as it was when she lived at home. As if she never left; as if she might be coming back.

"They'll still be on a shelf, Mom. What difference does it make?"

"They'll still be here, that's the difference." Eveline Liotta has a way of smiling that always makes Marigold feel as if it is she who's the child and needs protection. "I really can't bear the thought of you giving these away."

Since her mother doesn't know that Sadie exists, Marigold, of course, can't very well explain that this is a special case. That because Marigold loved these books so much she's hoping that Sadie will too.

"I know, Mom, but if some other kids whose parents can't afford to buy them books can use them, that's a good thing, isn't it?"

Not as good as Marigold thinks.

Her mother holds the books against her chest like a shield. "It's like giving away a piece of my heart."

The wrong move now could shove her mother into the very-bad-mood abyss. "Not really, Mom." Marigold's voice is gentle and coaxing. "They're just some good books that deserve to be read and loved by other kids."

"What about this?" Eveline looks like a little girl who thinks that she's clever enough to wangle an extra cookie. "What if I donate some money to the library so they can buy some new picture books, and we keep yours? Then everybody's happy."

Marigold almost always does what her mother wants. She has certainly never done anything to cross her mother. Not on purpose. Even on that long-ago Christmas That Almost Never Was, when she and Rose were finally called downstairs to open their presents Marigold acted as if nothing had happened because it would have upset her mother if she didn't. There is even a photograph of her, Rose and Eveline sitting in front of the tree together, as if it's eight in the morning not eight at night, and ahead of them is a day of love and laughter – not a day of Rose going over to her friend's and Marigold sitting in a closet eating Lucky Charms. But this time she doesn't do what her mother wants.

"I already promised." She snatches the books from Eveline's hands and jams them back in her bag. "I have to go, Mom. I don't want to be late for school. I'll see you later."

She doesn't turn back to wave. Just in case her mother is standing in the doorway in tears.

"Picture books?" Claudelia gives Marigold a quizzical smile. She was looking for a pen in Marigold's bag, but found something much more interesting. "Why are you lugging picture books around?"

"Happy endings," says Byron. "You know what Marigold's like."

Marigold ignores him. "They're for Sadie. I thought she might think they're more interesting than the books they have at the school."

"So do we have a Marigold Liotta success story here?" asks Will. "Gold spun from old shoelaces?

Marigold laughs. "I don't know about gold, but we may yet get a base metal of some kind. We are making progress. You know, one step at a time. That's what counts."

Asher, who has been eating with one hand and tapping on his notepad with the other, looks up and smiles as if he's about to ask the witness a trick question. "And you're growing as a person, right?"

"Yes," says Marigold. "Yes, I am." She's never in her life lied so much, been so unbending or resorted to such devious means of getting someone to do what she wants. Which means that Sadie Hawkle is making her grow as a person – though not necessarily in the right direction.

Georgiana is twisting her hair around one finger and looking thoughtful. "Maybe I should take one for my old bag," says Georgiana.

"Dr Seuss?" asks Will. "You really think that's her speed?"

"Oh, don't be such a jerk," groans Georgiana. "Obviously, I don't mean Dr Seuss. I mean a regular book. She'd have to shut up for five minutes if I was reading to her."

Will raises an eyebrow. "You can read?"

Georgiana sticks her tongue out at him.

"I thought you said she was an angel," says Claudelia.

Trust Claudelia to remember that. "She is. But she's a really chatty angel."

"What I find fascinating," says Byron, "is that Georgiana's met someone who talks more than she does."

"Oh God. *Et tu,* Byron," moans Georgiana. Things have moved on from Mrs Kilgour ignoring her, but not in a good way. "You wouldn't think it was so hilarious if you had to listen to her. She really never shuts up. I swear, zombies could invade St J's and she wouldn't notice or miss a word."

"And are you growing as a person?" asks Asher.

"Oh, that's really funny, Ash. Don't tell me the law's loss is going to be the world of comedy's gain."

Claudelia wants to know what Mrs Kilgour talks about.

"Are you kidding?" Georgiana looks almost affronted. "You think I don't have anything better to do than listen to her drone on? I mean, my God, it's like listening to static." Thank God for the World Wide Web and the cell phone or Georgiana might have lost her mind by now. "Seriously, she's like somebody digging around in an attic the size of the White House and constantly coming out with dusty old pieces of junk." She makes her voice shrill and raspy, which is not how Margarita Kilgour speaks, of course, but it is how Georgiana hears her. *"Oh, look at this! An earring from eighteen ninety! A picture of New York City before they put roads in! And here, here's a bottle from the first batch of Coca-Cola ever made!"*

Will helps himself to the half a cookie Georgiana's abandoned. "See, that is the one really good thing about plants. They're mega low-maintenance when it comes to emotional needs."

Asher raises his eyes from his notepad once more. "Count yourself lucky, George. At least she doesn't have any problems." Asher is starting to understand that the trouble with suffering humanity is that it suffers. Pretty much constantly. "You should come to crisis headquarters if you want your head done in."

"What do you mean she doesn't have problems? Of course she has problems." Georgiana's fork taps against the rim of her plate. "She's old, Asher. She's old and she's going to die soon. I think those are problems."

"Just how old is she?" asks Marigold.

Georgiana grimaces. "She's, like, practically ninety."

"Oh, right," says Marigold. But what she's thinking is: *Ninety's better than nine.*

Marigold is genuinely excited when she shows Sadie the books.

"These were my favourite books when I was little," she explains. "Especially this one." She puts *The Cat in the Hat* on the desk. "It always made me laugh. It still does. And if I was blue or in a bad mood or whatever, it cheered me up."

Sadie isn't so sure. "It's not in colour. Why isn't it in colour?"

"It is in colour." Marigold points out the colours. "There just aren't a lot of them."

Sadie isn't sure about the rhyming, either. "Songs rhyme," says Sadie. "Not books."

"But it is a little like singing," says Marigold. "It's really fun. I'll read you some and you'll see."

Sadie does get into the rhyme, but then she isn't sure about the story itself. "They're going to get in trouble," Sadie frets. "Their mom is really gonna yell at them when she gets home. She's gonna punish them bad."

Marigold glances over at her. She looks really worried. "You think so?"

"Uh-huh." Sadie nods, her frown as solemn as a funeral. "They're gonna be hit. Or not get supper. Or not be allowed to watch any TV." Her fingers rub against the edge of the desk. "Or … or something."

"It's going to be OK, Sadie," Marigold assures her. "I promise. I wouldn't love something so much that ends sad.

Let's keep reading and see what happens."

It takes a while. With each new page of chaos brought on by the Cat in the Hat, Sadie wiggles in her chair and her fingers rub harder, but she keeps reading and keeps turning the pages.

When they get to the end she falls back against her chair. "Whew," she breathes, and laughs. A sound Marigold has never heard before. "That was close." And then she actually smiles. "Do we have time for another one?"

Chapter Thirteen
A Match Not Made in Heaven

Looking at them, Georgiana and Mrs Kilgour seem as unalike as two members of the same species and sex can be. Age, build and hair colour aside, Georgiana (who does judge books by their covers) is stylish and fashion-conscious, and Mrs Kilgour (who always reads the book before passing judgement) has never been either of those things. Georgiana would wear a silk dress and six-inch heels to go to the deli for a box of cookies and Mrs Kilgour would wear jeans and sneakers to a Park Avenue party. How they dress reflects other things about each of them, of course. Georgiana is neat, organized and conservative by nature, while Mrs Kilgour, even before the years made her slower and even simple things harder to do, has always been slapdash, impetuous and anarchic. But there the dissimilarities end.

Unfortunately, the things they have in common aren't

things that make it easier for them to get along. Both of them are argumentative. Both of them are stubborn. They are both women of strong opinions – and, of course, their strong opinions are rarely the same. Indeed, between the obstinacy, the contrariness and the attitudes, putting them in the same room has a similar effect to mixing sulphur, charcoal and potassium nitrate: step back and watch your eyes! Nothing is so trivial or insignificant that Georgiana Shiller and Margarita Kilgour can't bicker about it. TV shows. The weather. How long it takes to drive from St Joan's to Shell Harbour. How to peel an orange. Movies. Books. The exact shade of Georgiana's skirt or Mrs Kilgour's sweater. Whether Christmas is better than Thanksgiving, or tomato juice better than grape. Which of the nurses is the nicest, which the most irritating, which of them probably owns a cat. How many times it snowed last winter… If they were dogs they'd fight over bones so small that no one else could see them.

And yet, unlikely as it may seem, Georgiana and Mrs Kilgour have developed a routine together that suits them both enough to make the other's presence bearable. They go for walks. Not around the easy-to-clean corridors of St Joan's, but long, leisurely strolls down wooded roads and quiet streets of unpretentious houses and into town. The walks were Mrs Kilgour's idea. Although at first she rejected Georgiana's suggestion that they do any such thing (rightly guessing that Georgiana's concept of a walk was nothing longer than to and from the car), when she thought about it later she realized that they could go much further than the borders of the centre. She'd be able to buy things she usually does without – her favourite candy, a magazine that is about more than celebrities and what they wore to some party, a bottle of wine. She'd be able to see things she never sees – children and houses and dogs sleeping in the sun. Being cooped up in her room for so long, she said, was sapping her will to live.

Being cooped up in Mrs Kilgour's room for an hour was enough to suck every particle of joy from Georgiana's heart. Even being able to perch on the bed and text or go online didn't help as much as you might think. The bathroom was private and quiet, as isolated in its way as being in a space capsule – albeit one that never left the ground – which meant that Georgiana could forget where she was until her phone told her it was time to go. Not so the bedroom. With the TV blaring or Mrs Kilgour talking, it was hard to forget she was in Room 10a at the St Joan's Nursing Centre. And she had to look up all the time to make sure the old bat hadn't noticed what she was really doing and was ready to start making sarcastic comments; look up and see exactly where she was and want to weep.

Not that Georgiana greeted the idea of leaving the grounds with a rousing cheer and a fistful of confetti. Even though she knew it had to be better than just sitting there like a tethered goat, she still found something to complain about. Georgiana said you'd think they were actually going somewhere nice – to a party, or a new super mall – and not just the one, dull parade of brick storefronts and parking meters of Main Street the way Mrs Kilgour carried on. Georgiana calls it the Fifth Avenue of Nowheresville.

"I mean really," said Georgiana, "it's not somewhere you want to go more than once, like Baja or Hawaii."

"I'm not saying it's Paris in the springtime," retorted Mrs Kilgour. "But there's only one season in this damn room, and that's bleak midwinter after the crops failed."

"More like bleak midwinter in a Russian jail." Georgiana does like to have the last word.

"After the crops failed." So does Mrs Kilgour.

Nonetheless, despite her grumblings and misgivings, the weekly walk has turned out to be better than Georgiana could have expected. True, she does all the pushing and the walking, but she has become something of an expert at shoving a wheelchair along with one hand while texting or keeping busy online with the other.

As the wheels crunch over drifts of leaves, everything she sees reminds Mrs Kilgour of the past. The falling leaves; the snap of cold in the air; the curling smoke of backyard fires; the houses decorated with jack-o'-lanterns, ghosts and witches, with bouquets of coloured corn, preening turkeys and ornamental squash. And all the while that the wheels turn, the leaves crackle and Georgiana communicates with people who aren't anywhere near her, Mrs Kilgour reminisces. How she always loved this time of year. The trees alight with colour; apple cider and bonfires; Halloween and Thanksgiving; that first sharp bite of winter in the air. The first Halloween costume she remembers was a cowgirl outfit. "Completely politically incorrect these days, I expect," she says. "But I thought it was wonderful. Thought I was Annie Oakley. I even had a holster and a cap gun. I suppose they must've been my brother's." But there were scores of other Halloweens and other costumes – that party in a New York loft where everyone came as Richard Nixon; scores of bonfires and first frosts; scores of Thanksgivings – one in a distant jungle where she was thankful just to be alive. She drifts from memory to memory like a butterfly in a field of flowers, rearranging years and places so that things that happened in Southeast Asia in the seventies jostle against things that happened in Europe in the fifties, wind around things that happened in South America in the sixties and eventually cross paths with things that happened in North America five or ten or twenty years ago.

Georgiana has heard none of this. Or very little. A word here and there – the name of a place she didn't know existed or of people she'll never know – each one darting past her so quickly that she forgets it instantly. As far as she's concerned, Mrs Kilgour might as well be whispering in Akkadian at a heavy-metal concert being played near the runway of a busy airport. This, of course, is why Georgiana likes these walks so much. Mrs Kilgour sits up in front of her, prattling on in her own little world, completely oblivious to the fact that, behind her, Georgiana is telling Claudelia what happened in her media class or ordering something online. It isn't as comfortable and convenient as locking herself in the bathroom for an hour (since the time they ended up in a hedge she's realized that she does have to look where they're going now and then), but it's good enough. At least she doesn't have to listen.

But today Mrs Kilgour is showing some reluctance to leave the centre.

"It looks like it's going to rain," she says. "Doesn't it look like it's going to rain to you?"

Georgiana has no intention of being trapped in the room where she has to actually pay attention to Mrs Kilgour, or at least be ready to seem as if she is.

"It always looks like that out that window," says Georgiana. "It's like permanent gloom. I just came from outside and it looked fine to me."

Mrs Kilgour continues to squint through the glass. "I've been feeling a little peaky today. I don't want to go out if it's going to rain."

Georgiana has no idea that "peaky" means unwell; she thinks it's just some lame excuse.

"It's not going to rain." Georgiana couldn't sound more certain if she actually controlled the weather. "It's a perfectly OK day." In truth, it would take Marigold Liotta to look up at that sky crowded with dark clouds and see sunshine. "It has all that fresh air that you like so much. And you said yourself that you'll grow roots if you spend any more time in this room. So let's just go." She doesn't add that at Mrs Kilgour's age she might not have that many more days left to go outside, but she thinks it.

"It's not that I don't want to go out," snaps Mrs Kilgour. "I'm just not sure that I'm up to it."

"What are you talking about?" Georgiana makes a give-me-a-break face. "You're not the one doing all the work. All you have to do is sit there."

Mrs Kilgour is much more quiet than usual. Occasionally she mumbles something, but aside from that the only sounds are the wheels of the chair and, if your hearing is exceptionally good, the gentle tap of Georgiana's finger on the touchpad of her phone. She and Claudelia are discussing the parties they're having over the holidays. Georgiana is giving the one for Christmas; Claudelia is doing New Year's. Because she is so busy (What to eat? What to wear? Can Byron put together three hours of Christmas music? Should the New Year's party be a masquerade?) she is completely oblivious to the abnormal silence. It doesn't start raining until they get to town.

Which is when Georgiana sees that the reason Mrs Kilgour has been so quiet is because she's fallen asleep. This sometimes occurs, of course. So long as Georgiana doesn't steer them into shrubbery or jump the kerb and nearly pitch the old woman onto the ground (which has also happened) the soporific movement of the chair can bring on one of Mrs Kilgour's narcoleptic episodes. Though it might occur to Georgiana that she's sleeping very soundly; even the rain doesn't wake her.

Georgiana's coat has a hood on it, but Mrs Kilgour has nothing but her Yankees cap to protect her. Georgiana is usually the kind of person who locks the barn door only after the horse has been stolen, shipped to another country and sold, but because she knows how much grief she's going to get for being wrong about the weather, she pilots them into Bargain World to get an umbrella for the walk back home. Forward planning at last.

Georgiana parks the wheelchair to one side of the entrance, out of the way, and goes in search of umbrellas, confident that Mrs Kilgour will never know she was gone.

Georgiana has never been in Bargain World before, and it takes her some time to find the umbrellas, tucked away at the back of the store. Bargain World has already started to put out its Christmas stock, and on the way back to retrieve Mrs Kilgour Georgiana is distracted by a display of really cute snowmen, elves and Santas that light up and play "Jingle Bells". She's still thinking about the musical lights as favours for her Christmas party when she sees the buzz of people gathered together at the front of the store. Most of them are just watching, but two of them are leaning forward. She can't see their faces, but their backs look concerned. The person Georgiana doesn't see is Mrs Kilgour. Where the hell is she?

The answer to that question, of course, is that Mrs Kilgour is at the centre of the swarm.

Georgiana starts to hurry.

"Is she breathing?" one person is asking, as Georgiana reaches them.

"Do you think she's had a heart attack?" asks another.

Someone else suggests a stroke.

She can't be dead. Not now; not here beside a window display of artificial Christmas trees in pastel shades. Georgiana won't allow it.

"It's OK. It's OK," says Georgiana, pushing her way through. "There's nothing wrong with her. She's just asleep."

"She doesn't look asleep to me," says the man who is bent over the slouched figure taking Mrs Kilgour's pulse.

"But she is," insists Georgiana. She has to be. "She does this all the time. She has that thing." She can't remember what it's called. What did Mr Papazoglakis – whose name, miraculously, she can remember – call it? "That narcotic thing."

The woman who is searching in her purse for a mirror looks up. "She's on drugs?"

"No, no, of course she isn't. She just falls asleep. You know, kind of whenever."

Someone else wants to know if the old woman is Georgiana's grandmother.

"God, no." And Georgiana, who thought she had no memory of the first Mrs Shiller, suddenly sees her clearly, holding out her hand because they're about to cross a street. Her grandmother was tall and heavyset.

She always dressed in grey or brown; her white hair was always twisted into a neat bun; there were gold and diamond rings on her fingers and brown spots on the back of her hand. She was nothing at all like Mrs Kilgour. "I'm just her visitor." Georgiana reaches out and shakes Mrs Kilgour by the shoulder. "Mrs Kilgour! Mrs Kilgour! Mrs Kilgour, wake up!" This has never happened before. Mrs Kilgour falling asleep is no more unusual than clouds passing overhead, of course, but when she's nodded off on the way to town, a gentle nudge and a "Mrs Kilgour, we're here!" has always brought her around. Though not this time, apparently.

The store manager bustles up to them, looking worried. "What's going on? Has anyone called an ambulance? Is she dead?"

"No," says Georgiana. "No one's called an ambulance, and she's not dead. She's just asleep. She could fall asleep standing up."

"She's definitely alive," says the man who took her pulse. "But it looks to me like she's had a stroke."

"She hasn't had a stroke." Georgiana is shouting now the way you do when no one will listen to what you're saying, but even that doesn't wake Mrs Kilgour. If anybody is likely to have a stroke, it's Georgiana. "She's old. She falls asleep. That's the whole story."

"I'm calling an ambulance." The manager looks at the pulse-taker. "Who's with this woman? You?"

The pulse-taker steps back quickly. "I never saw her before in my life."

"I'm with her." Georgiana is gripping Mrs Kilgour's shoulder hard enough now to wake her even if she were dead. She'd try shaking her out of the chair if she didn't think the manager would have her arrested. "But you don't have to call an ambulance. I keep trying to tell you, she's just asleep." Georgiana shakes some more. She leans closer and hisses into Mrs Kilgour's ear, "Wake up or they're going to call an ambulance. Wake up!"

"We can't just stand here hoping she'll come around." The manager takes out his phone.

Georgiana would like to believe that Mrs Kilgour is doing this on purpose, just to torment her. But she doesn't. It has finally occurred to Georgiana that "peaky" must mean not so hot. Deep down she knows that everybody who isn't Georgiana Shiller will blame her if Mrs Kilgour does die. She should have listened when she said she didn't want to go out. She shouldn't have insisted.

"Please, Mrs Kilgour," pleads Georgiana. She's on the verge of tears. "Please wake up. Please, please, please!"

Maybe it was saying please. Mrs Kilgour opens her eyes. She blinks several times, looking around. "What the hell is going on? Who are all these people? Why are they all gawping at me?"

"You gave us quite a turn," says the manager. "We thought you were having a heart attack."

Her nap has done nothing to sweeten Mrs Kilgour's personality. "And why would you think a dumb thing like that?"

"You fell asleep and you wouldn't wake up," explains Georgiana. "I tried to tell them you were OK, that you have that narcotic thing, but they wouldn't listen."

Mrs Kilgour's gaze falls on the window beside her, and then returns to Georgiana. "Didn't I tell you it was going to rain?"

Chapter Fourteen

Asher's Not Going to Let Mrs Dunbar Push Him Around Any More

Asher is smart. Besides being smart, he has been raised by one of the shrewdest lawyers in the country (which is saying something) and already has many of the skills he will need when he joins that important profession himself. One of the thousands of valuable things his father has taught Asher is that you have to get up pretty early in the morning if you want to outsmart a really clever lawyer; and even then you won't win unless your lawyer is even more clever – and just a little more ruthless.

Today, Asher gets up very early. Feeling extremely clever and worthy of his father's praise, he drives to the community centre not after his kung-fu class but before it. This is a manoeuvre Mrs Dunbar won't be expecting, and that makes it a manoeuvre that can't possibly fail. He doesn't like sneaking behind her back like this, but the direct approach doesn't work with the minister's wife. He has tried to reason and explain his way out of helping on Saturdays, but there's no use talking to Mrs Dunbar; he'd be better off talking to God. At least a person can convince himself that God is listening. Which is not the case with Mrs Dunbar. Even if he manages to get out two consecutive sentences, she just nods and tells him he's made a very good point or that of course she understands completely, and the next thing he knows she's giving him something else to do and lumbering off in the opposite direction, dropping things as she goes. But if he arrives *before* his class she won't be there. Nobody will. Most people will still be in bed, or at least huddled over a cup of coffee. He spent nearly a half-hour last night writing her a note he plans to slip under the door: *Dear Mrs Dunbar, I'm very sorry for the short notice, but due to unforeseen circumstances beyond my control I won't be able to make it today. I'll let you know if next Saturday works for me as I have a great many commitments right now. Yours sincerely, Asher Grossman.*

The main street is deserted except for a few birds and two dogs walking side by side in a hurry. Asher stops in front of the centre, so happy he feels like punching the air. Victory is his! He smiles to himself. Smugly. You have to be pretty sharp to defeat his father, and pretty sharp to defeat his father's son. Otherwise known as the chip off the old block.

Asher takes his letter from the glove compartment, lays it on the seat beside him and starts to unfasten his seatbelt. The clasp is stuck and he's trying to unjam it when a head suddenly appears in the window beside him. The head is wearing a red and black lumberjack hat. He can see the barrel of a rifle rising up beside it. It takes no thought to know that if someone were going to shoot him while he was sitting in his car, minding his own business, then this is the town where it would happen. He's so frightened his heart jumps as if someone kicked it and he somehow manages to hit the horn, causing his heart to make another leap for freedom. Not until she starts waving at him does he realize that the head and the gun belong to Mrs Dunbar. Christ Almighty, what's wrong with the woman? Dawn is still rubbing the sleep out of its eyes, and here she is running around town with a shotgun. Mrs Dunbar gestures for him to roll down the window, and, too traumatized to refuse, Asher rolls it down.

"Asher! I am so glad to see you." Holding a rifle is no obstacle to Mrs Dunbar clapping her hands in delight. "You won't believe this. I know you're a left-side-of-the-brain kind of person. And I can tell that you have a sceptical view of this kind of thing. But as I was having my breakfast I said a little prayer that you might show up early today. As a special favour."

"Really?"

She nods, the earflaps of her hat bouncing. Making her look like a very large, and clothed, spaniel. "Yes, I really did. It was more a hope than a plea, but I did mention to the Lord that it would be a great help if you came before you're supposed to." The earflaps bounce again. "Now isn't that something? And here you are!" She gives him a God-is-on-my-side smile. "I guess he realized it's an emergency." If Mrs Dunbar were a motor vehicle, she would be an ambulance, siren always on. "He certainly does work in mysterious ways, doesn't he?"

"Tell me about it," says Asher. Not so much mysterious as totally beyond belief.

"Come on, come on..." She opens his door without warning and he nearly falls on top of her. "I'll make us some coffee and explain what's happening."

Coffee. She's making coffee. In that cesspool they call an urn. She's determined to kill him this morning, one way or another.

She gives him a sudden squeeze. "Oh, I am so happy to see you, Asher! Come on, let's get inside."

Possibly because he's too shocked by the unaccustomed hug (his father doesn't go in for spontaneous displays of affection), Asher, the boy who has disputed every grade he's gotten below an A since elementary school, doesn't argue with her. Nor does he pick up the envelope from the passenger seat, thrust it into her hands, slam the door and roar out of town. He locks the car and follows her inside, agreeing that it's a beautiful morning.

The reason Mrs Dunbar was suggesting to God over her toast that it would be good if Asher showed up early is because a group of volunteers is Hunting for Hunger today. They might not be able to climb, carry, lift or bend but apparently they can all shoot. Which means that she's going to be more short-staffed than usual.

Is there nothing this woman says or does that doesn't surprise him?

"You're going hunting?" echoes Asher.

"Me? Go hunting?" The partitions shake with her laughter. "Oh, I don't think so. I'd be more likely to hit myself than anything else. Even if the deer came up and sat at my feet."

At least she's right about that.

"I just thought – you know, because you came armed…"

"Oh, the gun!" She pats the gun in question in what strikes Asher as a very reckless way. "This isn't mine. It's Carlin's. My husband borrowed it. I'm just bringing it back so Carlin can go on the hunt."

What astounds him more? That a minister borrowed a gun for some unknown reason? Or that he borrowed it from a man with addiction issues?

"I know it's none of my business, Mrs Dunbar, but—" Asher takes a deep breath— "but do you really think that's wise?"

"Giving Carlin back his gun?"

"No, not that. I mean … I just wondered if he can be trusted with a weapon like that."

"Of course he can. He's a damn good shot."

"I mean, in light of his drinking problem."

"What drinking problem?"

Although Asher hasn't seen him in that state since, he reminds her of his first morning, Carlin asleep on the couch, unable to help with the flood in the cellar. And his homelessness and chronic unemployment.

Between Mrs Dunbar's gait and her laugh, it's a wonder there's a partition still standing in the centre – or a building in the town. "Oh, he wasn't drunk, Asher. It's true he's having trouble finding work, but Carlin doesn't have a problem with alcohol. What he has is a bad back. Some days he's lucky he can walk."

"Oh," says Asher. "A bad back."

Mrs Dunbar picks up two moderately clean cups from beside the urn. "So, let's talk about today," she says. "I can get one of the mothers to take over story hour, that's no problem." She pours them each a cup of coffee

Superman couldn't see through. "But this is the Saturday we give CV and job application advice, and I have no one who can do that."

Asher stares into his cup. There's something in it besides melted tar, but he can't decide if it's moving or not. It can't be moving. This coffee would kill a cockroach.

"So what do you think?"

Asher looks up. "Excuse me?"

"About the job advice session."

Asher blinks. You can't take your eyes off this woman for a second. "Do you mean *me*?"

"You're perfect," crows Mrs Dunbar. "Look at you! Neat, well dressed, extraordinarily well organized, articulate, a straight-A student. And with a keen legal mind, used to thinking around corners and outside the box."

He's sure he never told her who his father is or about his own career strategy, but, somehow, she seems to know.

"Yeah, but I'm only a high-school student."

Mrs Dunbar bangs him on the shoulder, making him spill coffee all over his shoes. "These people aren't applying for positions at Harvard, Asher. You're more than qualified to help."

There isn't a napkin in sight. Of course.

"The thing is, Mrs Dunbar..." Asher looks right at her, trying to ignore his shoes and his fear that the brew can eat through leather. "The thing is that I have something else—"

Something else to do this morning, is what he is trying to say, but she cuts him off before he can finish his sentence.

"I know you have a lot of abilities and interests, Asher. You've already proved that. And I certainly don't want to dictate to you."

Heaven forbid.

"As you know, that isn't the way we work here. But these advice days only happen once every six weeks, and they are very important. Our people count on them."

Which means that it might be better not to have half your staff going out to gun down Bambi on a day when you've planned such an important event.

"Well, maybe things could be organized a little better," suggests Asher. Mildly. "You know, in the future." Hoping he sounds more diplomatic than he feels. "You know, to avoid scheduling conflicts like this."

"Oh, organized." Mrs Dunbar sighs. "You sound like my husband. He's a very organized man. Even his socks are arranged by weight and colour."

So are Asher's. She should see his medicine chest and DVD collection. Then again, perhaps she doesn't have to.

"But you are organized, aren't you?" Her smile

brightens. "I bet you could whip things into shape around here."

"Oh, Mrs Dunbar, I think you—"

"It's no use saying I should. Organization just isn't in my nature."

Now there's a revelation.

She shrugs in an and-so-it-goes kind of way. "And as I always say to Mr Dunbar, the lilies of the fields aren't organized, either, but they manage just fine, don't they?"

Asher is so blind-sided by the lilies of the field and their organizational skills that he finds himself following her to one of the larger cubicles with no further protest.

She knocks over a plastic cup filled with pencils, and pulls out the top drawer of the old file cabinet with such force that it crashes to the floor.

Asher positions himself out of range while she explains how the advice sessions work. If people have filled out an application or written a CV, you check it over for them. If they haven't, you help them do it. If they have questions, you answer them. As soon as Mrs Dunbar shambles off, the walls of Asher's cubicle shivering in her wake, he calls his kwoon to say he can't make it to class. His teacher is an international champion, a man who is something of a legend in the world of martial arts. To him, Asher can say no.

It's another day that could only seem longer if he were hanging by his ankles. Following the example set by the lilies out in the fields, there are no set appointments. He takes them as they come, one at a time. What surprises him is how many people show up. He expected them to line up for the free food – that's a no-brainer – but another thing Asher's father taught him is that people only listen to advice when they're paying a lot for it. And yet there they are, sitting stiff with nerves in the waiting area: men and women, young, not so young, and old. A few have even dressed up for the session, wearing a suit or a good dress, practising making a good impression. The sight of Asher, who is not only younger than any of them but who has never had so much as a job mowing lawns or washing cars, doesn't seem to throw them at all. They don't look annoyed; what they look is desperate.

It doesn't take much time for Asher to figure out where the desperation comes from. Never mind applying for a position at Harvard, most of these people would have trouble applying for a janitorial job at a community college. They have limited education and limited skills. They're too old or they're too young. They're under-qualified or overqualified. They have disabilities and difficult work histories. Some of them have never managed to get more than a temporary, marginal job that gave them little money and no benefits. Others had jobs for decades and were let go when the business outsourced, moved or went bust – leaving them with no pension, no savings, no health insurance. Most of them get no further on their applications than name, address and date of birth.

After the third person whose CV is as white as the snows of Siberia, Asher starts getting creative. Lawn-mowing and hedge-trimming become gardening. House-wife becomes accounting, administrative, cooking and cleaning experience. Babysitting is childcare.

"Every skill you have is useful," Asher hears himself saying. "Think of all the things you know how to do. Driving. The Heimlich manoeuvre. Putting up shelves. Anything. Put it all down." He finds himself suggesting that what they need are group workshops where they can practise being interviewed and give each other feedback.

Mrs Dunbar, who (no doubt called by her guardian angel) appears in the cubicle as this idea is flying off the top of his head, thinks it's great. "Fresh blood," she cries. "That's what we've needed! Fresh blood!" Not so much a crisis centre as a coven of vampires.

The last person Asher sees is Shelley Anne Rebough. Shelley Anne is thirty-two and has never had a job, unless you count babysitting when she was in high school.

"I had my kids kind of young," says Shelley Anne, "so, you know, that's what I've been doing. Taking care of them."

Instead of planning for the future. What did she think would happen to her without a career? Without investments? Without a solid pension and life insurance? With no portfolio? But none of these people plan for the future. They just stumble into it like blindfolded lemmings lunging over a cliff. And yet (another surprise for Asher) they're not the deadbeats and parasites he was expecting. He kind of likes them all. And not because they keep thanking him for his help as if he were some prince being nice enough to speak to them. Because they thank him and they mean it. Asher wishes he really could help them.

"And now they're older and you want to work?" he presses Shelley Anne.

How grown can they be? When did she have them – when she was twelve?

"Kind of," says Shelley. "Their dad died, so, you know, we need the money."

Asher doesn't have the heart to ask her how many children she has.

Chapter Fifteen
Waiting for Mrs Hawkle

There have been consequences for giving her old picture books away. Which, of course, Marigold knew there would be. This is why Marigold has tiptoed around her mother for seventeen years. It's bad enough when you don't go against her, let alone when you do.

As soon as Marigold stepped through the front door that night, Eveline started screaming – as if she'd been standing there, ready and waiting, all day long. Marigold's an ingrate. Marigold's selfish and self-centred. Marigold would just as soon stomp on her mother's heart in stilettos as do her mother the slightest kindness. Someday God will judge Marigold for her ingratitude and callousness. "Honour thy father and thy mother!" howled Mrs Liotta while Marigold stood stone-like in the hallway, still wearing her jacket and holding her book bag, barely daring to breathe. When her mother started sobbing,

Marigold started apologizing. Her mother thundered up the stairs and into her room, slamming the door behind her. Marigold made herself a sandwich and watched a comedy on HBO.

For several days after that the temperature in the house would have made an ice floe seem warm. Her mother spoke to her, but flatly and stiffly, like a robot with a limited vocabulary. There were a lot of frowns and disapproving looks. *Can't you put things back where you got them? I thought you were going to bring in the mail. Was it you who finished the cake? You didn't say you'd be so late.*

Marigold's budget doesn't stretch to diamonds, but, when she saw no thaw in sight, she bought her mother flowers and her favourite chocolates, and was finally forgiven. On condition. "Just promise me you won't do anything like that again," ordered Eveline. Marigold promised.

Despite all that, Marigold wasn't sorry that she'd taken the books. The books have definitely helped with Sadie. There has been a real breakthrough. It may not be as momentous as the "one giant leap for mankind" of the moon landing, but Marigold has finally made real contact with the distant, mysterious planet that is Sadie Hawkle. There is talking. There is eye contact. For the first time, Marigold feels that she and Sadie are both on the same side. And it is the books that brought about this change. Sadie is not a dancing-in-the-streets, ringing-bells, shouting-from-rooftops kind of girl. If enthusiasm were hair, Sadie Hawkle would be bald. But she likes the books Marigold gave her. She actually said so. "They're good," said Sadie. "And they're easy to read." She gets through one a night before she goes to sleep. "They're not even a little boring," judged Sadie. High praise indeed.

Now that she and Sadie are getting along so well – or, at least, so much better – Marigold doesn't rush off the second the session is over. And today has been especially friendly and relaxed. They've laughed. They've talked. Sadie read without prompting or pleading, and read very well. "I thought I was doing better," she said when Marigold praised her. And almost smiled.

Sadie, Bonnie Kupferberg and Marigold are the only ones still in the classroom when the janitor comes around to check that everyone has gone.

"Sometimes my mom gets stuck in traffic," says Sadie as the three adults look at the clock.

Marigold and Bonnie glance at each other.

"Then she must be coming via the expressway," mutters Bonnie. Traffic jams in Half Hollow being slightly less frequent than presidential motorcades.

They leave together, the janitor following to lock the

door. Mrs Hawkle is not running up the steps or racing down the street towards them.

Bonnie Kupferberg sighs. "I texted her, but she hasn't answered." Sadie's lost her phone and it hasn't been replaced. "I guess there's nothing to do but wait for her to show up."

It's been such a good afternoon that Marigold offers to stay with Sadie until her mother comes. "I'm sure she'll be here soon," says Marigold. "She must be on her way."

"Probably." Bonnie looks nervously from her to Sadie. "You sure you want to hang out here? I can do it." God knows she's done it plenty of times before. "I don't live far."

"We'll be fine," says Marigold. "We have stuff to talk about."

This turns out to be a wish more than a statement of fact. As soon as they're standing on the sidewalk the good mood of the afternoon disappears, and Sadie goes back inside her fully-armed, nuclear-powered tank of silence, standing with her arms wrapped around her and her eyes on the road.

Minutes pass, and then more minutes join them. Marigold hears the branches creak. It's not a busy street, and every time a car comes around the corner Sadie starts. Which is the only time she's seen to move.

"I'm sure your mom will be here soon," says Marigold.

Sadie nods, once more rigid as the lamp post under which they stand.

"You have the new books I brought today, right?" This isn't a question; it's something to say. Marigold knows where the books are – she put them in Sadie's backpack herself.

Sadie nods; her expression blank.

A few more cars and several more minutes go by. Sadie's pale face is ghost-like in the gloom.

"So what would you be doing now if you were at home?" asks Marigold. Brightly.

This question receives one of Sadie Hawkle's shifty looks.

"Would you be watching TV?" prompts Marigold.

Sadie yawns.

Yawns. Silence. Like a satellite, Sadie drifts out of reach.

"That isn't a trick question. Sadie, I was just wondering." Marigold leans down to make it easier for Sadie to see her without actually looking at her. "You know what I'd be doing? I'd either be doing my homework or talking to my friends." Marigold winks. "Probably I'd be talking to my friends."

Sadie's head turns towards her. Slightly. "You don't watch TV?"

"Oh, I watch TV. Everybody watches TV. But that would be later. After I do everything else." Marigold readjusts her own backpack. "You have a favourite show? What do you like to watch?"

Now Sadie looks right at her. Marigold's finally found something she's happy to talk about.

"Cop shows," says Sadie. "I really like cop shows." Her favourite is one called *Justice for All*. "Because people who obey the law deserve justice, too," explains Sadie.

Marigold says she's heard of the show, but she's never seen it.

"It's really awesome," Sadie assures her. "It's like you're right there. So sometimes you're really scared and holding on to the couch. And sometimes you're clapping. And the cop I like best is super smart." She turns again, so now she's looking right at Marigold. "I'm going to be a cop when I grow up," she announces. "Just like on *Justice for All*. I'm going to find out who did the crime and I'm going to catch them and put them behind bars, where they belong."

What a thought. Sadie doesn't move fast enough to catch a cold.

"And probably I'll get medals and have my picture in the paper," she goes on. "It'll be really awesome."

"It sure will," agrees Marigold. "That'd be a very cool

job. Really interesting and exciting."

Sadie nods. "And you're doing good. That's the best part."

"That's right. You'd be helping people. But wouldn't you be afraid of getting hurt? I know I would be."

"They teach you how to shoot," says Sadie. "And I'm going to learn kung fu, too. You have to know stuff like that if you want to be a cop."

"You know, my friend, Asher, he does kung fu. He's been doing it for years."

Sadie's all eyes now. "Does he have a black belt?"

"I'm not sure." She has no idea. "Probably. I know he's really good." Which is certain to be true. If Asher does something, he's good at it. "He has a class every week."

"Is he going to be a cop?" asks Sadie. "Is that what he wants to be, too?"

Marigold's almost tempted to lie and say yes. "Not exactly but kind of. He wants to be a lawyer. Like his father. He's a regular chip off the old block."

"What's that mean?"

"It means he's just like his dad."

"It's too bad he wants to be a lawyer." Sadie seems genuinely saddened by Asher's poor career choice. "But I guess that makes sense. 'Cause of his dad." She raises her chin. "My dad's a cop."

This is the first time anyone has mentioned Sadie's father. Ever. Marigold assumed that, although it stands to reason that she must have one, he is less involved in her life than the staff in the cafeteria. Probably doesn't even know she exists.

"Really? I didn't know that. That's pretty cool. No wonder you want to be a cop."

Sadie doesn't grin, but a tiny light goes on behind her eyes. "He's a detective. He's a really good detective. But sometimes he gets yelled at because he does things his way."

"He must be very smart if he's a detective," says Marigold.

"He is. He's very smart. Everybody says so. Even when they're yelling at him they say how smart he is. And he's brave. He's always saving people."

This is the longest and most in-depth conversation she's had with Sadie. Who says patience and tenacity don't pay off?

"And where is your dad? Does he live around here?"

"Oh, no, not here." Sadie sounds shocked that Marigold would think there are any very smart detectives in Half Hollow. "He's in New York."

"New York City?"

"Uh-huh. That's where he works. They have billions

of detectives there. But he doesn't live in the city. You know, 'cause it's really expensive. He lives in New Jersey."

"Right, New Jersey. Well, that's not too far from the city. Do you get to visit him much? Does your mom take you to see him? Or does he come out here?"

"No." Sadie's eyes are back on the road and her arms are folded around her again. "He's way too busy to come here. But he emails me all the time on my mom's computer. And he calls me. When he gets a chance. When he's not solving cases and stuff like that."

"It's too bad you don't get to see him, though," ventures Marigold. "You must miss him."

"Yeah. I do. 'Cause he's really funny. He always makes me laugh. But I see him sometimes." She kicks some leaves into the gutter. "I'm going to visit him at Christmas. I'm going to stay overnight. And we're going to watch movies and make our own popcorn. He lets me stay up as late as I want."

Marigold says that sounds like fun. "And what about your mom?" she asks. "Is she a cop, too?"

"Nooo." It's a what-planet-are-you-from sound. "She's a waitress."

"You know, I was just thinking. When I was your age I loved reading mystery stories." This is, in fact, a classic example of someone tampering with the truth. Marigold has watched a few police shows on television and seen a movie or two, but she's never actually read a crime novel. They're too depressing. "Do you like mysteries?"

"With cops?"

"Or detectives who aren't exactly cops. They're stories where someone's done a crime and the cop or the detective has to find out who and why."

"They have those in books?"

How does she not know that? You'd think this child was being raised in a cave in the Rockies by wolves.

"They sure do. And there are some pretty good ones around." She leans closer, lowering her voice. "It's fun to see if you can solve the mystery before the detective in the book does. I bet you'd be really good at it."

It would be an exaggeration to say that Sadie looks excited, but she does look interested.

"They really have books like that?"

"Uh-huh. Tons of them."

Sadie frowns. "But for grown-ups. Not for kids like me."

"No, for kids, too." Though not all of them can be like Sadie. "Maybe—" Marigold is about to say that maybe she could find a mystery for them to read together, but the sharp honking of a horn cuts her off. A car has stopped across the street. It's an old car, and although it's hard to be sure in the dark, one of the fenders seems to be a different colour to the rest of it.

"There's my mom!" shouts Sadie.

Marigold can see that there is, indeed, a woman behind the wheel, but her face is in shadow. She doesn't roll down the window to say *Hi* or *Thanks for standing in the cold with my child*. The horn bleats again. It sounds annoyed.

"I have to go," says Sadie. "She's waiting."

And, before Marigold can stop her, she launches herself into the road.

At least she remembered to look both ways.

Marigold watches them pull away, waving. No one waves back.

Chapter Sixteen
Georgiana Can't Find Her Phone

It is a peaceful afternoon in the parking lot of St Joan's Nursing Centre. A few birds glide overhead; a couple bearing a bouquet of flowers walks towards the entrance; a squirrel scampers over the lawn.

Sitting in her car, Georgiana closes her eyes and breathes deeply. *Think*, she tells herself. *Think hard. When was the last time you had it?* She pictures her phone, metallic red and illuminated, its bank of icons shining. She tries to imagine herself holding it in her hand. Where is she? What does she do next? This is a trick she read about in a magazine article on finding things you've lost. Much to her surprise, it actually works. She remembers exactly. When she got into the car after school she checked to see if she had any messages, and then she put it in her bag. She can see herself open the bag and drop in the phone. So where is it?

"Oh, for Pete's sake, it has to be in here somewhere." Georgiana dumps the entire contents of her bag onto the passenger seat and starts rummaging through it. "It has to be!" she repeats. Make-up bag. Nail bag. Several pens (most of which don't work). One unsharpened pencil. An assortment of hair clips and ties. A comb and a brush. Tissues. Her wallet. The business card from the store where she bought her father's Christmas present. A clump of sales receipts. Sunglasses. Two pairs of tights. One pair of leggings. One pair of socks. Gum. Several empty wrappers. Half a roll of breath mints. A toothbrush. A tube of toothpaste. Keys. More keys. A small sewing kit. A jar of correction fluid. Three Maglites with dead batteries. A container of dental floss. Several memory sticks. Breath spray. A fork. A handful of sugar packets. A paperback she was going to read in the summer. An old travel mug. A plastic Bart Simpson on a skateboard with wheels that really turn. Quite a few necklaces and bracelets. Seven earrings (none of which match). Reward cards from the coffee bars she frequents. The take-out menu from her favourite Chinese restaurant. The headset her mother's been looking for since September. But no cell phone. Resisting the urge to cry, Georgiana puts everything back by the handful, still searching, but it isn't tucked into a tissue or caught in the toe of her tights. She pats the pockets of her jacket for the sixth time, but it still isn't in any of them, either.

How will she get through the next hour and a half? After the Incident at Bargain World (as it has become known to Georgiana and her friends), she's not planning to venture into the great unknown with Mrs Kilgour again in a hurry. She needs another episode like that about as much as she needs dandruff. Indeed, after the Incident at Bargain World, she's assuming that not only will Mrs Kilgour not want to go out, but that she'll be asleep. What's Georgiana supposed to do if she doesn't have her phone?

Pondering, as many great thinkers have, the unfairness of life, Georgiana gets out of the car.

Although some people might think it's still a little early, St Joan's is already decked out for Christmas. Not with boughs of holly, of course, but with tinsel garlands and paper chains donated by the nearby elementary school. There is a small artificial tree on the reception desk. Georgiana compliments Alice Einhorn on the elf hat she's wearing and signs in.

All the doors along Mrs Kilgour's corridor boast some holiday decoration, no matter how small; all except the door to 10a. It is as it always is, but, because every other door sparkles or shines, it looks worse. Georgiana stares at it for several seconds. Surrounded by all the tiny Santas, snowmen, reindeer, poinsettias, bells and wreaths that line the corridor, it looks sad and friendless. Like Mrs Kilgour herself. As far as Georgiana knows, no one ever calls her; no one but Georgiana ever visits – which is as sad as spending your birthday by yourself with not even a cupcake or a single card. Did Mrs Kilgour ever have a life? Did she never do anything but wait to grow old and die?

Georgiana sighs, raises her hand and knocks. Softly. And, to her surprise, Mrs Kilgour answers.

"Who is it?" she calls.

"It's Abraham Lincoln," Georgiana calls back.

"Then you'd better come in," is the answer. "But make sure you're not being followed by that actor."

Georgiana opens the door, and stops as if she's walked into a six-foot Christmas tree with a singing angel at its top. Though, needless to say, that isn't what she sees.

What she sees is Mrs Kilgour, already in her chair and wearing an ancient pair of army fatigues, a bright green turtleneck, an orange duffel coat and a red beret. The antique camera bag she uses as a pocketbook is on her lap. If there's one thing you can say about Mrs Kilgour besides the indisputable fact that she's an old lady, it's that she doesn't dress like one.

Mrs Kilgour ready to roll does not fit in with how

Georgiana saw the afternoon panning out. "Are we going somewhere?" Her smile is as hesitant as someone peering through the ogre's window.

"Of course we are. We're going out. Why wouldn't we be going out?" Mrs Kilgour's smile is the smile of the ogre. "It isn't raining, is it?"

"I just thought ... you know..." The Incident at Bargain World unnerved Georgiana so much that she nearly mentioned it to Alice Einhorn. The only reasons she didn't were: 1. Alice Einhorn would probably laugh and say, "So what else is new?"; 2. If Alice didn't shrug it off but took it seriously, Georgiana would get the blame. "Because of what happened the other day..."

"Nothing happened," says Mrs Kilgour. "I fell asleep, and you actually did the right thing for a change."

"I did?" Mrs Kilgour has never accused Georgiana of doing anything right before. Maybe she really did have some kind of stroke after all.

"Yes, you did. You didn't let them ship me off to the hospital. At my age, if you go into the hospital odds are you'll come out in a box."

"Oh, I..." mutters Georgiana.

"And anyway, it was pretty funny." There is, as usual, a smudge of lipstick on Mrs Kilgour's front teeth. "Didn't you think it was funny?"

"Well…" It's really funny when Georgiana recounts the Incident at Bargain World to her friends, but she didn't think Mrs Kilgour was particularly amused – and it wasn't very funny at the time. Not with all those panicking adults ready to call an ambulance but not prepared to listen to Georgiana.

"Of course you did. I'm sure you have your friends in stitches over it. It's a wonder I didn't wet myself. Those men all rushing around like Hawkeye Pierce at a helicopter crash. They'll be dining out on that story for weeks."

"Like who at a helicopter crash?"

Mrs Kilgour's sigh is almost a groan. What patience she once had didn't live as long as she has. "Never mind. Before your time. The thing is that we're going out."

"But I don't know if that's such a great idea. I mean, if you haven't been feeling very well—"

"And who told you that? That big mouth Alice at reception, or one of those nosey nurses? Not any of them could mind her own business unless she was locked in a tower."

"You did." It was Alice. Alice said they called the doctor in. "Last week you said you were feeling peaky."

"That was last week," snaps Mrs Kilgour. "This week I'm dandy as candy. I've been looking forward to this all day."

"I didn't know you cared," Georgiana mumbles.

"Don't flatter yourself. Not because I was going to see you." Mrs Kilgour's hearing is clearly not as bad as Georgiana thought. "You may smell a lot better, but you're less company than a dead cat."

I'm not the only one, thinks Georgiana, but she gives a little laugh, so Mrs Kilgour will think that Georgiana thinks that Mrs Kilgour is joking.

Mrs Kilgour couldn't give a dead cat for what Georgiana thinks. She adjusts the bag on her lap; it's time to move. "Well, don't just stand there, girl. Shake those shapely legs of yours and let's get out of here."

They start off on their usual route, but today Mrs Kilgour wants to go left towards the river instead of right towards the town.

Leave it to Mrs Kilgour to find something even less interesting than this busted town with its one shopping street and cheap stores. "But there's nothing there," argues Georgiana. "Don't you want to get some chocolate? Or some wine?"

"What I want is to see the river," repeats Mrs Kilgour. "I used to go there all the time when I first moved here. But I haven't been there in years."

"I'm sure it hasn't changed much," says Georgiana. "I'm sure it's still made of water."

"And I'm sure there are plenty of small towns in Hell," says Mrs Kilgour. "I want to see some of the things I'm going to miss when I'm gone from this world while I still have the chance."

Scowling, Georgiana turns the chair to the left. When she's as old as Mrs Kilgour, if she hasn't seen them already, what Georgiana will want to see is the Taj Mahal or Venice or the Eiffel Tower or Hawaii – the things most people dream about seeing. Most people, but not Margarita Kilgour, of course. She wants to see dead leaves – dead leaves in the trees, dead leaves along the side of the road, dead leaves on the ground. It would be boring enough pushing the chair past houses and stores with nothing else to do, but pushing it along the narrow, unpopulated river road that is only woods and more woods brings boredom to an entirely new level.

The result of being stranded dead centre in the middle of nowhere with nothing at all to distract her is that Georgiana has no choice but to listen to Mrs Kilgour's ramblings as they walk along. Since God chose this day to make her phone disappear.

Tucked up in her wheelchair, occasionally breaking her monologue to shout out a direction – turn here, or go down there – Mrs Kilgour babbles on. She starts out talking about most towns being pretty much the same.

"Doesn't matter if they're made of brick, wood, bamboo or mud," says Mrs Kilgour. "They're like crocodiles. If you've seen one, you have a good idea of what the rest of them look like."

As if the great river-watcher has ever seen a town made out of bamboo. Or a crocodile.

She then moves effortlessly from mud huts and reptiles to communication. According to Mrs Kilgour, the world used to be more fun and a hell of a lot more interesting. None of this instant this and instant that. Everybody on their damn cells every minute of the day. In her day you only talked on the phone when you had something to say. "Like you," she says, the red hat bobbing. "Always taptaptapping like some damn woodpecker. I've known alcoholics who were less addicted to hard liquor than you are to that stupid phone."

Georgiana says nothing. Putting aside the fact that she didn't think Mrs Methuselah was aware of her emailing and texting, she is not going to argue with someone who was probably born before the telephone was invented. In her day they used tin cans joined by a string, or drums.

"I used to do a lot of communicating in my day," Mrs Kilgour jets on, "and believe me, it wasn't about telling everybody what I had for lunch."

Yeah, of course she did tons of communicating. Every

year she sent out a slew of Christmas cards, birthday cards and vacation postcards. Practically the one-woman NBC network.

"Left or right?" asks Georgiana.

The gnarled and bony hand points left.

"And travel," Mrs Kilgour rolls on. "Look at the way people travel nowadays. A week here. A weekend there. Moving all over creation like car parts on an assembly line. It's not natural. Thousands of miles in a few hours and all you see is a movie or the people sitting next to you. Everybody knows it's the journey that's important, not the destination."

She's right about that, thinks Georgiana as she stops the wheelchair. They have reached their destination. This is not the grand old Mississippi. It's a ribbon of water, more stream than river, running between two banks littered with beer cans and plastic bottles and bags. If ever a place was crying out for some community service, this is it.

Only that isn't what Mrs Kilgour sees.

She throws back her head and raises her arms. "Look at those trees!" she cries. "Aren't they magnificent?"

Georgiana looks. They're regular, old, everyday trees in late autumn. Most of their leaves have already fallen. Through the twisting branches she can see cars flash past on the old highway.

"You know what this has always reminded me of?" Suddenly, Mrs Kilgour's voice is unnaturally soft and almost warm. She might be speaking to someone else. She might be someone else speaking. "It's always put me in mind of that cabin we had in Oregon."

Oregon? Georgiana has heard about the late Mr Kilgour from Alice, the big mouth receptionist. He was born and raised in the town, and Alice heard that he didn't like to leave it very often. "I can't imagine how they ever hooked up," Alice confided. "I know she doesn't come from around here. I guess he must've left some-time." Alice, who also doesn't come from around here, didn't know what Mr Kilgour did for a living. Some kind of family business, she thinks. "Maybe a hardware store or something like that. He kind of looked like that type." He died at St Joan's after a severe stroke that left him paralysed, for which Mrs Kilgour must have blamed herself. She'd talked him into going for a weekend in New York to celebrate their thirty-fifth wedding anniversary. They never got there.

"We wouldn't see or talk to anyone else for days when we went there," Mrs Kilgour is saying now. "No radio, no telephone, just the sounds of the woods and the river. At night we'd sit on the porch and listen to the wolves howl and watch for shooting stars." Her sigh sounds the way a broken dream feels. "Like they would bring us luck."

"Oregon?" Georgiana tries not to sound too incredulous. She can't quite picture the skinny, balding, dull-looking man in the wedding picture on the dresser watching for shooting stars in the wilderness. "You and Mr Kilgour had a cabin in Oregon?"

"What?" She starts as if she'd forgotten Georgiana is there. "Oh, not Mr Kilgour. He loved cities. It was Anderson's cabin. His retreat."

At last, in the millions of words that have flowed from Mrs Kilgour like water from a broken fire hydrant, she has said four that grab Georgiana's interest. "Anderson?" She steps out from behind the chair to stand beside it. Curious. "Was that your first husband?"

"Husband? Oh no, no, no. Anderson wasn't the marrying kind." Georgiana isn't sure, since she's never heard it before, but she thinks the sound the old lady makes is a chuckle. "Neither was I. Not then. You couldn't have gotten either of us to the altar if you'd called in the Marines."

"Oh." Georgiana kicks at the leaves at her feet. "Oh, right. So Anderson was like your boyfriend."

"Very like. If things had been different, I suppose he might've been my first husband. If he'd been different." Mrs Kilgour stares at the sunlight, shimmering over the water like a ghost. "I was head over heels in love with him for a while there. Completely bewitched."

Georgiana looks at the old hag in the wheelchair – her thin, dyed hair; her dull, rheumy eyes; her sagging, shrivelled skin – trying to fit the words "head over heels in love" and "bewitched" to her. Trying to imagine what she was like fifty, sixty years ago retreating into Oregon with the man who was obviously the love of her life.

The two of them are silent, listening to the burble of the water and the rustle of the trees. A leaf drops into the river, lost as Mrs Kilgour's long-ago love.

"So what happened?" Georgiana asks at last. Expecting to hear that he left her. That he found someone nicer, or prettier, or more exciting. That he got tired of her and went away.

"He was killed."

"Killed? You mean like in a car crash?"

"No, it was nothing like a car crash." Mrs Kilgour's hands rub against the arms of her chair. "It was in Vietnam. He always was reckless. And fearless, I guess. Which amounts to the same thing." She closes her eyes, and when she opens them the river is still there. "The damn fool got himself blown up."

Georgiana knows two things about Vietnam. She knows that there was a war there (because it was mentioned in American history); and she knows that it is near Thailand (because, when they were on vacation there, her parents talked of going to Vietnam for a few days while they were so close, but in the end they chose to stay where they were. "Better the beach you know, than the one you don't," as Mrs Shiller put it).

Georgiana stares at the debris on the opposite bank. "He was a soldier?"

"No, not Anderson. He only shot things with a camera. He was a photographer. One of the best damn combat photographers there was. Won more awards than Westmoreland had medals."

A person would have to have a heart as hard as a diamond not to be moved by such a bittersweet story of love and loss, and when it comes to romance Georgiana's heart is about as hard as a pat of butter left out on the table on a summer day. Georgiana doesn't see the garbage along the riverbank, or the gnarled old trees any more. She sees Anderson dying on a foreign field, alone and forgotten in the cries of war. She imagines a beautiful, young woman, thousands of miles away, nervously waiting through the long, dark, lonely nights for the return of her one true love. Imagines her making plans and weaving dreams. Imagines Margarita anticipating her lover's knock on the door. Home at last, and safe in her arms.

Heartbreak tears fill her eyes. "So I guess you got one of those telegrams," she whispers.

"Telegrams?" Mrs Kilgour looks over her shoulder at her. "What telegrams?"

"You know, saying how they regretted to inform you that Anderson was dead."

"No, nothing like that." Mrs Kilgour, imagining things of her own, shakes her head. "Anderson died in my arms."

Later that night, Georgiana finds her phone in her book bag. Where she put it.

Chapter Seventeen

More Than One Kind of Mystery

Because Marigold knows only slightly more about mystery novels than she does about Iroquois culture and history (which is absolutely nothing), she asked around for recommendations. And was surprised at how many people she knows who are fans of the genre of cloaks and daggers. And, unlike Marigold's mother, they didn't mind parting with books they'd read years ago and were never going to read again. Which was totally unexpected. She asked for suggestions, not donations. Merry Christmas!

Byron sets his lunch on the table, pulls back the chair next to Asher and flops down. "Geebus, María and José." He eyes the stack of books beside Marigold. "What's all this? Somebody starting up her own library?"

"Not even close," says Will. "Marigold's looking for inspiration to commit the perfect crime." He grins, waggling his eyebrows. "She may act like she's all sweetness and light and God's answer to the discouraging word, but it's just a fiendish disguise. Behind that mild manner and angelic smile lurks the heart of a master criminal."

Asher's head has been busily bent over his notebook, but now he looks up. "Only they're not really perfect crimes, are they? They all get solved. By definition, no one would ever be able to crack the perfect crime. It might even never be detected. That would be a perfect crime. One no one ever knows has happened."

"That's why she needs to read up on ones that bombed, doesn't she?" counters Will. "So she knows what mistakes not to make." He taps his head. "It's all very diabolically clever."

Byron, who has spent the last hour in a computer lab – a world of logic that always makes sense – is still confused. "So what is all this?" he asks Marigold. "Is this what happens when you hang out in a place like Half Hollow? You decide to commit a crime?"

Claudelia groans. "Yeah, of course. Marigold's going to kill Barbie. She doesn't think she's cheerful enough."

Marigold laughs. "Don't pay any attention to them, By. These are kids' mystery novels people gave me for my Teach Sadie Hawkle to Read campaign." Without which she would probably have nothing new to bring for their session today. "Remember I told you she says she loves cop shows? So I figured mysteries might really interest her."

"I'm gutted." Byron puts on a hurt face. "You didn't ask me to give you anything."

"That would be because you don't actually read books."

"Yes, I do," he protests. "I read all the time."

"Tech books don't count," says Georgiana. "The operative words here are 'mystery novels'."

Byron points his roll at her. "I'll have you know that mathematics is the key to a trillion mysteries."

"I think we can wait till she gets beyond the one multiplication table before we spring that one on her," says Marigold.

Claudelia looks over the pile. "There's bound to be something in these she'll like. You have something for everybody." One features a boy detective, one a girl detective, one a terrible detective, one a genius detective – and one a detective who's been dead for five hundred years and one who's a dog. "If nothing else, they should keep her busy for a while."

"Are you kidding?" Marigold rolls her eyes. "The rate Sadie goes, she'd be lucky to finish half of them before she's fifty. But I'm not giving them all to her at once. I'm going to dole them out to her."

"Well, I guess that's better than giving her golf clubs," says Georgiana.

Even Marigold laughs.

Just a few short months ago this would have been only slightly less improbable than a burning river, but the fact is that Marigold has been looking forward to seeing Sadie this afternoon. It's their last session before the Christmas vacation because the after-school programme is being closed early to save fuel, and Marigold has picked three of the mysteries she's been given – the three that seemed the easiest and the most fun – for Sadie to take home with her. All day, Marigold's been imagining Sadie's face when she shows her the books. Not an enormous grin and shrieks of joy, maybe, but at least her mouth should twitch and those blank eyes open wide. Marigold's hopes are always high as the clouds, of course, but her hopes for Sadie learning to love books are bumping into the stars right now. She wants Sadie to find her way to other worlds. As Marigold did. Books allowed her to escape the anger and unhappiness at home, but they also allowed her to travel through time and space. There was nowhere she couldn't go. To San Francisco or to India. To Victorian London or to ancient Rome. To a cave in the mountains of Peru or to a junk on the Yangtze. She could cross the continent in a Conestoga wagon or fly to the moon. Past, present, future; reality and make-believe. It was all there, held in her hands, showing her that there is more to the world than the place where you live and the moment you're in. That's what Marigold wants for Sadie. She pictures her curled up on the couch, the lights of the Christmas tree shining on her, reading one of the mysteries Marigold gave her. Finally finding somewhere she feels safe; finally understanding that she isn't so alone.

This picture is so strong that when Marigold gets to the tutor room and doesn't see Sadie, she actually thinks for a second that she must be in the wrong place.

But there is Bonnie Kupferberg, marching towards her, shaking her head. "She wasn't in school today," says Bonnie.

The bag of books bangs against Marigold's leg. "Is she sick?"

"Who knows?" Bonnie shrugs. "Sadie doesn't exactly have a perfect attendance record. She always comes on your day, but the rest of the week... Believe me, if this was an airline and not a school she'd never get any frequent-flyer miles."

Marigold goes back to the street and just stands there by the lamp post where she waited for Mrs Hawkle with Sadie the night she found out about Sadie's interest in detectives. Marigold feels like a balloon that's been pricked with a pin. She's not sure why it means so much to her, but she really wanted Sadie to have the books for Christmas. What should she do now? Take them home and give them to her after Christmas? Go back upstairs and see if Bonnie Kupferberg might be able to give them to Sadie in school – if she shows up? The bag presses against her – as if the books are impatient to get where they're going, too.

Marigold takes out her cell phone and calls Byron.

"Apartment 1a, 116 Clarendon Road," says Byron when he calls her back.

"You're sure? Hawkle?"

"Positive. J. M. Hawkle, Apartment 1a, 116 Clarendon Road. It's the only Hawkle in town."

Which does make it likely that it's the right one.

"You have a pen handy?" asks Byron. "I have the map up. I'll tell you how to get there."

Clarendon Road turns out to be fairly near the school, in a neighbourhood of large old houses that were once the homes of the town's professionals. Though not any more. Now most of them have been broken up into apartments or rented rooms, and the ones that aren't falling down could definitely use some cheering up.

Number 116 was long ago painted blue with orange

trim. There are posts missing from the railing of the porch and a row of bells on either side of the front door, names taped below them on pieces of paper. Marigold is nervous about ringing the bell. She doesn't want to disturb Mrs Hawkle. A busy single mother with a sick child, the last thing she needs is some stranger showing up. Marigold gazes at the bell that says, *Hawkle – 1a*. She'll leave the bag by the door with a note, that's what she'll do. This isn't the kind of neighbourhood where anyone's likely to steal a few used children's books.

1a is the apartment on her left, the one with the flashing reindeer in the window and the cardboard in the missing pane. Marigold knows this because as she's getting a pen and paper from her bag the curtain moves and she looks up to see Sadie's fish-on-ice eyes appear in the opening. Marigold waves and the face disappears, but she hears a door inside open and feet hurrying down the hall.

The front door swings back, and there is Sadie – not in the robe and pyjamas of an ill child but fully dressed. Even more surprisingly, Sadie is smiling. "How come you're here?"

Marigold smiles back. "I wanted to make sure you're OK. Mrs Kupferberg said you weren't in school today. I hope it's nothing serious."

"No, I—" begins Sadie, but a sound that is partly human and partly angry beast cuts her off.

"Sadie! Sadie! Sadie! What the hell do you think you're doing? Get back in here this minute!"

The smile vanishes faster than a drop of water on a desert. Her entire body suddenly looks worried and wary. "My mom was sick and she needed me," Sadie whispers. And then, looking over her shoulder to where the door of 1a stands ajar, shouts back, "I'm sorry! I'm coming! I'll be right there!"

"I just stopped by to give you this." Marigold holds out the bag of books. "It's a present."

Sadie makes no move to take the bag. "What is it?" Her voice is so soft that Marigold, standing inches away, can hardly hear her. "Is it a Christmas present?"

"Kind of. It's just something I thought you'd like."

Sadie looks at the bag and then over her shoulder again as a stunning, youngish woman in a red silk kimono charges into the hall. Her feet are bare and she holds a mascara wand in one hand. Everything about her looks furious.

"Sadie! Are you deaf or just stupid? What the—" But as soon as she sees Marigold her expression changes. Unlike her daughter, she obviously smiles all the time. "Oh, I'm sorry. I didn't realize… You know kids…" She puts the hand holding the mascara wand on Sadie's shoulder so there isn't any doubt about which kids she's talking. "You have to watch them every second. Especially when they don't have much sense. You know? Anything could happen to them." She has no trouble talking, either. "Is there something I can do for you?" She notices the bag. "Are you selling something?"

If anyone had asked Marigold what she thought Sadie's mother was like she would have said like Sadie. Only older, of course. And taller. An average – probably below average – looking woman. Schlumpy. Dowdy. Drab. Rushing towards middle age, not so much letting herself go as pretty much already gone. But Sadie's mother is so unlike that – and so unlike Sadie – that for a few seconds Marigold thinks it's someone else, someone in no way related to Sadie Hawkle or her gene pool.

"No, I… I mean, yes, I…" As if she's caught Sadie's difficulty with speech, Marigold stumbles over her own words. "I just … I was at the school and…"

"You're from the school?" J. M. Hawkle stands up a little straighter; her smile deepens. "Look, I'm really sorry about today. I know she's missed some school this year, but she's very delicate and she had a fever when she woke up and—"

"No, no, I'm not from the school. I mean, I'm kind of

from the school, but not like that. I'm Marigold. Marigold Liotta? I'm Sadie's reading tutor in the afternoon programme." She doesn't add that she was the person standing in the cold with Sadie the other evening.

"Oh, the famous Marigold!" Mrs Hawkle claps her hands together and her bracelets jangle. "I should have known! She never shuts up about you. Marigold said this… Marigold said that…"

Marigold could be knocked over by a snowflake. Sadie not only talks, but Sadie talks about her.

Still gripped by her mother, Sadie looks as if a tank couldn't move her.

"I'm Justine Hawkle." She extends her free hand. "I was hoping I'd get to meet you."

Though not enough to wave from your car.

She points to the bag still dangling from Marigold's hand. "And I guess that's Sadie's, right? Little Miss Use-it-and-lose-it. I swear, the only reason this child has a head is because it's attached."

"Oh, no, she didn't forget anything. It's a present. From me. It's just some books I had at home that I figured she'd be interested in. Because she's a fan of mysteries—"

"Is she?" Justine Hawkle rolls her eyes and laughs. "The only mystery around here is Sadie."

Sadie stands there like a locked door.

"So anyway," Marigold pushes on, uncomfortable enough to consider making a run for it, "I thought I'd drop them by for her. You know, since she wasn't in today. So she could start one over Christmas. If she wants to."

"Well, isn't that sweet of you?" She gives Sadie a shake. "What do you say, honey? Thank Marigold for being so nice."

"Thank you," mumbles Sadie, but she still makes no move to take the bag.

Her mother gives her another shake. "Well, take the books, dopey. Marigold didn't come all the way over here just to show them to you." She laughs. "I just hope she knows what to do with them."

"Oh, she knows," says Marigold. "She's doing really well with her reading."

"Is she?" Sadie's mother looks more surprised than pleased. "Well, I guess it's like they always say: wonders never cease."

Chapter Eighteen
This Time Asher Really Isn't Going to Let Mrs Dunbar Push Him Around Any More

It's Thursday night and raining. It's been raining almost constantly for the last two days, and the forecast is that it will continue over the weekend. Asher doesn't care. They have a day off school tomorrow, making this a long weekend. Because he and Will both have a lot of other commitments – basketball for Will, anything to do with his career strategy for Asher – they haven't been able to go climbing, but this weekend they will. Nothing is going to stop them. A blizzard might – with sub-zero temperatures and a platoon of zombie yetis roaming through the woods – but not a little rain. Not even falling rocks will stop them. If the car breaks down he'll push it to the cabin if he has to. And Loretta Dunbar isn't going to stop them, either. Asher has written another note, explaining that he's very sorry but he has plans for the weekend and won't be able to help out at the centre.

I'll be in touch… he wrote at the end, which is his way of saying that he'll be in touch sometime in April. But forewarned is forearmed. This time he's delivering his note on Thursday night when he knows for certain that she won't be there, and just in case she happens to be driving through Queen's Park on her way home from choir practice or something he's taking the long way through the back roads and will park several blocks away.

The rain is heavy and Asher gets a little lost in the unfamiliar labyrinth of side streets between Shell Harbour and Queen's Park, the satnav directing him to more than one dead end and up some stranger's driveway. Asher leaves the car so far away from the centre that he may not be able to find it again. It's close to ten when he finally slips into the parking lot behind the old supermarket like a cat burglar wearing a sodden parka. The lot is empty and dark, the only light coming from the single caged bulb over the back door, presumably to discourage thieves. Silent as a shadow, Asher dashes across the asphalt. He isn't a yard from the building and is just reaching for the envelope in his pocket when the door suddenly swings open like the gates of Hell – and there she is, an apparition in farmers' overalls … but instead of a pitchfork and horns she's holding a bag of garbage and has a plastic bag on her head. "Asher!"

Caught off guard, he staggers backwards, banging into the dumpster.

"I really am beginning to think you're an angel from the Lord," says Mrs Dunbar. "It is truly uncanny how you always show up when I need you most."

The angel of the Lord rubs the back of his head. He's beginning to think she really is in league with the Devil. "Mrs Dunbar, what are you doing here?" If it were anyone else he'd assume her husband threw her out and he'd be ready to recommend a good divorce lawyer. "Did something happen?"

"Oh yes, indeedy, something happened. That's why I'm so glad to see you!" She heaves the garbage bags over him and into the dumpster. It's possible that she played basketball in high school. "It's Sod's law, isn't it? It never rains but the ceiling comes down!"

Of course it did. It's probably been waiting for this exact moment. *Should I collapse today? Tomorrow? Next week?* it asked itself. *No, no, not yet*, it answered. *Asher will be dropping by at ten at night in the middle of a monsoon to leave a note for Mrs Dunbar on Thursday. Wait till then.*

She looks behind him. "Where's your car?" He could ask her the same question, except he knows she probably parked out front. Divine guidance again. "You couldn't have walked here."

"No. No." He gestures vaguely to the left. "I parked a little way away."

"Well, come on inside out of the wet," she orders. And then, impulsively, gives him a hug that stops his breathing for a full second. "Carlin will be so glad for your help."

As he follows her in, Asher wonders whether, if Mrs Dunbar told him to kill his firstborn son, he'd do it. He figures he probably would. So maybe it isn't the Devil she works for.

"Everything was copasetic. I was just settling down with my book and my chamomile tea," Carlin tells him, "when suddenly I hear this almighty crash like the sky fell."

But it wasn't the sky, of course, it was the plasterboard drop ceiling over the old photocopier. Water must have been collecting there from a leak in the roof for months, and it finally gave way.

"It was like Niagara for a while there. That's why I called Mrs D."

Who immediately jumped into her overalls and rushed over.

"Lucky choir practice was cancelled because of the storm," says Mrs Dunbar with a God-thinks-of-everything smile.

Carlin moved the photocopier and put a garbage pail and several buckets under the drips.

"Temporary measures," says Carlin. "But now you're here to give me a hand, I want to clear the whole area. Maybe see if there are more receptacles in the cellar. And get up on the roof to see how it looks from up there. I'm worried more of the ceiling could come down."

Mrs Dunbar, getting ready to leave, shakes her head firmly enough to send the child's barrette she habitually wears flying past Asher's eye. "You can't possibly climb up there in this weather." She turns to Asher. "His back's acting up again. He could kill himself."

Asher knows where this is heading.

"So you want me to climb up and have a look." Obviously Asher can't kill himself; he's an angel of the Lord.

"No, no way." Carlin shakes his head. "I won't hear of it. It's too dangerous if you're not used to heights."

Asher should keep quiet. Asher should say that he can barely climb the stairs to his room without suffering vertigo. That just standing on a chair makes him dizzy. Anything except the truth.

"But I am used to them," says Asher. "I'm a rock climber. I've been doing it for years."

Mrs Dunbar beams. "You see? That's why he's here!"

Of course it is. Why else would he suddenly show up at this hour on a night like this?

After Mrs Dunbar shambles off, they clear the area

as best they can, find more receptacles and put them in place. Then they tackle the roof itself. Carlin holds the ladder while Asher goes up it.

"You OK?" shouts Carlin.

Asher doesn't hear him. It's just as well he's an experienced climber. Mrs Dunbar's connections in Heaven are doing nothing to improve the weather. The rain is coming down by the bucket. The ladder was a donation, like everything else at the centre, and is a foot and a half short of actually meeting the edge of the roof. The rungs are slippery and the gusts of wind are trying to blow him back to the ground. If this is how he dies, his father will never forgive him.

Asher hauls himself over the parapet and steps down with a splash. He takes the flashlight Carlin gave him from his pocket and turns it on. It doesn't work. Well, why would it? Nothing else at the centre does. Except Mrs Dunbar, Carlin and a handful of volunteers.

"What's wrong?" Carlin yells into the wind. "What's going on?"

Neither the wind nor Asher answers.

Asher, of course, is not a young man to leave much to chance; there's a Maglite on his keychain. He turns it on. How the roof looks from up here is like a marsh, only without the grasses, rushes, cattails and nesting birds.

The good news is that the corner where the leak is looks relatively dry. Which would be because most of the water is now inside. The drainpipe must be blocked, so Asher wades across the roof until he finds it. He has no stick or gloves; there's no choice but to shove his bare hand into the opening and hope he doesn't catch anything before he gets to his antibacterial wash at home. His face knotted with disgust, he manages to dislodge a nest of leaves, plastic and silt.

Leaning over the side of the roof, Asher gives Carlin the thumbs-up and starts back down the ladder.

It may be that Asher is better at going up than coming down, or that he's so cold and wet it makes him careless, or that the ladder being a little short throws him off balance – or it may simply be that the soles of his shoes are slick from the muck on the roof. What can be said with certainty is that he's lucky he loses his footing when he's in the middle of his descent and not at the beginning. Carlin breaks his fall.

Carlin gets up, wetter but miraculously uninjured. Asher can't stand without help.

"It's my ankle," he says. "I must've twisted it."

Carlin blames himself. "I never should've let you go up there. I knew it was dangerous."

But it isn't Carlin's fault; it's Mrs Dunbar's. For working

one of her spells and making Asher volunteer. *Oh, I'm an experienced climber, let me go up your broken ladder in gale-force winds. No sweat.*

Carlin helps Asher limp inside. He makes him take off his soaked clothes and gives him a sweatshirt and a pair of jeans to put on. Asher isn't happy about wearing someone else's clothes, but it can't be worse than putting his hand into toxic debris, and they do seem freshly laundered even if they haven't been ironed.

"I don't think it's broken." Carlin frowns at the foot, already so swollen it looks like a club. "But you can't drive home with that. You'd better call your folks to come and get you."

"Folk," says Asher. "It's just me and my dad, but he's not home." Albert Grossman is in Europe this week, doing something important. For no reason, or no reason that he can later remember, Asher adds, "My mom's dead. She died when I was little."

Carlin looks more thoughtful than he did examining Asher's ankle. "So what are you saying? That even if I take you home, there's nobody there to look after you?"

There is, at least technically. Mrs Swedger, the house-keeper, is there. But nearly midnight is well outside of Mrs Swedger's work hours. She wouldn't be happy to be woken now and asked to drive to Queen's Park, and

Asher wouldn't be happy to ask her. He doesn't want her involved. She'll want to know what happened, and then she'll tell his father, and then he'll have to explain about the community centre and what he was doing on the roof. The closest Albert Grossman has ever come to a roof is the terrace of someone's penthouse. His father will be disappointed in him. Asher can't even face the idea of that.

"No, it's just me right now. But if you can give me a ride I'll be OK. I can take care of myself."

"Like hell you can," says Carlin. "You can't walk."

"I can walk." He hopes he can. If he tries hard enough. That's what counts in life. Focus. Purpose. Determination. Trying.

"Really?" Carlin gives him a nod. "OK. Let's see you walk."

He can't walk, but he is able not to howl in pain.

"That settles that. I'm calling Mrs D, to tell her what happened, and then I'm going down to the gas station to get some ice for that foot, and then I'm getting my air mattress out of the car. You can have the sofa."

"No, really—" begins Asher.

"Yes, really," finishes Carlin.

After Carlin comes back with the ice and sees to Asher's foot, he makes them both a herbal tea. Asher has gone on record as believing that only old ladies and people who think the world is run by aliens drink herbal tea, but he takes his cup without comment. After all, he's already wearing used socks. And used clothes. And about to sleep on a used couch.

They sit in the waiting area at the front, Asher on the bed that's been made up on the sofa and Carlin on a plastic chair. There's a desk lamp on the table beside the couch. Also on the table are Carlin's reading glasses and a framed photograph of a younger Carlin with a smiling woman and little boy. Just like home.

"I don't want you to think I've moved in here or any-thing," says Carlin, seeing Asher look at his things. "But Mrs D, she lets me sleep here when the weather's bad or I'm in too much pain to manage in the car. And so I can keep an eye on the place."

"You sleep in your car?" The Grossmans' gardener lives in a trailer, but Asher has never known anyone who lives in an automobile. Not even a large one.

"Lost my job. Lost my house. My wife took our son and went back home to her folks. Nothing else she could do, really." Carlin smiles. Things can always be worse. "At least I still have the car."

Since they've already exhausted the topics of rain, leaks and flat roofs, Asher asks about Carlin's job. "So I guess you lost it because of your back," he ventures.

"Nah," says Carlin. "I lost it because of my big mouth."

Carlin worked for one of the largest construction companies in the country for over twenty years. He was project manager on a major infrastructure project for the government, and he raised some health and safety issues – first with his immediate superior and then with his immediate superior's superior and then with head office. He was ignored. Then there was a related accident that could have been prevented if they'd listened to him, in which several workers were injured and two lost their lives. The company denied any responsibility. The company doesn't allow a union, so when the survivors and the families of the men who died brought a suit against the company, Carlin gave them copies of the letters he'd written about the health and safety breaches and agreed to be a witness.

Carlin gives a little wave "And goodbye was all they wrote."

"I know a little about corporate law," says Asher, "and I'm pretty sure they can't do that."

"Oh, I think they did it." Carlin makes a such-is-life gesture. "Anyway, they didn't say that was why. They made up some stuff and fired me for that."

Even if everything Carlin says is true, Asher knows

that if a person wants a job a person will find a job. As his father often says, it's only the lazy and feckless who can't get work. "But what about other companies? I mean, with your experience and everything—"

"They have a list, man. Troublemakers' list. Nobody wants a troublemaker. Not even little, local places." Carlin shakes his head. "If it wasn't for Mrs D I'd've given up a while ago. She makes me feel like things can happen. I do odd jobs for her and for her friends, and I get by. Pretty soon I'll be able to get somewhere to live." He gives Asher the this-isn't-as-bad-as-it-could-be smile again. "You know, somewhere without wheels and with a bathroom."

It may be the rain beating against the windows, or the circle of light that makes it seem that they're alone in the world, but Asher finds himself thinking out loud. "She's kind of unique, isn't she, Mrs Dunbar?"

"She sure is," laughs Carlin. "She's one of a kind."

"Why do you think she's…" – one of the most stubborn people Asher has ever known; one of the most oblivious; a woman with a complete disregard for reality; a woman who forces things to be the way she wants them to be – "like she is?"

Carlin's mouth shrugs. "I guess it's because she believes."

"You mean in God?"

"I guess so." This time it's Carlin's shoulders that shrug. "She is married to a minister, so it figures, doesn't it? But what I meant was people. Mrs D believes most people are good and want to do the best they can if they have half a chance. It's hard to disappoint somebody like that. You know? It'd be like shooting your dog when it's staring up at you with its tail wagging."

Asher has been taught that sentiment has no place in business. He falls asleep with the rogue thought: *Would my father shoot the dog?*

Chapter Nineteen
Georgiana's Lost Lover

It is not, of course, Georgiana's lover who is lost. Georgiana has yet to find a lover, never mind lose him. It is Mrs Kilgour's lover. Anderson. The daring, dashing war photographer (as Georgiana imagines him). The man who (as Georgiana also imagines him), shattered by the cruelties and horrors of battle, retreated to the woods of Oregon to listen to the timeless flow of the river and stare up at the stars. Only to become a victim of those cruelties and horrors himself. Killed in the prime of his life. Lost in time and lost to his one true love. And, it seems, lost to Georgiana as well. Mrs Kilgour, like a secretive government, is refusing to release any more information.

As they walked back to St Joan's after the revelations by the river, Georgiana asked her what she was doing in Vietnam. "You weren't in the army, were you?"

"Yes," answered Mrs Kilgour. "I was a brigadier

general. It would amaze you how many deaths I was responsible for."

So that good mood's over, thought Georgiana. Aloud, she said, "I would've figured you more for a sniper."

"Takes one to know one," Mrs Kilgour shot back.

But Georgiana wasn't about to give up. She might not have the drive of Asher or the determination of Marigold, but she has a belief in romantic love that makes Juliet and Romeo seem cynical. For Georgiana, meeting someone with a real, racing-heart love story – the sort of story that could fuel a thousand damp-eyed dreams – is like a devout monk meeting Jesus. Georgiana has no doubt that her parents love each other, but in an eat-from-the-same-fork way. You couldn't describe their relationship as a death-defying passion of blazing hearts and mated souls. It's more the comfortable matching of similar backgrounds and a mutual fondness for a game of golf. The Shillers are a light shower on a summer day in the backyard; Mrs Kilgour and Anderson are a tempest in the middle of an endless sea.

"So what were you, a nurse?" Georgiana persisted. "Is that why you were there?"

"I'm tired now." Mrs Kilgour turned the chair so her back was facing Georgiana. "You better go."

Anderson... Anderson... Anderson... Faceless and

unknown. But, decided Georgiana, not necessarily unknowable. He may be lost to time and Mrs Kilgour, but that doesn't mean he has to be lost to her. The World Wide Web exists now, where, if you know how and what to ask, any question you have can be answered just by tapping a few keys.

Unfortunately, Georgiana hadn't realized how very long the Vietnam War was. It went on and on and on. Nor had she realized how many people are named Anderson – quite a few of them photographers, and a surprising number involved with that particular conflict. Because those are the only three things she knows about Mrs Kilgour's tragic lover, it takes Georgiana several hours before she finally finds him. Anderson Littlejohn, born June 15, 1925, in Seattle, Washington, died July 2, 1967 in South Vietnam. She finds several pictures he took for *Life*, but no photograph of him. All that represents him are a woman fleeing with a baby in her arms, a burning village and bombs exploding among the palms.

Georgiana thinks about Anderson for the rest of the week. She can't seem to stop. He is every hero she's ever read about, heard about or seen on the silver screen or on the Shillers' personal entertainment system – from William Wallace to Jesse James.

Anderson… Anderson… Anderson… Man of ardour

and adventure. She sees him leaping over walls and jumping out of helicopters. She pictures him as ruggedly handsome and overpoweringly charismatic. Renegade and impetuous. Principled and brave. And such is the power of imagination that she creates a young and beautiful Margarita Kilgour to match him. The heroine of an epic, a tragic figure fated to an empty, lonely life. Georgiana knows that this Margarita, all these years later, is still in love with Anderson, and guesses that the old camera bag Mrs Kilgour uses as a purse belonged to him, and wonders if any traces of Anderson's blood are still on it. Because Margarita has never stopped missing him. Longing for him. Grieving for him in her broken heart. Georgiana also knows that Margarita's marriage to Mr Kilgour was an act of defeat and despair. If she couldn't have the man she loved why not marry a man she could never love? Be safe in the suburbs. Be buried alive. Since her soul was already dead.

Moments featuring Anderson and the young, beautiful and doomed Margarita run in Georgiana's head like a movie. They sit by the fire in Anderson's cabin retreat, whispering love. Hand in hand, they stumble over minefields through storms of bullets, never letting go. They cling to each other while their helicopter spins down into the lush, chattering jungle. They dance in the moonlight, alone in a world of love. There is, however, one very major difference between Georgiana's remake of Mrs Kilgour's life and the original. In Georgiana's version Anderson lives. As he lies in Margarita's arms on the dusty road, her tears washing the blood from his face, she whispers, "Don't die." And he whispers back, "I won't, my darling. I'm never leaving you." Happily ever after. Georgiana channelling Marigold at last.

For days Georgiana is distracted by these fantasies. If only Mrs Kilgour were more forthcoming. All these months she's been going on and on about the most boring and uninteresting things, and now that she actually has something to talk about that Georgiana wants to hear, she shuts up as if she's taken a vow of silence. She has the twisted mind of a torturer.

In school, Georgiana's thoughts wander, so that at the end of each class she has no idea what's been going on and is always surprised by the bell. She brings her history text to maths, and her Spanish notebook to her media class. Mr Marks finally gets her attention by leaning on her desk and putting his face right in front of hers. "Well?" he asks. "Yes or no?" Georgiana says yes, causing the rest of the class to laugh hysterically. She only finds out afterwards that the question Mr Marks asked her was whether he was being more boring than usual or whether she was so deep in thought because she was trying to resolve the financial crisis.

At home, she puts salt in her coffee instead of sugar. She puts her phone in the refrigerator instead of the margarine. She parks the car in someone else's driveway. Her mother wants to know if she's taking drugs.

"Of course not," says Georgiana. "I just have something on my mind."

Georgiana's mother's eyes lock on her like laser beams. "And what would that be?"

It is as she's gazing back at her mother that Georgiana finally has the idea that could solve her dilemma. A brilliant idea. She rarely flat-out lies to Adele Shiller because there isn't any point. Georgiana's mother is a very successful PR consultant. She is not only an expert at manipulating information, she can spot a lie the way a bloodhound can pick up a scent. But if Georgiana tells her the truth – that what's on her mind is a man who's been dead for nearly fifty years – Mrs Shiller will have her in therapy faster than you can say "Agent Orange". However, if she handles this right, there's a chance that her mother – whose other useful talent is that she is very good at putting people at their ease and getting them to talk – could help Georgiana find out what she wants to know about Anderson. She opts to tell her almost-the-truth.

"Mrs Kilgour," says Georgiana. "You know, the old lady I visit at St Joan's?" She frowns with concern. "I don't know, I can't help worrying about her with Christmas coming up. You know, everybody celebrating with their friends and families... But Mrs K has no friends ... and no family... and she doesn't mix with the other people at the centre..."

"And you feel bad for her, being all by herself," finishes her mother. Understanding the human psyche is part of her job.

Georgiana nods. "Yeah. I guess I do. It just seems kind of sad."

As Georgiana knows very well, Adele Shiller is a doer, not a worrier or a talker as many of us are. For her, problems are there to be solved, not fretted about. She nods, too. "I have an idea. Why don't we invite her to join us for Christmas Day?"

"Oh, I didn't mean..." protests Georgiana. Adele Shiller could make a corpse tell her its life story, but she won't do it if she suspects that's why Georgiana wants Mrs Kilgour to come. Manipulators don't always like being manipulated themselves. "You have so much to do already. It would be a big imposition."

"One person isn't going to make any difference." Mentally, Adele is already laying another place at the table and roasting a few more potatoes. "It's just Bruno and Liz coming this year. And you know what they say: the more the merrier."

Not if one of the more is Mrs Kilgour, but Georgiana definitely isn't going to tell her mother that.

"Um… I'm not so sure. Maybe it's not such a great idea." What she's not sure about, of course, is how Mrs Kilgour would react to an invitation from Georgiana. Just saying hello can cause an argument. "She might think it's strange, you know—"

"Well, if you think she might feel a little uncomfortable, I could call and ask her myself. Say I've heard so much about her and I'd really like to meet her."

"*You?* Are you serious?"

"Of course I am." Adele taps her fingers together. Thoughtfully. "I know what I'll do. We probably have to clear it with St Joan's anyway. I'm sure they do have to know where their residents are. You can't just waltz off with an octogenarian under your arm. So before I talk to your lady, I'll call them and work it all out. That way I can find out if she has any special dietary requirements. There are so many different allergies these days. Remember that luncheon last year where one of the guests had to be rushed to hospital because there were nuts in the pasta sauce? And perhaps they can tell me if there's anything she needs that we could give as a little gift."

And here is something that Georgiana, dazzled by her own brilliance, overlooked. Adele Shiller likes to control things. (On a vacation in Rome she actually took over the tour when the guide showed up drunk.) Mrs Kilgour, on the other hand, doesn't like to be bossed around.

"Oh, but you're so busy, Mom. Maybe I should talk to Mrs Kilgour first. See if she even wants to come."

Adele Shiller is shaking her head. "No, I think it's better if I talk to her. I want her to feel that the invitation comes from all of us, not just from you."

"She still might not want to come. She's a very private person."

But as Georgiana also should know, there is no such thing as a private person in the world of PR.

"Don't be ridiculous," says Adele. "We're having her over for Christmas dinner, not putting her life story on Facebook. What's the number for St Joan's?" Her phone is already in her hand.

Chapter Twenty
Asher's Lost Weekend

Claudelia, Marigold and Georgiana are in the student lounge on Monday morning, catching up on what happened since the last time they talked on Sunday night. They are so engrossed in their conversation that they don't see Byron, Will and Asher come in until they're almost on top of them.

"So how was mountain-goat week—" begins Georgiana, but stops when she notices that Asher is limping and leaning on an old wooden cane. "Holy Christmas! What happened to you?"

"Oh my God, Asher!" Claudelia is trying to sound concerned and not laugh at the same time. "What'd you do? Fall off a rock?"

"No, a roof," says Will.

Asher corrects him. "Actually, it was a ladder."

"A ladder?" repeats Marigold. "You mean at the cabin?

What were you doing on a ladder at the cabin?"

Will puts a hand on Asher's shoulder. "I'm afraid Mr Grossman never made it to the mountains. I went with my brother, and we had an awesome time, in case anyone's interested."

No one is.

"So what were you doing up on your roof?" asks Georgiana. "Don't you have a guy who does that stuff?"

"It wasn't at home. It was at the community centre."

"The community centre?" It hasn't escaped Claudelia's attention that Asher not only spends every Saturday at the centre, but that he also spends a lot of time organizing schedules and sessions on his notepad when he isn't there. She just didn't think he went there during the week as well. "What the hell were you doing there?"

"Tell the truth, man," laughs Byron. "They're paying you, aren't they? They have you on some kind of retainer."

Will winks at Asher. "Personally, I'm still not convinced that Mrs D isn't so hot flames come off her."

"Give me a break, OK?" Asher says to Will. "You know that's not true." He turns back to Claudelia, who seems to be glaring at him. "I just stopped by Thursday night to leave a note saying I was going away for the weekend."

Georgiana asks how, if he was leaving a note, he

wound up falling off a ladder. "Is the mailbox on the roof?"

"No," says Asher. "The leak was on the roof." And explains that the centre's handyman couldn't go up because of his back. "It's just a sprain," he says in summation, "but it really hurt for a day or two."

Claudelia is looking at him as if he's a puzzle. "Hang on," she says. "Are you telling me that you were home alone all weekend, and you didn't call me to help you or at least come keep you company?"

"I was OK." He stares at the toes of her shoes. They're a little scuffed. "And, anyway, you know... I wasn't exactly at home."

"Right." Claudelia nods and the feathers hanging from her ears nod along. "So where exactly were you?"

Thursday night, when Carlin went to get some ice, Asher called Will and told him what had happened and said to go climbing without him. But he let Will think that he was already back at home. To be fair to Asher, he thought he'd go home the next day, but that was before Mrs Dunbar arrived at the centre at seven o'clock on Friday morning, bringing an ACE bandage, Epsom salts, a cane, breakfast and sunshine. Asher wasn't going to explain any more, but he knows from the look on Claudelia's face that she's hurt that he didn't call her. Hurt is just a heartbeat away from mad. He's got enough problems without having her mad at him.

"I was at the centre."

"At the centre? Are we talking about the community centre? What did you call it? The birthplace of chaos?" Claudelia almost smiles. "That's where you stayed?"

"Dude!" Will leans towards him. "The whole weekend? I thought you said you were at home."

"Mrs Dunbar insisted I stay there." This is true. After breakfast she bandaged his foot with a skill and gentleness he wasn't expecting, and said that he should stay off it for a couple of days. Carlin had told her there was no one at home to look after him so she thought he should stay where he was. "I'd bring you to our house," said Mrs Dunbar, "but we have the in-laws staying and there really isn't any room." Which, for Asher, meant that there definitely is a God.

"But you said the centre's a total dump," says Will. "You said the only reason it doesn't have rats is because rats have higher standards."

It's pretty astounding how – when it comes to something like this, but not when he suggests they carry their own hand gel or start thinking about life insurance – everybody remembers everything he's ever said down to the tiniest detail.

"Yeah, well, I didn't really have a choice. You know,

since I couldn't walk or drive. I kind of had to take what I could get."

Byron wants to know where he slept. "OK, they give out free food, but it's not a homeless shelter, is it? They don't have beds."

"No," admits Asher. "No beds."

Everybody is looking at him.

"So?" prompts Claudelia. "Where did you sleep?"

Asher glances at his watch, hoping to discover that the bell is about to ring, but time seems to have sat down if not actually come to a dead stop. "There's a sofa."

"A sofa!" Will laughs so loudly that heads turn. "*You* slept on a sofa? On somebody else's germ-ridden old sofa? Were you drugged?"

He slept badly his first night. His foot hurt every time he moved, the sofa was as lumpy as a cobbled street, Carlin's clothes and blanket made him feel as if he was in someone else's bath water, and instead of the howling of coyotes in the mountains there were drunks singing "Dancing Queen" on Main Street. But on the second night he fell asleep as soon as they turned out the light and didn't wake until morning.

"I did have some herbal tea."

"Oh well, there you are," says Byron. "Sofa? Herbal tea? The man must've fallen on his head."

"And what about clothes and stuff?" asks Will. "You expect me to believe you didn't change your underwear for three days?"

"Of course not." On Friday afternoon, when he could hobble around enough to be considered ambulatory, Carlin drove him home to get his toothbrush, his laptop, his phone charger and clean clothes.

"I just don't get it." Claudelia sounds like an archaeologist who has opened a three-thousand-year-old tomb to find everything wrapped in plastic bags. "I would've come and gotten you if you'd asked. You could have stayed with us. We have beds with mattresses."

"Any of us could have picked you up," adds Georgiana. "And given you a bucket of water to soak your foot in."

"But at least you weren't hurt really bad," says Marigold. "And you were being looked after. I mean, it's lucky that guy was there. You could've been laying there in the rain all night."

"Marigold," says Byron, "if that guy hadn't been there, Asher wouldn't have gone up on the roof."

But nothing is going to distract Claudelia. "So why didn't you call one of us, Asher?"

"I didn't think of it, that's all." Which sounds stupid, but happens to be the truth. "You know what they say about inertia. I was there already – and I was in pain and trying to rest my foot…" And Mrs Dunbar brought them breakfast and supper, and at night he and Carlin played backgammon and hung out. As Carlin would say, everything was copasetic.

"Yeah, but what'd you do all day?" asks Georgiana. "You must've been bored out of your mind."

Asher takes another quick look at his watch. Is the bell broken or something? Have they drifted into some parallel universe where you stay in the same moment for ever? It has to be time for classes to start. He's been here hours. "Oh, there was stuff to do."

"What?" Claudelia again. "While you were in so much pain and resting your foot you found something to do?" Maybe she's the one who should be a lawyer. A prosecuting attorney.

"Mrs Dunbar found some desk-work for me."

Mrs Dunbar said that he didn't have to feel that he was missing out on a fun weekend. "There's more than one way to climb a mountain." He could start preparing his first job workshop while he was laid up. "We'll schedule it for right after Christmas," she announced. "Start the new year right." Asher didn't know what job workshop she was talking about. Mrs Dunbar reminded him that it was his idea. Group workshops where their clients could practise being interviewed and give each other feedback. Build their confidence; make them feel that they aren't alone. Didn't he remember? Only vaguely. Mrs Dunbar, however, remembered it vividly. And she didn't think it mattered that Asher had never actually had a job interview himself, either. Her only worry had been that there would never be any time to get it together because there was always so much else to do, especially with Christmas coming up. It's not just a busy time of year for Santa Claus. "And here we are," she joyfully declared, "with the perfect opportunity to get it all done." *Don't say it*, Asher silently begged. *Please don't say it.* But she said it anyway. "God really does work in mysterious ways."

But from the expressions on his friends' faces now it would seem that the person who works in mysterious ways is Asher Grossman.

"So let me make sure I understand this," says Byron. "You've been at the community centre since Thursday." He counts off on his fingers. "One ... two ... three ... four nights."

Asher nods. "Because I couldn't walk. And this morning's the first time my foot was really OK enough to drive."

"And it never occurred to you to call one of us to say where you were or what happened," says Claudelia.

Asher nods again.

"I guess you're going to be real glad to get home," says Marigold.

Asher says, "You bet," as the bell finally goes. If he could stand on his foot, he'd run from the room.

The day Carlin drove him over to pick up his things, Carlin was amazed by the size of the Grossmans' house. He got out of the car and stood there for a few minutes, just staring at it like a tribesman from a remote village who's never seen a skyscraper before. "This is some place you have here," he said at last. "No offence, but I couldn't live in a house this big. I'd feel like I was in a dinghy on the ocean when I was here by myself. You know, kind of lost and lonely. But I guess you're used to it."

Asher said he was.

But when he pulls up to the garage on Monday afternoon it is Asher who gets out of the car and just stands there for several minutes, staring at his home. He's been living in a space the size of the downstairs shower room for two days, and suddenly the house he grew up in looks too large. Too large for two people. Even if they had dogs and cats and a talking parrot it would be too large.

That's when he hears Marigold in his head saying, *I guess you're going to be real glad to get home...*

Now he isn't so sure.

Chapter Twenty-one
Christmas Present,
Christmas Past

Jack Frost nips at noses, silver bells ring, and cash registers hum. Lawns and houses blaze with coloured lights; smiling Santas wave from rooftops, wink from windows and peek out of chimneys. There is a manger in front of three of the local churches, a lighted tree on the town green, and Frosty the Snowman and a posse of elves roam through the mall handing out candy canes and coupons. Artificial snow falls outside the entrance of Toys for Tots. It's Christmas-time in the suburbs.

And nowhere is it more Christmas-time than at 24 Wolff Drive. The dove of peace has been nesting on the Liottas' roof for the past couple of weeks, cooing and stretching its wings. This visitation, so in keeping with the holiday season, has a lot to do with the fact that Mr Liotta has been away on business since the beginning of December. The Liottas have always gotten along a lot better when they're not together than when they are. It's difficult to carry on the hand-to-hand combat of domestic warfare when one of the fighters is in a hotel three thousand miles way. Their nightly phone calls are pleasant and affectionate. Mrs Liotta catches her husband up on what's happening in Shell Harbour without once raising her voice or bursting into tears. When he's home, Mr Liotta sometimes complains about his family or things that happen in the house, but when he's not his complaints are all about other people and the things they've done wrong. All of which makes a nice change. When they've finished talking, Marigold is called in to say hello and goodnight to her father. He always asks her how school is and what she's been doing, as if she's ten. "I'm really looking forward to Christmas," he says every night. "I miss the two of you so much." They tell him that they miss him, too. They can't wait for him to come home.

All of which also makes it easy to forget that he is a man who has been known to punch a hole in a wall, and that she is a woman who has been known to hurl a hot chicken pie across the kitchen at his head (narrowly missing). And Marigold does forget all that.

Because, despite the number of times it has ended in tears (or possibly because of them), Marigold has always loved Christmas. Everything looks so much prettier and brighter. Happier. And people are happier, too. 'Tis the season to be jolly, after all. They smile. They hum along with the radio. They shout out, "Happy Holidays" to everyone they meet. Marigold throws herself into the preparations with enough enthusiasm to sail a sled across the skies. Christmas music plays morning, noon and night. She dashes around the mall with Claudelia and Georgiana, dodging elves and ticking things off a list. She buys enough gift paper to cover the Pentagon. She spends hours deciding what to wear to the holiday parties. She and her mother bake gingerbread cookies and decorate the house inside and out, even going so far as to put lights around the rear window of the car and around the birdhouse on the front lawn. Mrs Liotta signs and addresses dozens of Christmas cards while Marigold, a halo of silver tinsel on her head, decorates the tree and the Crystals sing "Santa Claus Is Coming to Town".

"Even though Rose can't get home, this is going to be the best Christmas ever," says Marigold's mother. "Don't you think so, honey?"

"You bet," says Marigold. They will Skype Rose on Christmas Day, waving at each other from the screens of their laptops. "It's going to be awesome."

It would have to work pretty hard to be the worst Christmas ever.

But, of course, neither of them mentions that.

On the day Marigold's father comes home, Marigold stays behind while her mother drives to the airport to pick him up. It will be hours before they return. She makes herself a snack, then goes into the TV room and settles down to watch a movie. The movie she puts on is an old version of Charles Dickens' *A Christmas Carol* (old enough that it was originally made in black and white). The story is so familiar that although Marigold has never watched any version from beginning to end she feels as if she has. Which means that she doesn't have to give the movie her undivided attention. While the ghost of Jacob Marley visits Ebenezer Scrooge, Marigold finishes writing her cards. As the Ghost of Christmas Past arrives, Marigold wraps the last of her gifts. She begins painting her fingernails red and green during the visit of the Ghost of Christmas Present.

It's right at the end of this ghost's visit that he pulls back his robes to reveal two emaciated children crouched beneath them.

Marigold looks up, holding the red nail polish brush in mid-air.

There was one other thing that Marigold put completely out of her mind while she was shopping, wrapping and stringing cards across the mantel. And that one other thing is Sadie Hawkle. It is only now, staring at the haggard faces of Ignorance and Want with their wide, dark, deadened eyes, that she remembers her.

That afternoon when she took the books over, it was such an uncomfortable meeting that she couldn't get away fast enough. And as soon as she was on the sidewalk, she called Claudelia and talked to her all the way home, putting Sadie so far out of her mind that she couldn't find her way back. Until now. Now, of course, Marigold can't stop thinking about her. She tries to concentrate on finishing her nails, but she can't get rid of the sad and sallow face of Sadie Hawkle staring at her like the ghost of some poor Victorian flower girl who froze to death in the snow. Sadie standing beside her mother on the afternoon Marigold went to her house. Silent and still as a corpse.

As that image comes back to her, with it come all the questions Marigold didn't ask herself at the time. Was Sadie lying when she said her mother was sick the morning that she didn't go to school? Or was Sadie's mother lying when she said that Sadie was sick? But why would Mrs Hawkle lie? She certainly didn't look sick. She looked as if she was going out. But Sadie didn't look sick, either.

She looked as if she'd already been out. And why did Sadie rush to the door when she saw Marigold, then act like she'd been struck dumb? Why was it so hard to get her to take the books?

Almost as if she's being directed by some external force, Marigold suddenly turns off the television, and goes over to the cabinet where her mother keeps the old photo albums. She goes through half a dozen before she finds the one she's looking for. The picture taken late in the evening of the Christmas That Almost Never Was. She sits back on the floor with the album on her lap. There they are, she and Rose, sitting side by side in front of the tree, each of them wearing one of their gifts and holding another. She can hear her mother saying, in her chirpy, cheerleader voice, "Come on, girls. Give me a really big smile!" And they do. Both of them are smiling. But only with their mouths. If their expressions were a sound, it would be a cry for help.

Now who does that remind her of?

Chapter Twenty-two
Merry Christmas, Mrs Kilgour

Although she knows her mother can be very persuasive (Adele Shiller can take almost anything back to the store and get a refund, even if whatever it is has been opened and used), Georgiana didn't really expect Mrs Kilgour to accept the invitation to Christmas dinner. She had no trouble imagining what Mrs Kilgour would have to say about the invitation – or with how much sarcasm and contempt. Why would she want to spend the day with a bunch of strangers? What was she, the last charity case left in town? Had they run out of one-legged dogs and one-eyed cats? Did it make the Shillers feel good to drag some poor old lady into their home and make her eat food she has trouble chewing that's too rich and not good for her? What were they hoping, that she'd drop dead and they'd see an angel? Are all the soup kitchens going to be closed for the day so that they can't go to one of them and bother the homeless?

But what Georgiana overlooked was that Mrs Kilgour isn't just as stubborn as blood, she also enjoys being difficult. Contrary. Doing exactly what Georgiana doesn't expect her to do. According to Adele Shiller, when she extended the invitation Mrs Kilgour said none of the things Georgiana imagined. She didn't even hesitate and ask for time to think it over. She said, "Thank you very much, Mrs Shiller. I'd love to come."

When her mother reported this conversation, Georgiana stood beside her mother's workstation for several seconds, watching reindeer dance across the screen and trying to process what she'd just been told, squeezing out a smile the size of the last drop of toothpaste in the tube. "Did you say she accepted? She said *yes*?"

"Of course she said yes. She was thrilled to be asked. And we had such a nice chat."

A nice chat? With the woman who makes the Grinch seem jolly? Was that even possible?

Mrs Shiller shook her head, not the first parent to be baffled by the ways of her child. "You never mentioned what an interesting woman she is. How charming."

"Gee whiz." Georgiana slapped her forehead. "How could I forget that?"

"Well, I really don't know." The maternal head was

shaking again. "She's extremely intelligent and knowledgeable. If I didn't know her age, I'd've thought she was a much younger woman."

Georgiana laughed. Her mother must have spoken to some other old lady. Whoever was on reception must have put her through to the wrong room.

"Take my advice," said Adele. "Don't ever take drugs, Georgie. God only knows what you'd be like if you did."

On Christmas morning, Georgiana is sent to pick up Mrs Kilgour. Naturally, she hasn't told her mother how difficult their guest can be. Partly because she doesn't want to discourage her, and partly because her mother wouldn't believe her. Especially not after she found Mrs Kilgour so interesting and charming over the phone.

But on the way to St Joan's misgivings about the day ahead start to settle in Georgiana's heart like pigeons on a wall. There are a few things about their guest that it might have been useful for Adele Shiller to know. Maybe Georgiana should have told her mother – a woman known for her sophistication and fashion sense – about Mrs Kilgour's car-crash style of dressing. Maybe she should have mentioned how ungrateful and complaining she is. How she has the personality of a stink bomb. How she thinks Georgiana is shallow as a stream in a drought and has poor-quality air for brains. How she never has a good word to say about anyone. How she falls asleep. The image of Mrs Kilgour, dressed in a mixture of plaids, stripes and floral prints and a baseball cap, sound asleep at the dinner table, her head nodding dangerously towards the roast potatoes, dances in Georgiana's head all the way to St Joan's. It is only the thought of finally finding out more about Anderson that stops her from turning the car around and telling her mother the old lady wasn't feeling well and couldn't come after all.

Mrs Kilgour is sitting on her bed, waiting, wearing a velvet suit that doesn't clash with her hair, a corsage of tiny bells and balls and plastic holly and a string of pearls. Beside her are her walking stick, a sober grey coat and hat, and a canvas bag.

"What's wrong?" she asks, heaving herself to her feet. "You look like you were expecting someone else."

Georgiana isn't sure that she didn't get someone else. Mrs Kilgour looks as if she was once First Lady. "Nothing. I've just never seen you dressed up. You look nice."

"Well, how did you think I'd be dressed? It is Christmas, isn't it? Not Groundhog Day."

"I guess I figured you'd dress like normal." And Georgiana is caught so off guard that she says, "I didn't really think you'd come."

"Why wouldn't I?" Mrs Kilgour grabs her cane and thumps it on the floor. "It has to be better than staying here eating turkey roll and listening to them all sing 'Away in the Manger' off key."

Georgiana certainly hopes so.

In another surprising move, Mrs Kilgour doesn't once criticize Georgiana's driving the way she often criticizes her pushing of the wheelchair. Instead, she chats away happily, pointing out things that weren't there before – that development, that business park, that shopping centre – and things that have disappeared, mainly trees.

When they reach the Shillers', she greets Mrs Shiller with a hug. "I can't tell you how much I appreciate this," she says. "I haven't been in a real home since I moved into St Joan's. It's like being in jail, but the food's slightly better."

Mrs Shiller says the pleasure is all theirs. She's really been looking forward to meeting her.

Mrs Kilgour settles onto the sofa, exuding peace and goodwill and complimenting the Shillers on their lovely home. "And you also have a terrific daughter, of course," says Mrs Kilgour. "She's a real credit to you."

Georgiana gawps at her, smiling and holding a glass of sherry. Like the First Lady at a reception for foreign dignitaries. She doesn't sound as if she's being sarcastic.

"When you get to my age, people treat you like you're

a very young child or just very stupid. But not Georgiana. She treats me like I'm a real person."

"You mean because we always argue?" asks Georgiana.

Everybody laughs.

Georgiana's aunt and uncle arrive with their dog, Hank, two seasonal shopping bags and hugs all around.

Liz and Bruno also find Mrs Kilgour charming and delightful.

"Now it really feels like Christmas," says Liz, squeezing Mrs Kilgour's hand.

Bruno, who owns an antique store, is interested in the vintage corsage pinned to her jacket. "I haven't seen anything like that in years."

"Has to be at least sixty years old," says Mrs Kilgour. "I probably bought it in the five and ten."

Hank sits on Mrs Kilgour's lap. Apparently she's always loved Jack Russells. And they her.

Mrs Shiller bought several small gifts for Mrs Kilgour. Georgiana told her not to bother. "She can be kind of fussy," said Georgiana. Meaning that she wouldn't like them. "And it'll be embarrassing that she has no presents for us."

"It's more embarrassing for her to sit there like a hostage while everybody else opens theirs," countered her mother.

But of course Mrs Kilgour, who is determined to

disprove everything Georgiana knows about her, loves her gifts.

"How thoughtful," she coos over the slipper socks. The bolster cushion is just what she needs for reading in bed. And a box of chocolates, what a treat! She hasn't had Belgian chocolates since her last visit to Brussels. "Which, believe you me, was a very long time ago."

In the canvas bag are presents for the Shillers.

An antique silver fountain pen for Mr Shiller.

"It's a beaut," says Mr Shiller. "It reminds me of one my grandad had."

"Spanish." Bruno turns it over in his hand. "Early nineteenth century."

"It belonged to my husband's father," explains Mrs Kilgour. "He never used anything else."

A pale blue glass vase for Mrs Shiller.

"It's exquisite." Mrs Shiller holds it up to the light, the glass so fine it seems spun out of air.

"I picked it up in Venice," says Mrs Kilgour. "God knows how we got it back here in one piece. But my husband was a genius at packing."

A hand-embroidered Chinese wedding blouse for Georgiana.

Once again, Georgiana can't hide her surprise. A wedding blouse! It has to be the blouse Mrs Kilgour would have worn if she'd married Anderson. For once, Georgiana has nothing to say except, "Thank you."

Even Bruno has never seen anything like the wedding blouse before.

"I was hoping I'd find the right person to pass it on to. I'd hate to think of it just going to the Goodwill. But you should save it for a special occasion."

"You must have done a lot of travelling," says Mrs Shiller.

"In my day," says Mrs Kilgour. "Mr Kilgour and I worked as a team for many years. We were always going somewhere."

All the while the presents were being opened, Liz kept looking at Mrs Kilgour. As if she thought she knew her. Now she says, "Kilgour... Kilgour... You know, that name is so familiar. From when I was a kid, I think." Liz grew up in the area. "I'm sure my parents knew someone named Kilgour." She shakes the red bow she's still holding in her hand. "Their name was Fieldstone. Ring any bells?"

"Richard and Agnes!" says Mrs Kilgour, as if she'd only been waiting to be asked. "Your father had the newspaper store at the junction. My husband was Mordecai. They played poker together."

"Mordecai!" Liz claps her hands. "That's it! Mordecai Kilgour. Morty. He did magic tricks. And he ran the *Valley Herald*."

"That's right. We'd been living in New York when we weren't on assignment, but we came out here and took over the paper when Morty's father passed."

"That's right," says Liz. "I remember my mom talking about it. You were a reporter before that, weren't you?"

So at least now Georgiana knows what Mrs Kilgour was doing in Vietnam.

But Mrs Kilgour doesn't mention Vietnam. She just nods.

"The *Valley Herald* was a fine paper," says Bruno. "One of the best small presses in the country. It was still going strong when I moved out here. Didn't you win a Pulitzer?"

In fact, the *Valley Herald* won three Pulitzer Prizes when the Kilgours owned it: two for local reporting and one for public service.

"We loved the *Herald*," says Mrs Kilgour. "We both did a lot of things we enjoyed or were proud of. But the *Herald* was the best on both counts."

Georgiana sits back, listening and thinking. She's learning a lot about Mrs Kilgour, but none of it, of course, is what she expected to find out. Not even close.

Unless universal peace were declared or Santa himself made an unexpected appearance, the day couldn't go better. There are no awkward moments, no embarrassing scenes, no tempers snapping like turtles. No one dozes off over her roast beef. By the time dinner is done Georgiana's pigeons of misgiving are all sound asleep. Georgiana, however, is wide awake, mesmerized by this new Mrs Kilgour. Who is easily the star of the day. Where hasn't she been? She's crossed the Himalayas, driven across Europe, sailed the Java Sea. Whom hasn't she met? Presidents and peasants, celebrities and criminals, generals and gangsters. Her stories are more interesting than most Hollywood movies, and more entertaining. Georgiana's only disappointment is that she never mentions Anderson. She never says, "When I was in Vietnam" or "When I was with Anderson". Never suggests that anyone ever died in her arms. The pain must still be too great.

After dinner the men take Hank for a walk. Moving into the living room with coffee and cookies, the women start chatting about Christmases past. Favourite relatives. Funniest stories. Best memories. It's that kind of holiday, of course. Georgiana can see that she's not going to hear anything about Mrs Kilgour's lost love now, and excuses herself to take a call from Claudelia. Because it includes a list of what presents they got, it's a long conversation. When she returns, Adele Shiller is talking about Georgiana's grandmother. There's something in the tone of her mother's voice that makes Georgiana stop rather than stride into the room. Not eavesdropping, but definitely paying attention. No one seems to notice that she's there.

"It was just terrible," her mother is saying. "It was a Saturday morning. We'd only gone into town to do some shopping. When we got back, my mother-in-law was at the foot of the stairs, dead, and Georgiana was beside her, holding her hand and crying. Poor Georgiana. She was only four."

Apparently someone did know she was there. Mrs Kilgour looks over at Georgiana, rooted to a spot just outside the door. "What a terrible thing for you," she says.

From somewhere very far away, Georgiana mumbles, "Yeah."

But she has no memory of that morning at all.

Until this moment – her mother, aunt and Mrs Kilgour now all looking at her, the tree lights blinking, the sunlight leaning against the living-room window – Georgiana had always thought her grandmother died when she was a baby. Hundreds of miles away.

So now she not only knows why Mrs Kilgour was in Vietnam, she also knows why she's always been so afraid of old people falling down and dying – so afraid of death.

Chapter Twenty-three
Another Christmas Not a Million Miles Away

It's Christmas morning. All over the country children are shrieking, lights are shining and presents are being unwrapped. Though not in the Grossmans' house. The only sign of this joyous season are the cards Mrs Swedger has put on display in the living room on silver ribbon. Most of them are from companies and corporations. There's no tree, no lights, no Yule log in the window and no wreath on the door. Why bother? When Asher was little they always had a six-foot tree and blue lights strung along the edge of the roof. More recently, however, Asher and his father usually stay in New York over the holidays because Albert has so many social engagements to attend, and that tradition has been abandoned.

But this year they aren't staying in the city, either.

Asher, still in his pyjamas, pads into the kitchen in his bare feet. He makes himself a cappuccino and puts on the radio. Bing Crosby starts singing about a white Christmas.

There are seven large and very expensive hampers lined up on the kitchen table. They contain smoked hams and sausages; exotic cheeses, fruits, chutneys and jams; tins of crackers and cookies and chocolates; jars of nuts, pickled fish and unexpired caviar. The hampers are presents from some of Albert Grossman's satisfied clients. They come every year, as much a part of the Christmas ritual as the tree at Rockefeller Center. If Albert Grossman were here, he'd take out what he wanted and regift the rest, but Albert Grossman isn't here. This year Albert's in Dubai and can't get home.

"You'll be all right on your own, won't you," he said to Asher after he broke the news. It wasn't a question. "You can go to friends."

"Sure, of course I'll be OK," Asher assured him. "There are a couple of parties happening. Claudelia'll be at her grandmother's in Massachusetts, but I can go to Will's on Christmas Day."

"I'll make it up to you," Albert promised. "Soon as this business is settled."

"That'd be great, Dad." But the thought that skulked into Asher's head like an uninvited guest was: *When?*

Asher has been ignoring the hampers for several

days, but now he stands, cup in hand, gazing at them as if they're a flock of birds trapped in an oil spill and wondering what to do about them. He's already given one to Mrs Swedger to take to her family, and he can bring one to the Lundquists', but what about the other six?

And then he has the very vivid image of Mrs Dunbar, running around the centre in a Santa hat, handing out the oranges and miniature candy bars she managed to talk one of the big supermarkets into donating to the under-fives. It's a no-brainer! Why didn't he think of her before? The centre is closed today, of course, but every year the Reverend Dunbar's church makes a Christmas dinner for people who claim to have nowhere else to go. Mrs Dunbar will be able to use the hampers. He picks up his phone from the counter, not so much as glancing at the time. He's pretty sure that Mrs Dunbar never sleeps.

This is how Asher had planned to spend the day. He would mooch around the house in his pyjamas all morning – maybe watch a movie or catch up on the news, check his emails, call his aunt in Toronto. At around one he'd get dressed (black suit, red shirt, green tie, suspenders decorated with reindeer and elves) and drive over to Will's for dinner at three. He'd spend the afternoon and some of the evening there, and then he'd come home and call Claudelia at her grandmother's. A perfect day. Peaceful. Calm. Festive but measured.

If he'd had more foresight and included giving the hampers to Mrs Dunbar in these plans he would have arranged to drop them off on his way to the Lundquists'. When he was on a tight schedule.

"I'm at the church," says Mrs Dunbar, after she stops thanking him. "You better bring them right over so I can see what we can use today and what can be put aside for something else."

Asher looks at the coffee machine with longing. He was going to have a second cup. Since it's Christmas. "Now? But it's not even nine o'clock."

"It's all systems go here," says Mrs Dunbar. "Our first sitting's at 1.30 p.m. If you have some hams in those hampers they could really come in handy. Looks like we're going to have them lining up in the street."

"I'll be there in half an hour," promises Asher.

Carlin is waiting in the parking lot to help him unload the car. They go down to the basement and into the dining room, where trestle tables have been set up on either side of the room. Paper chains cross the ceiling from all directions, and on every table there is a centrepiece – tiny trees or tiny wreaths – each handmade by the ladies of the church. The paper tablecloths feature poinsettias. There's a small but real tree in one corner of the room, decorated with paper doves.

In the kitchen several harried-looking women and men peel, chop and stir, moving from stove to counter and counter to stove as if they're on wheels. They are all wearing either antlers or elf hats. Organ music drifts down to the basement from the church above.

He and Carlin set the hampers down on a table in one corner.

Mrs Dunbar rushes over. She is wearing an apron with a Christmas tree and at least half a pound of flour on it, and a mop cap of the type favoured by Mrs S. Claus and Betsy Ross. She has a dripping spoon in one hand.

"Will you look at all this! I can hardly believe my eyes! What isn't in these baskets?" Mrs Dunbar flips open the lids, excited as a little girl opening her Christmas presents. Asher's not sure if she's flushed from the heat of the kitchen or from amazement. "It's incredible. They're like mini gourmet delis!" She has that God-works-in-mysterious-ways look on her face as she turns to Asher. "How can we thank you? It may not quite be the miracle of the loaves and fishes, but it's close enough for us. I have to tell you the truth. I was really worried. I've been up since four trying to figure out how we'd ever manage to feed everybody."

"Glad I can help," Asher mumbles, and automatically starts to back away.

Mrs Dunbar slaps a floury hand down on his shoulder. He should never have worn the suit. "Where are you going?"

Where does she think he's going? To check the sheep?

"It's Christmas, Mrs Dunbar." As if she doesn't know that. Even Carlin is wearing a festive tie with his usual flannel shirt.

"But surely your family doesn't eat this early. It's still morning."

The suit is supposed to be his insurance policy. That's why he wore it. So it's obvious that he's going somewhere and she doesn't think of something else for him to do. Only it doesn't seem to have worked.

"Yeah but—"

"Oh, I know. I know." She thumps his shoulder again. "It's Christmas. You have things to do." She waves the spoon at him and the hampers. "And you've already done so much. I was just hoping that maybe you could spare an hour to give Carlin a hand."

Say no! Asher urges himself. *No! I can't give Carlin a hand. I have to go! For Christ's sake, it's Christmas!*

"A hand with what?" asks Asher.

Carlin is delivering meals to those who can't make

it to the church. Archie Shiplock was supposed to help him, but Archie's car won't start.

"Carlin can do it by himself," says Mrs Dunbar, "but it'd be so much quicker if the deliveries could be split in half."

"I don't know…" Everyone's looking at him as if he's trying to steal Christmas from the orphans. Asher Grinch.

"I'll pay for your gas."

"You don't have to do that, Mrs Dunbar. It's not the gas. It's just that… How long will it take?"

"Oh, not long!" Mrs Dunbar claps her hands together, whacking him with the spoon. "With two of you doing it? An hour. An hour and a half tops."

When they get outside, Carlin tells him to go on home. "I'll handle this, Asher. Mrs Dunbar will never know. Your dad's waiting for you. You should be with him on Christmas Day, not driving all over Queen's Park."

Possibly because they're standing outside the church, Asher hears himself telling the truth. "Actually, it's not my dad. He's … he's away. You know, for work. I'm having dinner at my friend's."

Carlin's nod is non-committal. "Same difference. Your buddy's waiting for you."

"Yeah, but it is still early." Asher makes a show of

checking the time. "I have hours yet. They don't expect me before two."

"Well, that would be very copasetic," says Carlin.

The morning goes quickly. Everybody is so glad to see Asher, you'd think he was a long-lost son or grandson. Grandson mainly. In one case, a great-grandson. Everybody wants to talk. How are the roads? Did he see that special on TV last night? Does he know anything about computers? They offer him cups of tea and coffee, cans of soda. Tell him how the arm was broken and why the daughter or the sister couldn't come this year. Some of them try to give him a tip.

Nonetheless, by one o'clock he has only one more delivery to make. And for the first time Asher recognizes the name on his list. Shelley Anne Rebough was the last person he saw when Mrs Dunbar roped him into doing the job application advice session. The one with the children, whose husband died and who has never worked outside the home.

Shelley Anne is living in a trailer. A small one.

Shelley Anne recognizes him the second she opens the door. And she, too, is glad to see him.

"Hey, I remember you! Merry Christmas! How're you doing?"

Asher says he's doing fine.

Which is more than can be said for Shelley Anne. She hasn't found a job yet, and they lost their house. "But, really, I can't complain," she says. "We're pretty lucky. At least we have a place to live." She nods to the box in his hands. "And Christmas dinner."

Inside, the trailer looks even smaller than it does on the outside. Possibly because there are four people and a dog living in it. There are Christmas lights around the walls of the living area, and the tiniest artificial tree he's ever seen on the coffee table.

"This is great," says Shelley Anne as he puts the box down on the counter. "You tell Mrs Dunbar thanks like ten million. I would've liked to come to the church for the dinner – it'd be nice for the kids to get out." She shrugs. "But, you know, it's a pretty long walk into town and there's no bus today."

The other thing they lost was the car.

Asher looks at the kids, sitting on the couch in a row. A few minutes before they were staring at the TV, but now they are staring at him. The dog, sitting on the lap of the smallest Rebough, is also staring at Asher. The whole trailer would fit into the Grossmans' kitchen (though you'd have to take out the utility island first). And this is the Reboughs being lucky.

"Well, you know," says Asher, "if you want, I could drive you all to the church for the dinner."

"Oh no." Shelley Anne shakes her head. The children all raise theirs. "No, we couldn't ask you to do that. I'm sure you want to get home to your own dinner."

"It's not a problem," says Asher. "Really. We're not eating till later."

"Thanks, but I really couldn't impose like that."

The children haven't moved but it feels as if they're sitting on the edge of their seats.

"Look." A new thought has occurred to him. "If you're worried about getting back, I can bring you guys home. That's not a problem, either."

"No, that—"

"I'm telling you the truth, Mrs Rebough. My family's not having Christmas dinner till way later."

Depending on when Albert Grossman finally has time, it could be next year.

A chorus of "Please, Mommy, please" erupts from the sofa.

"I don't know…" If the rope in a game of tug-of-war could make a face it would be the one made by Shelley Anne. "Well, if you're sure…"

"Sure I'm sure."

While the Reboughs are getting ready, Asher calls

Will to tell him he's going to miss dinner.

"I'm not even going to ask," says Will.

Asher doesn't arrive at the Lundquists' until long after dessert.

Will answers the door. "Geebus, María and José, dude," says Will . "What the hell happened to you?"

Asher's suit is rumpled and decorated with a variety of stains, he's lost his tie and he's wearing antlers.

Asher hands him the hamper he's brought them. "It's a long story."

"Asher!" Mrs Lundquist appears in the hall. "You finally made it! Come on in. Merry Christmas!"

"Merry Christmas," says Asher, and steps inside.

Chapter Twenty-four
Just When Things Seem to Be Going So Well

Sadie Hawkle is having a brand-new year. She's reading by herself at home a little each night. She's been enjoying the mystery she and Marigold read together every week. And, although she can still get that who's-the-informer look on her face and answer in monosyllables, most of the time she talks to Marigold as if she wants to (not the way she used to, as if someone was holding a gun to her head). She's full of stories about school. About her teacher and her classmates and her friends. Sometimes her teacher is really unfair and picks on her. Sometimes the boys tease her. She likes a girl named Charlie and one called Lil, but she doesn't like Kitty Johnston; Kitty Johnston's really mean and stuck-up.

Sadie also talks a lot about her dad. She had so much to say about her visit to him at Christmas, you'd think she'd been there a month. He thinks it's great that she's into detective stories. He called her a "chip off the old block". "That's what he said, 'a chip off the old block'," Sadie repeated. "Just like him." He took her to a bookstore and let her choose a book to read when she visits him. His present to her was a bright pink cell phone, and he must be calling her more, because she is full of things he said and did; things the two of them are going to do together. "What I like about him best," says Sadie, "is that he never yells at me."

On this afternoon, Marigold closes the book with a happy smile. "Only one more chapter to go, Sadie. That's a whole novel you've done. You'll have to pick what we read next."

"I did. The one with the ghost detective. That one looks cool."

This is another night when Sadie's mother is late picking her up, so they walk out together to wait in front of the school for her. At least, that's what Marigold thinks they're doing.

That's not what Sadie thinks. As soon as everyone else has gone Sadie says, "It's OK. You don't have to wait with me. My mom said I should just go home."

Marigold looks down at her. "By yourself?"

"Yeah." Sadie nods. "She lets me. I know the way. It's not far."

It isn't far; a couple of blocks.

"But it's dark." Marigold points at the sky as proof. "You can't walk home in the dark by yourself."

"Yeah, I can. I know what to do." She pats her pocket. "That's why my dad bought me a new phone. For protection."

What's she supposed to do? Throw it at the kidnapper?

"I still don't like the idea of you going home all by yourself," says Marigold. "Why don't I just walk with you to your door? Since it's only a couple of blocks."

Sadie says she guesses that's OK. But not enthusiastically.

"So how's your dad like his new apartment?" asks Marigold as they start off from the school. He moved right after New Year's to a brownstone in Brooklyn where Sadie now has her own room. "He all settled now?"

"He thinks it's awesome. It's way better than his old place." In the old apartment, the oven didn't work, the lights would dim when you turned on the hot water and you couldn't leave a window open even in the summer because there was a squirrel that would squeeze through the window gate and steal cookies. It was especially fond of Oreos. "And when I go at Easter we're going to paint my room any colour I want. Even stripes. Or polka dots. And he's going to get me one of those beds that isn't on the floor."

They discuss interior decoration for the rest of the walk to Clarendon Road.

There are no lights on in 1a.

"It doesn't look like your mom is home," says Marigold.

"That's OK." Sadie pulls something out of a pouch on her backpack and holds it up. "I have a key."

Marigold looks from the key to the unlit window to Sadie's face. She doesn't know what she should do. She can't leave Sadie by herself – that wouldn't be right. On the other hand – she's not exactly a friend of the family and can't just barge into the house, that wouldn't be right either. "So do you think she'll be back soon? Did she say why she couldn't pick you up today? Did she have somewhere she had to go?"

"I don't remember." Sadie shifts from one foot to the other. "Maybe she's taking a nap. She gets really tired." She swings her backpack, hitting the wall. "Or maybe she felt sick."

And maybe there's a note in the kitchen: *Have a migraine. Sandwich in the fridge.*

Marigold peers through the window, hoping to see a light at the back of the house. Another hope dashed. "I really don't like leaving you all alone."

"I'll be OK," Sadie assures her.

"Well, why don't you just check to see if your mom

is in there? Maybe you're right and she's lying down. My mom does that a lot."

"Really?" This information seems to perk her up. "Your mom gets tired, too?"

"She sure does." Exhausted by life. Marigold follows Sadie into the main hallway. "I'll wait here," she says, and stands outside the apartment door while Sadie turns on lights and goes to see if her mother is lying down.

Sadie may be reading better and talking more, but she doesn't move any faster. She's gone long enough to go back to the school to see if Justine Hawkle has shown up there after all. Leaving Marigold gazing into the apartment like someone with no money staring through a restaurant window.

It isn't just cats that are curious. Marigold leans over the threshold. The living room looks cosy. She leans a little further. A door and a corridor lead off it at the back. There are posters on the walls of the corridor. She takes a few more steps into the room, just to see what the posters are. She can glimpse the kitchen at the end.

Sadie, who has changed out of her school clothes, is coming out of a door on one side, just as the front door opens and her mother starts shouting.

"Sadie! What the hell's going on? Why is the apartment wide open? How many ti—" She freezes in the doorway just as Sadie has frozen in the middle of the hall. Only Justine is smiling. "Oh, hi. It's Marigold, right?" The smile comes so quickly that Marigold isn't sure she saw the rage on Justine's face half a second before. "I'm sorry I shouted like that. You know how dozy Sadie is. I figured she forgot to shut the door." She laughs a little. "She's always doing stuff like that."

"I hope you don't mind. I walked her home because it was dark. But I didn't mean to barge in or anything. I was just waiting for Sadie to see if you were … if you were in."

"No problem." Justine comes in and drops her bags in the nearest chair. "It was really nice of you to walk her home, but you didn't have to bother. I told her if I'm not there when you're closing up to just come home. It's not that far." She's still smiling, but now it's a goodbye smile.

"Yeah, well…" Marigold glances over at Sadie, whose only movement since her mother arrived has been to blink. "Well, I guess I better go."

Back in the outer hallway, she turns to wave goodbye to Sadie just in time to be able to say, when she describes what happened to her friends, that the door was slammed in her face.

Almost immediately, Justine Hawkle starts screaming again. *Who said you could bring strangers in my house? Why can't you ever do what you're told? Maybe you shouldn't go to the after-school programme if it makes you act like this...*

Marigold lets herself out, making sure she shuts the house door loudly behind her. But she stays on the porch until the screaming stops. Then she slowly walks down the steps and onto the sidewalk. She glances back at the house as she passes. Sadie is standing at the window, staring out at her as if she's watching the last rescue boat pull away from the shore.

Marigold waves, but Sadie doesn't wave back.

Chapter Twenty-five

A Few More Things That Georgiana Didn't Know About Mrs Kilgour

It seems that Mrs Kilgour doesn't like deep winter. "Bleak as a battlefield after the battle," said Mrs Kilgour. "If you ask me we should be like bears and hibernate till the spring. We'd all be much happier if we spent January to April with a quilt over our heads."

And so, as the new year starts, Mrs Kilgour stops. Every time Georgiana is supposed to visit, Mrs Kilgour cancels. She isn't feeling up to having company. They can't go out because of the weather. "I haven't noticed that anyone's invented a wheelchair on skis," she says. "How are you going to push me in the snow?" If she had a choice she wouldn't want to sit in her room, why should Georgiana?

Humans, of course, are not especially known for being consistent. They say one thing, and then do something else. They believe in one thing, and, before you can blink, they believe in its opposite. They're always changing their minds. Georgiana is not an exception to this rule. Having complained so much about having to see Mrs Kilgour and about Mrs Kilgour herself, now that Mrs Kilgour has stopped her from visiting, that's the one thing she really wants to do.

"Are you for real?" asked Will. "Now you're annoyed that you can't go see her?"

"I guess I got used to her," said Georgiana. "You know, like you get used to shoes that are a little tight."

"The way you griped about her it was more like you were wearing concrete blocks on your feet, not too-tight shoes."

"God, Will," groaned Georgiana. "You really do exaggerate."

But it's more than just getting used to her. Somehow the weeks seem incomplete without Mrs Kilgour. Like fries without ketchup. The fries still taste good, but not *as* good.

And then, for no obvious reason, Georgiana starts to worry about Mrs Kilgour, not just miss her. She remembers what a good time she had at Christmas and pictures her sitting in that miserable blue room all alone. Seeing no one. Talking to no one. Having no one to argue and bicker with. You can't really talk back to the TV.

There's an old saying that goes like this: if you don't ask the question you can't get the answer you don't want to hear. So Georgiana doesn't ask, but arrives at St Joan's one afternoon without warning, carrying a bag of things to brighten up the winter gloom.

The receptionist is glad to see her.

"I never had a chance to say how great it was that your family had Mrs Kilgour for Christmas," says Alice. "She really had a good time. I can't remember when I saw her that happy. It would've been a real shame if she'd had to spend the day all alone in her room."

"We had a good time, too."

"I was afraid we'd seen the last of you," Alice goes on as Georgiana signs in. "I'm glad she's feeling well enough again."

Georgiana decides against mentioning that she isn't expected. "Yeah," she says. "Me, too."

But if Mrs Kilgour is glad to see Georgiana, she hides it well.

She is sitting up on her bed, wearing jeans and a T-shirt advertising the New Orleans Jazz Festival of 1998. There is a large, red cardboard box on the floor beside her, and so many things on the bed that you can hardly see the spread. She's just reaching into the box for something when Georgiana knocks, and looks up as

Georgiana appears in the doorway. "What are you doing here?" she demands. "I thought I told you not to come."

"That was last week. Anyway, I'm here now." Georgiana smiles as if this might be welcomed news. "Aren't you going to invite me in?"

"I don't want you in. I told you I wanted to be alone. I've never known anyone so contrary. Or so stubborn."

Georgiana steps inside and shuts the door behind her. "You know, I could say the same about you."

"All I want you to say is 'goodbye'."

"But I brought you presents." Swinging the bag in front of her, she walks towards the bed. "Look at what I got." She sets the bag on the table beside the armchair and starts taking things out. "Magazines. Those boring ones you like so much. And flowers to cheer up your room. And look at these!" She holds up a baker's box. "Fancy cupcakes."

"Thank you. That's very thoughtful of you. Now if—"

"So what's all this?" It's a small room, and Georgiana is already standing beside the bed looking at the things laid out all around Mrs Kilgour. Bundles of papers and letters. Scrapbooks and albums. Manila envelopes filled with newspaper clippings. Odds and ends, and this and that.

"Nothing. Just old things."

Georgiana cranes her neck. "Like what?"

"Just old things." Mementos of Mrs Kilgour's eighty years. A lifetime in a cardboard box. "Pictures mainly."

Pictures. Georgiana's heart doesn't actually skip a beat, but it does stumble. Pictures from Mrs Kilgour's past. And now Georgiana knows why she had the urge to come today. It was Fate. Fate sent her here. Fate was whispering in her ear: *You want to see Anderson? You want to hear the greatest love story never told? Go to St Joan's! Go now!*

With astounding calm for someone whose heart has stopped stumbling and started stampeding, Georgiana says, "Can I see?"

"You wouldn't be interested in this old junk."

"Yes, I would."

"I'm sure you must have somewhere else to be."

"No, I don't. I wanted to see you. I miss…" Georgiana tugs at her hair. "I miss our afternoons."

Mrs Kilgour doesn't look at her. "Well, I guess if you're really interested…" she mutters. "I was just sorting through this box." She leans over and pulls out a pile of photographs. "I haven't looked in it in years."

Georgiana perches on the edge of the bed, prepared to have Mrs Kilgour knock her off.

"When you get bored you can leave," says Mrs Kilgour. But she doesn't tell her to move.

Georgiana doesn't get bored. They go slowly through

the pile of photos. Mrs Kilgour's birthday party when she was four… The house where she grew up… Her parents on a beach… Her high-school graduation… Her first apartment… The dog she had when she was a child… The cat she had when she lived in New York… Mrs Kilgour holds up each picture, and Georgiana looks. Mrs Kilgour explains each picture, and Georgiana listens.

And then, under a photograph of a young Mrs Kilgour in front of a delicatessen on the Lower East Side of Manhattan, is a black and white snapshot of a man in a pin-striped suit, light-coloured shirt and floral tie standing at the railing of a ship, the wind blowing his hair. He's laughing. "Who's that?" asks Georgiana.

"That's the picture I was looking for!" Mrs Kilgour snatches up the rectangle of paper. "That's him!"

That's him! It could only be one person. The great love of Margarita Kilgour's life.

"Anderson," says Georgiana.

"Anderson?" Mrs Kilgour looks up at her as if she's said it's a picture of George Bush. "Of course that's not Anderson. That's Morty."

"Morty? You mean your husband?"

"Yes, I mean my husband. I hardly have any pictures of him because he was the photographer – always behind the camera, never in front of it."

"He was a photographer, too?"

"Didn't I say? That's how we met. Not war, like Anderson. He managed to stay out of the war, but he was everywhere else something was happening in the sixties and early seventies. Then, when we got married, we decided neither of us wanted to get shot, so we teamed up and did profiles on people and places for magazines. Until we came here and took over the paper. Then he became editor-in-chief." Mrs Kilgour smiles down at the man who seems almost to be smiling back at her. "This was the day we got married. We took a honeymoon cruise on the Staten Island Ferry." She closes her eyes. "It was the happiest day of my life."

"But I thought—"

The eyes open. "What?"

Georgiana shakes her head. Nothing. Everything she thought was wrong. "So your bag? The camera bag? That was your husband's?"

"It went everywhere with him. It's the closest thing to having him with me." She smiles down at the photo again. "Every year we'd ride the ferry for our anniversary." She sighs the way a twig snaps. "I'd give anything to do it again, just once more before I die."

Georgiana, trying to come to terms with the fact that Anderson wasn't the love of Mrs Kilgour's life, Mordecai

Kilgour was, is only half listening. "Well, maybe you will. You're not going to die yet."

"I wouldn't be so sure of that," says Mrs Kilgour.

The encouraging smile that was on Georgiana's face vanishes. "What? What are you talking about?" Things that she hadn't put together fall into place. The walk to the river. Coming to Christmas. The special gifts. Searching through the box for the picture of her husband. And these last few weeks of not wanting to see her. What was it Alice Einhorn said? *I'm glad she's feeling well enough again.*

"I haven't been too good lately," says Mrs Kilgour. "You can't believe doctors, but sometimes they get things right." She lays the photograph on the table beside her. "That's why I decided to sort through the box. While I still can."

Later that night, lying in bed with the lights out, moonlight spilling in through the window, Georgiana finally remembers her grandmother. And starts to cry.

Chapter Twenty-six
Things Are Bad, Then Things Get Worse

It's snowing. There hasn't been much snow all winter and now, when it should be thinking of stopping or at least slowing down, it's coming down by the shovelful. Asher – booted, hooded and wearing insulated gloves – stands outside the community centre, banging on the door and trying to peer through the blinds. Assuming that another part of the ceiling hasn't collapsed, he thinks he sees light inside but the door is locked, and so far no one's answered his knock. If this kind of thing had never happened before he might just go home, but, of course, it has happened before. Asher bends down and shouts through the mail slot, "Mrs Dunbar? Mrs Dunbar, are you in there? It's me! Asher! Are you all right?"

He presses his ear to the door, listening for footsteps – and pitches forward as it suddenly swings open just enough for him to be yanked through.

There was a time, not a million years ago, when making this kind of entrance would have discombobulated Asher, but now he simply straightens up and says, "What's going on?"

"Thank God you're here," says Mrs Dunbar. "I was afraid you might not come because of the snow." She puts her hands together as if she's about to burst into prayer. "We have a little crisis."

So what else is new?

Asher stomps the snow from his feet. There is a light on, but it's a small one and in the furthest cubicle. "Another stalker?"

Two weeks ago Mrs Dunbar locked him out because she was hiding a woman and her two children who had run away from a violent husband only to discover that the women's refuge had been shut down and there was nowhere for them to go.

"Kind of. But not exactly." She puts the chain on the door. "Why don't you come inside and warm up? You look half frozen."

No, he doesn't. Asher's jacket is so thickly padded that what he looks is as if he were made out of marshmallows. Navy-blue marshmallows.

Asher glances from her to the chained door then to her again. "Um, Mrs Dunbar… What are you doing?

Shouldn't we be opening up? The others'll be here soon." He peers into the dimness. "Where's Carlin? Don't tell me he slept in his car last night."

"Of course not. He slept at our house. And the others aren't coming. Not in this weather."

Asher frowns. He is not his father's son for nothing. "You mean you told them not to come."

"Let's go in the back, Asher." She won't meet his eyes. "What about a nice hot cup of coffee? What could be nicer on a morning like this?"

Asher moves less than a tree. "So why didn't you call me and tell me to stay home if you told everybody else?"

"Asher, please. Just come in the back, will you? Sometimes you're as stubborn as the Lord himself." With which she grabs his arm and leads him down the hall.

She takes his coat. She hangs it up. She makes him a cup of coffee. She offers him one of the day-old dough-nuts donated by the bakery down the street the day before. She asks him if he had any trouble driving in the snow. And all the while she's talking, her eyes are on his ear, or his forehead, or his chin.

Asher takes a large swallow of coffee without even sniffing at it first. "OK, Mrs Dunbar. What's going on? What's 'kind of a stalker but not exactly'?"

She gives him her trust-in-God smile. "A state marshal."

Possibly because his brain was slightly chilled, standing outside waiting for her to let him in, it takes Asher a second or two for these words to settle in his mind. "A what?"

"A state marshal. You probably haven't had too much to do with them, but take it from me they tend to be pretty persistent."

Asher takes another slug of coffee. "A state marshal? Are you saying you have the place all locked up because you're expecting a state marshal? What's he going to do? Arrest you?"

"That's right." Mrs Dunbar nods. "The township wants to evict us. They're serving us with one of those Summary things."

"Summary and Complaints."

"That's it. Summary and Complaints. I knew you'd know all about this."

"I don't know all about it," says Asher. "But I did intern in the mayor's office, and I know they can't do that. First they have to give you a Notice to Quit."

Mrs Dunbar waves a dismissive hand. "Oh, they did that. They've been doing that for months."

Asher laughs, not because he thinks Mrs Dunbar is

making a joke but because she never ceases to amaze him. The only reason he believes she's real and not some kind of elaborate hoax is because he doesn't think anyone could make her up.

"Notice to Quit? They've been giving you them for *months*?"

She half fidgets, half shrugs. "Well, maybe not *months*. But I'm sure we've had a couple. I didn't actually count them."

"And you didn't do anything else about them, either? You know, like reply?"

She smiles again, still trusting in God. "I was hoping that they'd stop."

So one of her prayers has been answered.

"And did you tell anybody else about the notices? Your husband maybe?"

"Oh, no." She shakes her head, and something falls out of her hair. "Not Archie."

Of course not. The organized Reverend Archibald Dunbar would have made sure she answered the first one right away.

"Well, what about Carlin? Or the other volunteers?"

"Oh no, not them, either." She shakes her head again, and spills coffee over the desk. "We've had such a hard time this last year or two. So many problems. And no money. Everything's been such a struggle. I didn't want the others to worry."

"That was really thoughtful of you, Mrs Dunbar, but don't you think they might worry anyway – when they find themselves standing out on the street?"

"I have been praying," Mrs Dunbar assures him. "I really didn't think it would come to this."

Asher resists the urge to sigh. "I'm assuming that the township wants to evict us because we owe them rent."

"That's only an excuse," says Mrs Dunbar.

Besides the township's own problems with deficits and debt, federal and state funding has been cut and is going to be cut again. The township needs to save millions of dollars. To do this it is reducing school staff and slashing after-school and remedial programmes; closing two libraries, two parks, two beaches and the municipal pool; and selling assets. Among the assets it's selling are the buildings that house the two women's refuges, the homeless shelter and the community centre.

"They've already put the shelter over on Sullivan up for sale," says Mrs Dunbar. "Which is why we have these desperate women coming here. They have nowhere else to go. What's going to happen when we're all gone and there's no one to help the poor and the unlucky? It's like dominoes, isn't it? You knock over one, and that knocks over the next one until everything's collapsed."

"I see your point," says Asher. "But the fact is that if we're behind with the rent—"

"Fiddlesticks," says Mrs Dunbar. "It was only a token rent. Because the building's falling down around our ears. That was the deal. Peppercorn rent and no maintenance."

"Only we haven't been paying it." The law, of course, relies on logic.

But so, in her way, does Mrs Dunbar.

"Well, how could we?" she demands. If her voice were a glass it would be about to break. "We don't have any money. The little bit of funding we've been able to scrounge has got smaller and smaller, while more and more people have to come to us for help. We have a greater need than ever and even less to give."

He can't exactly argue with that, can he? They don't have any money. He has no idea how she manages to pay for the phone or the electricity. And she's right about things going from bad to worse and then really worse. It *is* like knocking down a line of dominos by pushing over the first one. *Clunkclunkclunk.*

"Be that as it may," says Asher. "We have a legal responsibility—"

"Legal responsibility, my grandmother's garters. What about our moral responsibility?" And now her voice breaks like a Venetian goblet thrown from the roof. "These aren't the people who caused this crisis. These are the victims. The ones who are paying for someone else's crimes. What are they supposed to do if there's nowhere to turn? Just disappear?" She puts her head in her hands. Her shoulders start to heave.

"Mrs Dunbar? Mrs Dunbar, are you crying?" Asher hasn't had much experience with tears. He must have cried himself when he was little, but he doesn't remember that. He has seen people cry, but aside from the occasional outburst from one of the girls and the time Will fell from the climbing wall and broke his foot, the tears Asher has seen shed have been mainly in movies and on TV. Lawyers don't cry, and corporate lawyers cry even less. Asher doesn't know what to do. "Mrs Dunbar, please don't cry."

Mrs Dunbar's response to this plea is to sob even harder. "What are we going to do?" she wails. "Not just the centre, but all of us. The women's shelter. The food bank. The church groups that have been doing what they can—"

Asher gets up and stands next to her, patting her shoulder. "Mrs Dunbar, please try to calm down."

She raises her head, snuffling and wiping the tears with her sleeve. "But what are we going to do?"

Asher knows that she isn't really asking him, but he feels compelled to answer. "Well, what if we all get together? You know, all the charities and organizations and groups. Maybe even the people who are losing their jobs in the cuts. If we presented, you know, a united front—"

"Asher!" He watches her expression change from hopeless despair to hope-filled joy. "Asher! You've found the solution. That's it!" Mrs Dunbar pulls him to her in a hug that nearly lifts him off the ground. "You're a genius. I knew the Lord sent you to us for a reason! That's exactly what we have to do!"

Asher steps back, straightening his shirt. "Well, I'm glad you—"

"We'll make them listen to us. Them and everyone. We'll bring the issues to the attention of the nation. Maybe the world." She is so excited she jumps to her feet. "We'll get everyone together and we'll occupy the town hall!"

It's just as well Asher isn't drinking coffee now, or he'd choke.

"We'll do what?"

"Like the ninety-eight per cent did! Like Occupy Wall Street! You're so right. There's strength in numbers. Nobody listens to one voice. But if it's all of us… That's what Martin Luther King taught. And Gandhi. Civil dis-obedience. Passive resistance. No change happens if you don't force it to happen."

This, of course, isn't what Asher meant. He meant a petition. Or possibly a letter in the local paper. Not every do-gooder in the township camping out in the mayor's office.

"Maybe you shouldn't get too excited," says Asher. "I mean it might not be so easy to—"

"No, this is the right thing to do." She hits her chest. "I feel it here! I'm sure it's what Jesus himself would do. He always stood up to authority." She gets to her feet and makes another lunge for him. "Thank you, Asher. What would I do without you?"

Asher is saved from answering by being smothered in another hug.

"And don't you worry," says Mrs Dunbar. "If it's the right thing to do, the Lord will help us."

Asher certainly hopes so.

Chapter Twenty-seven
Detective Liotta on the Case

After their last session together, Marigold dreams about Sadie for the next two nights.

In the first dream, Sadie arrives in the tutor room dressed in the uniform of a New York City patrolman. The uniform is a little big for her; she has the sleeves rolled back and the hat keeps sliding down over her eyes. She says she only came to tell Marigold that she can't stay because she has to go on duty. "Law and order must be maintained and justice must prevail," says Sadie – using at least two words Marigold has never heard her say in reality because she probably doesn't know them. "But what about the book we're reading?" asks Marigold. "I thought you wanted to find out what happens next." Sadie pushes her hat back up on her head, and says they'll have to read it another time. "Duty calls louder than pleasure," says Sadie. She waves a pair of handcuffs over her head and disappears.

In the second dream, Marigold leaves the school to find Officer Sadie Hawkle on the street outside, arresting Justine Hawkle. She has her handcuffed to the railing and is reciting the Miranda Act while Justine cries and pleads to be released. Marigold hurries over to ask Sadie why she's arresting her mother. Sadie turns her fish-on-ice eyes on her. "Because she's always yelling at me," says Sadie.

Marigold is not a qualified psychologist, of course, but she has a pretty good idea why she's having these dreams. She has started to understand the Sadie Hawkle signs. It used to be that if Sadie was having a hard time at school or at home and was feeling vulnerable she'd be quiet and withdrawn at their sessions. Some might even describe her as sullen, staring at you silently with that small-animal-about-to-be-squashed-by-a-truck expression. But now it's different. Now if Sadie's miserable she talks about her father. This week when they met, it seemed as if Sadie mentioned her father every five minutes. He'd finished making her new bed. He wanted her to come and pick out the paint for her room. He was thinking of getting a cat. Then there was a very long story about how he found a little boy who was missing for a week. Everyone thought he'd been kidnapped or killed. The family was afraid they'd never see him again.

The parents cried on TV. It was really sad because even though the cops kept on looking, they didn't think they had much hope of finding the missing boy alive. Only Sadie's dad thought he'd run away on purpose. Because he was always being yelled at for doing everything wrong. It was Sadie's father who talked to everybody in the neighbourhood – even other kids – and figured out where the little boy was. When he brought the boy home everybody said that Sadie's dad was a real hero. He had his picture in the paper and got a special medal and for once he wasn't in trouble with his boss. When this epic finally ended, Marigold asked how Sadie's mother was. Sadie's gaze went straight to the floor. "She's OK. She gets tired."

Marigold wakes up on Saturday morning, still thinking about Sadie. She's getting ready to meet Byron to go shopping for an anniversary present for his parents when Bonnie Kupferberg phones.

Although Marigold always assumes the best, this is such an unprecedented occurrence that she doesn't greet her with a cheery *Hi, Bonnie!* She says, "Bonnie? What's wrong?"

Bonnie doesn't waste time on pleasantries, either. "I just had a call from Justine Hawkle. It seems that Sadie's gone missing."

"What?" Marigold is standing at the basin, checking her make-up with nowhere to sit down, but she feels as though she's collapsed into a chair. Or been knocked into it. "When?"

"Justine said she wasn't in the apartment when she got up this morning. At first she figured Sadie'd gone to the store for a bag of chips or a candy bar. She does that. So she waited, and when she didn't come back, Justine went after her. There was no sign of Sadie and nobody'd seen her."

But the habit of hope is hard to break. "Maybe they just didn't notice her," Marigold suggests. "You know if they were busy with other customers or something, they might not."

"That doesn't answer the question of where she is, though," says Bonnie.

"So I guess Mrs Hawkle checked everywhere." This is a question.

"Of course she did. She said sometimes Sadie hides just to make her worry. You know, if they had a fight or she yelled at her about something. Usually she's in a closet or under the bed. And one time she found her in the cellar. Last time she pulled this, she was in the garage at the back of the house."

And that, of course, is Marigold's silver lining in this

particular cloud. "Well, that's probably it, isn't it?" Nothing awful has happened to Sadie. She's done this before. They obviously had a fight last night, or Justine yelled at her about something, and Sadie went into a sulk and hid somewhere.

"Only her mom hasn't found her." Bonnie never expects the best. "She searched every inch of the apartment, the house, the grounds and the garage, and all she came up with was the pair of new sneakers Sadie lost last summer. She was hoping Sadie was with you. Or that you heard from her."

"Me? Why me?"

"Because Sadie's so fond of you."

"But she doesn't know where I live or have my phone number." She probably doesn't even know Marigold's last name.

"Well, it was worth a shot. Her mother says she doesn't really have any other friends. Not someone she might go to like this."

"Is there anything I can do?" *Everything will be all right*, Marigold tells herself. *Sadie wasn't abducted. She can't have gone far.* "Maybe if I talked to Mrs Hawkle?"

"Oh, I don't think that would be a good idea," says Bonnie. "You may be Sadie's favourite teenager, but you're not her mother's."

"I'm not?"

Justine wasn't happy that Marigold went into her house like that.

"But I wasn't really *inside*. I just—"

"It's OK. I got the picture. And, trust me, I know how touchy Justine Hawkle can be. But she has a hard time. It took a lot of persuading to stop her from demanding a different reading tutor. That's why I said I'd call you and see if you knew anything."

"I wish I did." Never has she meant that more. "But I'm sure there's nothing to worry about." Marigold has said these words hundreds, possibly thousands of times before; but this is the first time that she realizes how much like her mother they make her sound.

"Oh, there's always something to worry about," says Bonnie Kupferberg.

Sadie doesn't know Marigold's address, but she does know in what town she lives, so Byron detours on the way to the mall and takes the route the bus takes from Half Hollow to Shell Harbour. Just in case a pale, scrawny, afterthought of a little girl is walking along the side of the road with a sour expression on her face and no idea of where she's going. Marigold's head swivels from one side to the other, like a weather vane caught in a strong wind, and Byron drives so slowly that people behind them honk and make rude gestures as they pass.

"If she came this way she either walks real fast or she's wearing a coat that makes her invisible," says Byron. "Unless she took the bus."

Marigold keeps her eyes on the road. "I don't think she'd do that. I don't think she'd know how."

Byron darts a look at her. "I know you're not going to like this, but you don't think she'd take a ride from a stranger, do you?"

Marigold considers this for a few seconds, but shakes her head. "No. I really don't think so. Sadie's dad's a policeman. I'm sure he'd've warned her about things like that. Besides, she watches a lot of cop shows. She knows the drill."

"Really, a cop?" Byron laughs. "So we don't really need to be looking ourselves. He'll have half the force out by now."

"Oh, not around here. In New York." And Marigold, possibly to distract herself from worrying about Sadie, starts telling Byron about Sadie's dad. How he just moved to Brooklyn so Sadie has her own room. How he's a really good cop but always in trouble because he bucks the system. How he got a special commendation for finding a missing child.

"Geebus," says Byron. "This guy sounds like he's out of a movie."

"I just hope it's one with a happy ending," says Marigold.

According to Byron, who seems to be timing her, Marigold checks her phone every four minutes while they're shopping, and every three minutes during lunch.

"It's just that Bonnie said she'd call if there was any news." Marigold pushes her plate aside. "I'm really worried."

"What did you say?" Byron puts a hand to his ear, leaning towards her. "Did I just hear Marigold Liotta say that she's worried? Marigold? Liotta? The girl who would say Armageddon was going to turn out all right?"

Her frown deepens. "You don't think I should be worried?"

"Of course I think you should be worried." Byron puts an arm around her shoulder. "I'm just substantially astounded that you think so, too."

It starts to rain hard in the afternoon.

Marigold stares out of the living-room window. She pictures Sadie sitting in someone's garage, surrounded by cobwebs and spiders, clutching her beat-up pink back-pack and waiting to be found. Sadie might not be in a garage, of course. She could be in a deserted building. God knows there are plenty of crumbling, rat-infested deserted buildings in Half Hollow. How long would it take to search them all – them and every garage in town? Wherever she is, she'll be cold.

Marigold tries to comfort herself with the fact that her sister Rose used to run away all the time when she was little. She'd pack her overnight bag and march out of the house, vowing that she was never coming back. Marigold was always afraid that she really would never come back, but Eveline would stand on the stoop and wave her goodbye. Sometimes she was gone all day. But Rose always went to the same place: across the street to the Bestermans'. Edie Besterman was her best friend. Mrs Besterman would walk her back home in time for supper.

The rain continues to fall; the day continues to crawl along like a badly wounded soldier over rough terrain. It's already getting dark when Bonnie finally calls. Justine has reported Sadie missing. She's never stayed away this long before. She usually gets hungry after an hour or two.

"What about her dad?" asks Marigold. "Mrs Hawkle doesn't think maybe Sadie went to her dad?"

"Her *dad*?" Bonnie couldn't sound more surprised if Marigold had asked if Sadie could have gone back to her home planet. "But, Marigold, Sadie doesn't have a dad."

Yes, she does. He's a New York City policeman and he lives in Brooklyn. Marigold laughs nervously. "Everybody has a dad."

"Not one that's alive," says Bonnie.

"Her dad's dead?" That's not impossible. City cops are always being killed. "I had no idea." Marigold's voice is its own ghost.

Bonnie sighs. "Did Sadie tell you that her dad's alive?"

"I–I guess I misunderstood." How could Sadie make her father so believable? So completely real? It's not as if she's bent under the weight of a great imagination. "I just thought…"

"I didn't think she even remembered him. She was very young when he was killed."

And Marigold, convinced that Sadie's story must be based on truth, says, "Killed? You mean in New York? In a robbery or something?"

"New York? A robbery? No, of course not. Sadie's father was blown up in Afghanistan."

"Afghanistan? You mean he wasn't … you mean he was a soldier?"

"It was a terrible tragedy. He was a week away from coming home. Can you imagine? It was six years ago, but Justine still hasn't recovered. That's why I try to cut her slack with her timekeeping and … and other stuff."

"I'm so sorry. That's awful. I—"

"Yeah, well, that's life," says Bonnie.

Marigold can't concentrate. She doesn't want to hang out. She doesn't want to do homework. She doesn't want to watch TV. She doesn't want to play cards with her mother and Mrs Besterman. She doesn't even want to read. Where could Sadie be? But to ask that question is to start her mind picturing dozens of places where Sadie might be – and none of them are safe and warm and full of sunshine and laughter. To ask that question is to start her mind constructing dozens of stories about what's happened – and none of them have happy endings. Marigold has completely run out of silver linings.

Because her rainbow has vanished, instead of going to her room where there would be nothing to distract her dark imaginings, she sits on the sofa in the living room where she can put the TV on for company and hear the women talking in the sun porch. She puts her phone down on the coffee table next to the stacks of old magazines and TV guides, turns on the set and sits back.

She puts on a movie – a comedy that she remembers liking a lot the first time she saw it, but now it just annoys her. It's silly. It's shallow. Even if she hadn't already seen it, she'd know exactly how it would end. Happily. All problems solved. All bad things banished into someone else's film.

Restless, Marigold picks up a TV guide and flicks through it. She tosses it aside and picks up another. In the third one she happens on an interview with one of the stars of *Justice for All*, Harlan Colt.

Marigold has never seen this show, and has no interest in it, but because it is Sadie's favourite she starts to read. Harlan Colt plays Detective Fabio Ramirez. Harlan likes Ramirez because instead of being one of these hard-drinking loners, he's divorced and is very involved with his little girl. Harlan Colt feels that this gives Ramirez an added dimension and a greater ability to empathize with others. Marigold is about to close the magazine when she sees that Detective Fabio Ramirez lives in Brooklyn.

No wonder the stories about Sadie's dad didn't sound like something she could make up.

Marigold has to trawl through several weeks before she finds the episode she's looking for: the one where Detective Ramirez finds the boy who has run away.

Marigold is on her feet and in her boots and jacket before she actually thinks about what she's doing. She stands outside the coat closet for a few minutes. She can hear her mother and Mrs Besterman talking and laughing in the sun porch. Her mother's bag is on the hallway table. Marigold has never gone out without telling her mother where she's going; and she has never taken her mother's car without permission. But to do either of those things would entail a lot of explanations, and she doesn't have the time right now. She can't even imagine where she'd begin. Her mother has never heard of Sadie Hawkle; she still thinks Marigold's working at the library.

Still clutching the TV guide, Marigold opens the bag, takes the car keys and slips out the front door. She starts the engine and backs out of the garage. She isn't halfway down the driveway when her mother comes charging through the front door with a coat flung over her head and shoulders and a face like the Day of Judgement.

"Marigold! Marigold!" she shrieks. "Marigold! What are you doing? Where do you think you're going?"

Marigold's automatic response on seeing her mother is to stop the car and start apologizing. She locks her door but opens the window. "I have to go, Mom," she calls as Eveline skitters down the walk. "It's an emergency."

"Don't you dare leave!" Eveline's screams are sharp as a siren. "You hear me, Marigold? You promised. After you took those books! You swore! How can you do this to me!"

"I'm not doing anything to you. It's not about you.

There's this little girl who's lost. I have to find her. It's really important."

"More important than your mother?"

"Mom, please. I'll explain everything later."

Eveline's reached the driveway and is about to grab for the car when Mrs Besterman appears at the front door. "Eveline!" she shouts. "Is everything all right?"

Distracted, Marigold's mother turns.

Marigold puts the car into gear and goes. Her phone rings even before she's out of the driveway. As soon as she's out of sight of the house she pulls over and takes it from her pocket. *One missed call: Mom.* She turns it off.

Marigold has hardly driven a car in sunshine since she killed that pigeon, never mind heavy rain, but she is too focused on finding Sadie to worry about a detail like that. Visibility is poor, and in the battle between Nature (in the form of the storm) and Man (in the form of the windshield wipers), Nature has the slight advantage. Marigold keeps all her attention on the road, looking out for kamikaze pigeons in the curtained dark and concentrating so hard that she is nearly out of Half Hollow before she realizes she's even in it.

She turns into Clarendon Road and parks in front of 116. She doesn't even stop to lock the car but runs to the house and rings the bell. Almost instantly, the door to apartment 1a opens and Justine Hawkle comes running down the hall and pulls open the front door. Her hair isn't brushed, she's wearing no make-up and she looks as though she's been crying. It's obvious from her expression that Marigold isn't the person she was expecting, and definitely not the person she was hoping for. "Marigold? What is it?" Her voice sounds like a snapping pencil. "Have you heard from Sadie?"

"No, no I haven't, but I—"

She breathes heavily. "Look, I'm sorry. I appreciate you coming over, but I really don't have time for this now. I'm waiting to hear from the police." She starts to shut the door.

"But, Mrs Hawkle, I think I know where Sadie might be."

Hope is the sudden light in Justine Hawkle's eyes. "What? Where?"

"It's only a guess. And it is kind of a long story…"

"Oh, a guess. And a long story." She smiles sourly. "It would be with you." The door moves forward again. "I told you, I don't have time for this now."

But Marigold hasn't come all this way in this weather to give up now. "Please, Mrs Hawkle. Just let me explain." And Marigold begins, talking so quickly that her words fall over one another like people escaping from a burning building. Sadie's stories about her dad being a cop. How he found a boy who had run away. How it all came from her favourite police show.

"So you what?" If Justine Hawkle could laugh right now, this probably would be the moment. "You think she's in the cellar? Is that what you think? Well, she isn't. The basement's practically the first place I searched."

"Not the basement. Under the porch. The little boy in the show was hiding in the crawl space under the porch."

Justine Hawkle looks at the floor under Marigold's feet, as if she can see there is nothing under it. "So you think that's where Sadie is. Because she saw it on TV."

"It's worth looking," insists Marigold. "There's nothing to lose."

Sadie's mother doesn't seem convinced, but she does know she has nothing to lose. "You need a flashlight?"

"I have one." Marigold holds up a Maglite.

Justine Hawkle steps out onto the porch. "You're a regular Girl Scout."

"It's my mother's. She keeps it in the glove compartment."

Justine wraps her arms around herself and watches as Marigold steps back into the downpour.

"Sadie?" she calls. "Sadie, it's me, Marigold. Sadie, are you there?"

The space under the porch of 116 Clarendon Road is small, even if you're crawling, and there is no one in it with less than four feet.

Sadie's mother leans over the railing. "You satisfied now?"

But Marigold can't believe she's made a mistake about this. She has to be right. Anything else would be so wrong.

"OK, Sadie's not under your porch," reasons Marigold, "but every house in this neighbourhood has one. She could be under any of them. We have to keep looking. She can't stay out all night in this."

"And she could be under none of them," says Justine. "Why don't you leave this to the real cops? I'll tell them your idea, all right? I promise. You better go home now, Marigold."

Which is, of course, a polite way of saying, *Mind your own business.*

"But I have such a strong feeling—"

"Marigold, really. You should go, or your mom will be worrying about you next."

Marigold sighs. The habit of obedience is also a hard one to break. She goes back down the steps and returns to the car. She gets in, and sits staring out at 116. Justine Hawkle closes the curtains of the room at the front; the light goes off in the hall. The falling rain blurs the edges of the house ... of the street ... of the world. People die in storms. Marigold gets out of the car.

The good thing about the rain is that almost everyone is inside, not driving around, or walking along the sidewalks, or gazing out of their windows. There is no one to see Marigold shuffle through the rain, up one path and down another, crouching down as she circles each verandah. Looking for breaks in the latticework that surrounds the spaces beneath them. Calling, "Sadie! Sadie!" and shining her flashlight into the depths.

She does every house on the block, but with no success. There are other blocks and other porches, but there is no way she can do any more now. The night and the weather are against her. Justine Hawkle was right: it's a job for the real cops.

Finally defeated, Marigold kneels down next to the last house on the street. "Oh, Sadie, where are you?!" It's almost a wail.

And then she hears it, not beside her, but from behind her, a small voice that sounds as frightened as Marigold feels. "I'm here. Marigold! Marigold, I can't get out."

Marigold scrabbles to her feet. "I'm coming!" she calls as she races around the house. "I'm coming!" And there it is, a back porch! It never occurred to her to check if there were back porches as well as front ones.

The other miracle, of course, is that Sadie ever managed to find a way in. There is a broken panel, but it's so blocked by a close-growing shrub that you could only see it if you knew it was there. And even if you do know it's there, if you've been cowering in the dark for hours, it's easy to forget where it is.

Marigold rips out the panel with her gloved hands. She holds the Maglite in her teeth as she reaches in and pulls the shivering child into her arms.

Both of them are crying as Marigold carries Sadie back up the street.

"Is my mom going to be really mad at me?" whispers Sadie as they near her house.

Justine must have been watching out of the living-room window because the front door opens before they even turn off the sidewalk. Coatless, she races into the rain.

"No," Marigold whispers back. "She's not going to be mad at all."

Who says there is never a happy ending?

Chapter Twenty-eight
A Short Cruise, a Long Journey

Mr Papazoglakis says that they'll be growing lettuce on the moon before he'll allow Mrs Kilgour to travel all the way to New York City in her condition. Though he doesn't phrase it in quite that way, of course. What he says in so many words is, "I'm very sorry, Georgiana, but, as I told Mrs Kilgour only yesterday – and, I believe several times before – I'm afraid it's completely out of the question. She can't go into the city by herself."

This happens to be precisely what Mr Papazoglakis did tell Mrs Kilgour. Mrs Kilgour said he made her feel like a captured lion in a zoo in Wisconsin, trapped in a cage thousands of miles from the savanna, forced to forget it ever had another home and waiting to die. "You make sure you live your life while you can, Georgiana Shiller," warned Mrs Kilgour. "They can mess with your present and your future, but they can't do anything about the past." It was the part about living your life that sent Georgiana to talk to Mr Papazoglakis herself.

"But she really wants to go," she argues now. "It's really important to her." It's all she's talked about since they looked at the pictures together. She wants to ride the Staten Island Ferry one more time, just as she did when she was young and in love. "And she won't be by herself, either." When she stands up very straight Georgiana is almost as tall as the administrator. If she'd known he was going to be so unreasonable she would have worn her highest heels. And looked down on him. "I'll be with her."

"Unless I'm very mistaken, Miss Shiller, you don't actually have any medical qualifications." His mouth shifts into one of his choose-your-coffin smiles. "Unless you've been holding out on me." Anyone who didn't know better would think he was making a joke.

I have been holding out on you, thinks Georgiana. *I'm really a brain surgeon disguised as a high-school student. Gotcha!*

"We're only going for a few hours," Georgiana explains with the patience a sanctity of saints might hope to copy. "We'll be back before it gets dark. And I'll drive. And she'll have her wheelchair."

Mr Papazoglakis fingers the gold ring on his left

hand. "You do realize how ill she is, don't you? We're talking about days here – weeks at the most – not months or years."

And Georgiana, always so squeamish about the way life ends like a bubble popped by a pin, says, "Of course I know that." She would like to drop buckets of ice water over him and his dark suit and his mortician's compassion, but she beams back on him like a summer sun. "That's the whole point, Mr P. New York's where some of her best memories are. This is her last chance to see it again before she dies. So what's the problem? If she's going to die soon anyway, why not let her go? She doesn't exactly have anything to lose."

"But I do. The reputation of the centre," purrs Mr Papazoglakis. And then, just when Georgiana has decided that he doesn't have a heart, adds, "Surely she must have photographs of those days. She can look at them."

Georgiana keeps smiling. *I'd like to photograph you.* "If a photograph was the same as being in a place," she says, not only patient but sweet as well, "then nobody would ever go on vacation, would they? They'd just stay home and look at magazines."

Mr Papazoglakis spreads his hands in the air, palms down. It's not in his control. He's running a business. There are rules. "Be that as it may, photographs are what

Mrs Kilgour is going to have to be content with. She is not going to New York. And that, I'm afraid, is final."

Georgiana shrugs as though conceding defeat.

But what she's thinking is: *We'll see about that.*

The weekend receptionist looks up as Georgiana pushes Mrs Kilgour into the foyer. "Why, don't you look nice!" she exclaims. "Is this a special occasion?"

Mrs Kilgour does look nice. She's wearing a floral skirt and jacket under a red coat and, although it's not strictly the season for it yet, a jaunty panama hat. She has her old camera bag on her lap, and a silver star balloon tied to her chair bobs over her head.

"It's my birthday," says Mrs Kilgour. "Georgiana here is doing something special for me."

As it happens, both of these statements are true. Mrs Kilgour is eighty-one today and Georgiana is going out of her way to make it an exceptional occasion.

Georgiana, who is wearing the wedding shirt Mrs Kilgour gave her and who also looks very nice, says, "My mom's making a celebration lunch."

This statement, as it happens, is not true. It was Georgiana who, pretending to be Adele Shiller, called to get permission for Mrs Kilgour to leave St Joan's for the day. Her mother is in San Francisco with a client and has no idea what day this is or how she's supposed to be spending it.

"Well, you have a wonderful birthday." The receptionist smiles. *Since it's your last.* "Both of you enjoy yourselves."

They both assure her that they will.

In a historic moment of agreement, Georgiana and Mrs Kilgour came up with today's master plan together.

"Our mistake was in telling Count Dracula and his acolytes what I wanted to do," said Mrs Kilgour. "You'd think at my age I'd know better than that. My God, I've dealt with them all. From politicians and newspaper honchos to movie stars and generals. It's always best to lie to people in authority. It's only fair. They lie to us. What we have to do is tell them we're doing what they're happy for us to do, and then do what we want."

Georgiana tilted her head to one side, with a look on her face that on a cow means nothing but on a human signifies thinking. "They loved it when you came to my house for Christmas. You could've dropped dead then and they wouldn't've cared. They would've said at least you'd died happy."

Mrs Kilgour rewarded her with a smile. "You know, I think you have something there!"

The idea was that Georgiana would arrange for Mrs

Kilgour to have a day out, and pick her up from the nursing centre. They would drive to New York and have lunch in an Italian place the Kilgours used to go to so often when they lived in the city that they and the waiters knew each other by name. After lunch they'd make their way to the tip of the island and board the ferry. They would stay on the boat when it reached Staten Island and return to Manhattan and then drive back home. Mrs Kilgour would be back in her room at St Joan's before nightfall, and no one would ever be any the wiser. As plans go, there have been a great many worse ones in human history.

Georgiana, of course, is a girl who has always specialized in seeing the downside of every situation. Had she been present when Jesus strolled across the Sea of Galilee, all she would have noticed was that his feet were getting wet. And yet it isn't until they're on the road that she starts to see the drawbacks to what she thought was a strategy without flaws.

As soon as they get on the Interstate Georgiana realizes how little like a good idea this was. She has been to New York City three times in her life, but she was never the person driving the car. Nor has she ever driven on the Interstate before. Traffic tends to travel faster on the highway than it does in and around Shell Harbour.

She has, of course, heard the phrase "white-knuckle ride" before, but this is the first time she's really understood what it meant. *My God*, she thinks as cars fly past, *it's like we're in a race.* And not a race she's likely to win. When she drives around Shell Harbour other drivers – being friends and neighbours and in no particular hurry – often smile and wave. Even if she doesn't know them personally, it's such a friendly, laid-back community that no one makes a stink if you signal left when you want to go right or have to make a sudden stop or have a little trouble with your parallel parking. And if you're lost or unsure of what to do at the next intersection you can always pull over and ask for directions. The Interstate is not so agreeable. Everyone seems either to be going to some serious emergency or going to save-the-world meetings for which they are already late. Instead of smiles and waves there are offensive (if descriptive) hand gestures and threatening scowls. If it were possible to stop suddenly without causing a major accident – which it isn't – traffic would plough right through you. If you make a wrong signal horns shriek and you can tell what the driver behind you is shouting even if you don't lip-read.

"You'll be fine," Mrs Kilgour assures her right before she falls asleep. "You have that satellite thing."

While Mrs Kilgour snores away the miles, Georgiana

hangs on to the steering wheel, afraid to take her eyes off the road for even half a nanosecond to check the exit signs or the image on the satnav. She might as well be driving through a minefield. She clenches her teeth to stop herself from gibbering. She has no idea where she wants to get off, and she isn't convinced that the "satellite thing" does either. *Turn left*, it advises, where left is the divider. *Turn right*, it orders, where right is a wall of trees. If Georgiana could take a hand off the wheel long enough to fish her phone from her pocket she would call Claudelia or Will for moral support if not actual help, but doing that seems no less risky than hitting the divider would be. She could, of course, pull onto the shoulder and call from there, but this course of action has its own set of problems. She can't figure out how she can slow down enough to pull over without being rear-ended by the car behind her. Were she able to pull over and stop she would never be able to rejoin the traffic again. If she didn't rejoin the traffic she would be stuck on the shoulder until she was either rescued or (if you believe the stories Georgiana has seen on the news) hit by a very large truck.

When Mrs Kilgour wakes up, they are off the Interstate and parked on a wide and busy road. She rubs her eyes and looks over at Georgiana. "Where the hell are we?"

Georgiana, pale and perspiring more than she ever

has in phys ed, is staring at the map in the hopeless way of someone who has just been dropped out of a helicopter into an unknown country and doesn't speak the language in which the map is written. She and Claudelia have talked about doing a cross-country trip after graduation, but now she is doubting the wisdom of that project. They could spend the rest of their lives in Nebraska. Or never get past New York.

"I don't know. I think I must have missed the exit." Her voice is low and grudging because she's trying not to cry. "But I kind of don't think this is Lower Manhattan."

"That's a pretty good guess." Mrs Kilgour peers out of the window. "From the licence plates alone I'd say you've managed to bypass New York and go straight to New Jersey. And from the fact that we're on Kennedy Boulevard, I'd say we're probably in Jersey City." She points to the small and largely unhelpful screen. "See if that thing can figure out where the Holland Tunnel is."

Mrs Kilgour dozes off again as soon as they see the sign for the tunnel.

Georgiana has never driven in a tunnel before, either. Gripping the wheel as though it's a set of reins and she's trying to stay on the horse, she follows the line of cars under the Hudson river, and, for some reason assuming that the car in front of her is going where she wants to go, drives out of the tunnel and over a bridge.

This time it is hitting a pothole that wakes up Mrs Kilgour. "Now where are we?" she wants to know.

"Brooklyn," sighs Georgiana, and she pulls into the kerb.

It takes a few minutes for Mrs Kilgour to stop laughing enough to be able to speak. "Just what's your plan?" she asks. "Sneak up on New York and catch it by surprise?"

"I think we have to hope it'll surprise us," says Georgiana.

Eventually, and against many odds, they do find the West Village and somewhere to park.

"This is where we were coming the day Morty had his stroke," Mrs Kilgour explains. "It was our wedding anniversary. Thirty-five happy years. We were going to ride the ferry like we used to. And visit the old neighbourhood. Morty even had a friend who was lending us an apartment on Eleventh Street for the weekend. It was going to be our second honeymoon." She smiles. Mrs Kilgour is no stranger to the ironies of life. "Turned out to be the beginning of the end."

Georgiana remembers what Alice told her. "You feel like that was your fault?" she asks.

And is rewarded with a look like a spear. "Who told you that? That gossip on reception?"

Georgiana, manoeuvring the chair over a kerb, says nothing.

"Of course I didn't feel guilty. I didn't give him that stroke. I just wish it could've waited till we were on our way home."

Mrs Kilgour sits slightly forward in her chair as they stroll through her old world, directing them from one street to the next. Streets she used to walk down and shop on, streets where she knew the storekeepers and the man who made the best egg creams in the city. Most of the places and all of the people she knew so well are gone now. The deli is a phone store; the coffee house is a taqueria; the bookstore is a nail salon. The Italian place is a vegan restaurant.

"We're having an adventure," says Mrs Kilgour. "If we can detour through Jersey we can eat tofu."

After lunch they go to the red-brick townhouse where the Kilgours used to live. "That's our apartment on the top floor." Mrs Kilgour stares at the building as if she expects to see herself come out of the front door. "Sometimes we'd eat up on the roof. Candlelight and wine and music from the transistor radio." Her smile is for nothing that Georgiana can see. "We had some very good times here."

She starts to talk about the neighbours. The actors

and their parrot who lived underneath them. "That bird rang like a telephone morning, noon and night." The Polish refugee in the basement who played his violin in the garden on summer nights. "We all used to sit out on our fire escapes to listen. It was like our own private concert." The couple on the first floor who never stopped fighting. "And then you'd see them on the street, with their arms wrapped around each other like they'd invented love." The woman on the second floor who came from Wisconsin to be a Rockette. "Ended up the only tapping she did was on a typewriter at NYU." She remembers the summer of the blackout and the winter it snowed so badly people were skiing down Fifth Avenue. She remembers Horn and Hardart's Automat and subway tokens. Remembers musicians, writers, poets and painters that Georgiana has never heard of who were once as famous as the city itself, who walked these streets and worked in the downtown lofts and lectured at the universities and played in the bars and argued in the cafes.

"I feel like I'm watching a movie," whispers Mrs Kilgour. A movie of her life. "It's all so vivid. The memories. As if I'm really there. I almost can't believe that if we rang the bell to my old apartment Morty wouldn't stick his head out the window to see who it is."

Georgiana can't believe it, either. Has to stop herself

from asking why they don't try. Why they don't ring the bell and see what happens.

It starts to rain, breaking the spell.

"I don't suppose you brought an umbrella," says Mrs Kilgour.

Although she doesn't want to leave – doesn't want Mrs Kilgour to have to leave – Georgiana suggests that they go to the ferry. "It is getting kind of late."

Mrs Kilgour gives herself a shake. "Don't look at me. I'm not the one who doesn't have enough sense of direction to walk around the block."

Despite the weather, Mrs Kilgour insists on sitting outside. "We always sat outside. It's more romantic."

"And wetter," says Georgiana, but largely to herself.

They watch Manhattan recede as the boat chugs towards Staten Island. They take a picture of themselves, their arms around each other, smiling with the skyline of the city behind them.

"I almost brought Morty's ashes to throw in the bay, but then I thought better of it. They can dump his wherever they dump mine." She smiles one of her life-is-ironic smiles. "Together at last."

On the return journey, they stand at the rail to watch the lights of the city approach in the gloaming.

Georgiana turns to her companion. "It is roman—"

She stops herself and moves closer. It's hard to tell because of the rain, but Mrs Kilgour's eyes are filled with tears. "Are you crying?" whispers Georgiana. "Because everything went wrong and I got us lost?"

"Don't be ridiculous," snaps Mrs Kilgour. "I'm crying because I'm happy. This is the best day I've had since Morty died." She reaches over and pats Georgiana's damp hand. "You know, if I'd had a grandchild I'd want her to be like you." She pats the hand again. "Only with a better sense of direction. And possibly not so tall."

Chapter Twenty-nine
Asher's Career Trajectory Takes an Unexpected Turn

Since Asher accidentally put the idea of civil disobedience into Mrs Dunbar's head, she has been driven by the examples of Martin Luther King and Mohandas Karamchand Gandhi. "They should be everyone's inspiration!" Mrs Dunbar proclaimed. "If they could do it, we can do it!" Asher reminded her that both the Reverend Martin Luther King and Mr Gandhi were assassinated, and she reminded him that Our Lord was also assassinated. "Right. Well, that makes me feel a lot better," said Asher.

Perfecting her plan, Mrs Dunbar has spent the weeks since the idea first stumbled out of Asher's mouth meeting with every other charitable organization in the area, plotting their strategy as furiously as the revolutionaries of colonial America plotted theirs (minus the muskets and powdered wigs). Asher was in on every meeting.

Because he has worked in the mayor's office, Asher knows where everything is, which sections close early, which departments are likely to be understaffed, when specific offices are busy and when they're not. What he doesn't know he can find out easily enough. And because he has worked in the mayor's office, he not only knows a lot of the staff, they know him. "It's like having an undercover agent!" gloated Mrs Dunbar. She also managed a recruitment drive that the army could only envy, and organized workshops in passive resistance so that everyone would know what to do when the police tried to move or arrest them.

Today is the day when the talk stops and the action begins. Which is why Asher, sitting at the breakfast table with his father, is putting every ounce of energy he has into trying to act normal. He's not sure why he's doing this. He enjoyed the plotting, but he's not sure he'll enjoy the actual occupation as much. No matter what Mrs Dunbar, James Madison, the Bill of Rights, Martin Luther King and Gandhi have to say about the rights of ordinary citizens, Asher isn't the kind of person to wind up on the wrong side of the law. Which would be the opposite side to the one his father's on. The thing is – the thing that Asher can't ignore – is that Mrs Dunbar and the others aren't criminals. They're ordinary people. Good people.

People who try to practise what's preached to them.

Nonetheless, Asher has told no one about what's going to happen – not even Claudelia or Will. There's no sense in making them accessories.

"Damn!" Somehow, between lifting his cup and moving it to his mouth, Asher manages to spill coffee all over his breakfast.

"No harm done." Albert Grossman finishes stirring precisely half a teaspoon of sugar into his own cup. "Mrs Swedger can fix you more eggs."

"It doesn't matter." Asher pushes his plate away. "I'm not really hungry anyway." His stomach is so knotted he may never eat again.

"Something important happening at school today? Some big test? You seem a little tense."

A little tense? If he were any tenser he'd snap in two.

"No, just a regular day at school." This, at least, is one hundred per cent true. What is also true – and what he doesn't mention to his father – is that he won't be at school to enjoy it. For the first time in his entire life, Asher Grossman is playing hooky. "But, you know, it's the end of the year and there's a lot going on. The prom… And graduation." Depending how the day goes, both of those are things he may never see. "So I guess I'm just a little wired."

"Well, that's understandable. Who wouldn't be a little 'wired'? You've worked very hard." Albert smiles as if he's just won a difficult case and a commensurate bonus. "I told you to take more responsibility and handle things yourself, and you did. You've done me proud."

Perhaps he's taken on more responsibility than his father meant. Since that smile and those words are two more things Asher may never experience again.

"Yeah … well … thanks, Dad." Asher glances at his watch. "Sheesh. Look at the time. I better get moving." He looks at his father. Hopefully. "Don't you have to get to the office?"

"Not today. I'm working at home." Of course he is. It's not enough that, for a change, Albert Grossman is in the country, in the state and in the town, he's also decided not to leave the house. Today. Of all the possible days in the year. "I thought we could try that new steakhouse tonight. I've heard good things about it."

"Yeah," agrees Asher. "That'd be great."

Assuming, of course, that he makes it home.

It isn't just Mrs Dunbar who asked herself "What would Jesus do?" and decided that the answer was "Occupy Town Hall". In his younger days the Reverend Dunbar spent time in South America with liberation theologists, and he has joined in with his wife's scheme with all the enthusiasm of our Lord tossing the moneychangers out of the temple. It was the Reverend Dunbar who ran the workshops in passive resistance, and it is he who now drives the protestors from the community centre to the town hall in the church minibus, humming an old gospel song under his breath. He and his wife have more in common than Asher suspected.

The atmosphere in the bus is matter-of-fact and calmly excited, as if they are on their way to a picnic. As he should have known, most of the centre people have been on demonstrations before – against the war, against torture, against GM crops, against banker bail-outs. Only Asher, who has been more a poster boy for obedience to authority than its challenger, is new to it. He texts his father to say he may be home late.

Mrs Dunbar turns in her seat to face her troops. "Everybody knows what they have to do, right?"

Everybody knows. The Reverend Dunbar is a very good teacher.

"Let's synchronize our watches and our phones." She looks at the watch on her arm. "It's now two minutes past noon. Everybody got that?"

The staff in the various branches will have started taking their lunch hours. Some services will be closed.

Others will have long lines that move less quickly than a dozing snail. Waiting areas will be crowded. The security guards will be thinking about sitting down and eating a sandwich, not whether or not the afternoon is likely to descend into chaos. The protestors will enter the building as though they are ordinary citizens (which, of course, they are) who have come to apply for a licence or to ask about building regulations or tax deadlines (not stage a sit-in). They will linger and loiter, and spread through every floor and department. The protestors from the shelters and the food banks and the many church groups will be doing the same. At exactly 2.15 p.m. the Occupy Town Hall people will bring out their signs and sit down. Some will handcuff themselves to doors and railings; some to each other. Meanwhile, another group will have assembled outside, and by then the local papers and radio and television stations will have been alerted and reporters will be on the scene.

Mrs Dunbar and several other women from the centre – all of whom look as if they spend their spare time knitting baby clothes for their grandchildren, not breaking the law – head for the floor where the councillors and the mayor have their offices. And where the Thursday meeting of the town council is scheduled to begin at two and will this week feature an unexpected speech by Mrs Dunbar.

Asher, Carlin and Reverend Dunbar, inspired by the time Greenpeace activists scaled Big Ben in London, are occupying the roof. They have an enormous banner to hang over the side of the building that says: *Government of the people, by the people and for the people. We are the 98%.* The other thing that inspired this idea was the fact that Asher knows how to get onto the roof. When he worked in the mayor's office the roof was where the staff went to smoke, and sometimes he had to go after his supervisor when she was taking a break.

As they are getting into the elevator, Mayor Duggin is coming out.

"Why, Asher Grossman! It's good to see you." He claps Asher on the shoulder. "How's your father?"

Asher smiles back. "He's well. Busy."

"I know what you mean." Mayor Duggin winks. "No rest for the wicked, hey?"

"You can certainly say that," says Reverend Dunbar, smiling like a saint.

Everybody laughs.

"So what are you doing here?" asks the mayor. "Have you decided to work for government again?"

"Kind of," says Asher.

"Well, that's good to hear." Mayor Duggin gives him another shoulder thump. "Your efficiency and thoroughness have been sorely missed, let me tell you. Though I'm sure you've brought those qualities to whatever you've been doing."

"Oh, that he has," mutters Carlin. "By the truckload."

"Give my regards to your dad," Mayor Duggin calls through the closing doors of the elevator.

It would seem that the angels are on their team today; the door to the roof is bolted on the inside, which means that they have the roof all to themselves.

They spread out the banner and get it into position, ready to fling it over the parapet at 2.15 p.m..

The three of them sit out of sight from the ground with their backs against the wall.

The day is chilly but sunny and pleasant. Carlin says he hasn't felt this positive in a long time.

Asher, although no stranger to stress, can't remember ever feeling this anxious before. "You mean you think we're going to win?"

Carlin rubs his hands together. "Oh, I don't know about that. It just feels good to be doing something. Instead of just watching things happen to you. Like you're nothing but an observer in your own life."

"I know what you mean," says the Reverend Dunbar. "And I have to say, I'm feeling pretty excited myself. It does feel good to be acting rather than simply reacting."

He turns to Asher. "What about you, son? You're the one filled with youthful rebellion."

The only thing Asher is filled with right now is fear. "Tell you the truth, I'm feeling pretty nervous." They're both looking at him; he looks at the bird droppings scattered over the roof. "I've never done anything like this before. And, you know…"

"Your father's a lawyer," fills in Carlin. "So he probably isn't going to think this is a good extracurricular activity. Not like working for the mayor."

"Yeah." Asher nods. "You know, I've kind of grown up to respect the law." And yet here he is, sitting on a rooftop, preparing to break it.

"Laws are made by men," says Carlin. "And not always for the sake of justice."

"As Edmund Burke said," says the minister, "'It is not what a lawyer tells me I *may* do; but what humanity, reason, and justice tell me I ought to do.'"

"I don't think my father knows that quote," says Asher.

At fourteen minutes after two they all take up their positions and Reverend Dunbar starts counting down.

It isn't until he says, "Three … two … one… Now!" and they hurl the banner over the edge that they see the crowd already gathered below. Demonstrators. News people. Spectators and passers-by. And police. A cheer goes up, and Asher, Carlin and Reverend Dunbar all wave. Which is the image that is later shown on national news.

A few hours pass before Asher calls his father.

Albert wants to know where he is.

"I'm in Queen's Park," says Asher. "I've been arrested."

His father laughs. "No, really, Ash. Where are you?"

"In jail. You're my one phone call. I need you to bail me out."

"In jail?" repeats his father. "What the hell are you doing in jail?"

"My community service."

Albert Grossman is not a screamer and shouter. Logic and reason are his weapons; that and always being right. Indeed, he is so calm and relaxed when he arrives to get Asher that he might be picking him up from a game and not a police station. You would have to be his son to know he's angry. The only comment he makes as they leave the building is, "Well, this will be a story to tell my grandchildren. Hopefully, I'll be able to laugh about it then."

Because Asher's father likes to concentrate when he's driving, they don't discuss what happened until they get home.

"I can see Dr Kilpatiky's reasoning," says Albert after Asher explains about the changes she made in the community-service placements. "There's no harm in giving kids a push. But you should have told me. I could have done something."

Asher shrugs. "You said I should stand on my own two feet."

"Not on the roof of the town hall, I didn't."

"No," Asher mumbles. "That just kind of happened."

His father positions himself in front of the fireplace as if he's pleading before a judge, his hands clasped behind his back. "So did these people force you to join them today?"

"You mean at gunpoint?" asks Asher. "The Reverend Dunbar and his wife?"

"There's no need to be facetious. I know that young people your age need to flex their muscles as it were, but I don't really understand why you would break the law like that."

Albert Grossman exudes confidence and wellbeing. As he should. He has it all: professional success, status and money. So much so that he could be an advertisement for the benefits of Western civilization; *Living the Dream*. But as Asher looks at him, it is not the well-dressed, well-fed, well-respected businessman he sees, it is Shelley Anne Rebough and her children at the Christmas dinner at the church, so happy you'd think they'd won the lottery.

"Because a lot of people need help, that's why," says Asher. "And everything's being shut down and taken away."

"That's the way the world is," says his father.

"That doesn't mean it's the way it has to be," says Asher.

Albert laughs. "It isn't? You really think your little protest is going to change anything?"

If there is one thing Asher's learned in the last year it's that the world isn't run by or made for Shelley Anne Rebough and her children; it's run by and made for Asher's father and men like him. "Probably not," Asher admits.

Albert laughs again. "Then why do it?"

"Because it's the right thing to do."

Epilogue
A Conversation at the Beginning of Summer

Coloured lights have been strung across the Shillers' backyard; chairs and small tables dot the lawn. The umbrellas from Thailand have been arranged to shelter the buffet of food and drink near the house. A banner saying *CONGRATULATIONS!* hangs over the patio doors and music plays from speakers fixed to several trees. The roses are in bloom.

This is the last weekend in June. Soon summer jobs and family vacations will begin. Marigold will be counselling at a summer camp for inner-city kids, Asher will be working at the community centre, and Georgiana, Byron, Will and Claudelia are doing a road trip, but right now they all sit together at a table near the koi pond. Dunkin lies under the table. The humans are dressed up for the party. Dunkin is wearing a bow.

"Man, I can hardly believe it," says Will. "We

actually made it. We graduated!"

Claudelia picks up a nacho from her plate. "Is it me," she wonders, "or has this year gone really fast?" It seems to her that it was only yesterday they were sitting by the pool and Georgiana was complaining about going back to school, and now it's all over.

Though that is not the way it seems to Asher. "I don't know about fast." There were some parts of the year that seemed to Asher to move so slowly they were standing still. For instance, the day of the demonstration. Just the wait at the police station for his father to pick him up and the conversation that followed lasted a couple of years each. Long, unpleasant years. "But I suppose that at least it's been pretty interesting."

Will flicks a potato chip at Asher's head. "*Interesting?* Is that what you call it? Asher Grossman, future president of our nation, is filmed defying the government, and you call it *interesting*?"

"I wasn't defying the government." Asher throws the chip under the table to Dunkin. "I was participating in it." A point that Albert Grossman accepted the way we all accept bad weather. Just as he's accepted the fact that instead of working in his law firm this summer Asher will be working at the community centre. Albert, of course, is hoping his son isn't serious about not studying corporate law after all, and is just going through a phase. Even he, in his rebellious teens, spent two weeks in India. "But maybe 'different' would be a better description of this year."

"Well, my year was definitely interesting," says Marigold. Asher wasn't the only one to get his picture in the paper. Marigold's exposure wasn't national, of course (and not filmed), but the article in the local paper went a long way to making her mother forgive her for running off with her car and upsetting her like that. In fact, Eveline later said that if she'd known why Marigold was behaving so badly she would never have been upset in the first place. This, of course, isn't true but it is the closest her mother has ever come to admitting she might be wrong. Marigold smiles. "Didn't I say that placement would broaden my horizons?"

Byron laughs. "And the great thing is, you're still your old, sunny, optimistic self."

Marigold laughs, too, but for a different reason. "Yeah, well, I kind of think I got lucky. I mean, everything worked out OK, but it didn't have to." It could have been a disaster. She could have failed to get anywhere with Sadie. She could have been so defeated by Sadie she gave up before a month was out. She might never have found Sadie under that porch. Sadie could have been inspired by a different show and been somewhere a lot worse. "Things don't always turn out the way you expect them too."

"Tell me about it," says Georgiana. As far as a year of firsts goes, no one can beat her. OK, Asher broke the law and Marigold suddenly turned into Action Girl, but Georgiana did something she never thought possible. On the Saturday when Alice Einhorn called to tell her that if she wanted to say goodbye she better hurry, instead of freaking out, Georgiana went straight to St. Joan's. She arrived in time to have Mrs Kilgour snap at her for crying. "What are you making such a fuss about? You know I don't like a fuss." Georgiana was holding Mrs Kilgour's hand when she died. It turned out, however, that Mrs Kilgour had one more surprise up her sleeve. She had named Georgiana as her next of kin, which meant that Mrs Kilgour's ashes were released to her. She and Byron took them and Mr Kilgour's ashes to New York, and threw them over the side of the Staten Island Ferry. "But you know what?" says Georgiana. "When stuff doesn't turn out how you expect, that's not always a bad thing."

"No," says Asher. Nothing is turning out the way he thought it should. And certainly not the way his father wanted. "But everything is copasetic anyway."

"Watch it, dude…" Will shoots another potato chip at him. "You're starting to sound like Marigold."

Their laughter causes Dunkin to wag his tail in his sleep.